W9-BBX-616

Hot Box in the Pizza District

by

Thomas W. Keech

Baltimore, 2015

ISBN 978-0-9836990-2-6 Hardback

Library of Congress Control Number
2015940771

Published by
Real Nice Books
11 Dutton Court
Baltimore, Maryland 21228

Publisher's note: This is a work of fiction. Names, characters, places, institutions, and incidents are entirely the product of the author's imagination or are used fictitiously, and any resemblance to actual persons, living or dead, or to events, incidents, institutions, or places is entirely coincidental.

Printed in the U.S.A.

Cover art and design by Vanessa Snyder

For Dan and Julie

Also by Thomas Keech

The Crawlspace Conspiracy
Prey for Love

Chapter 1

She was – what, about 25? Black hair glowing with a rainbow iridescence like gasoline spilt on a wet asphalt road. No furniture or curtains on the first floor. The light was hitting her figure from a big window in the empty room to the left as she paced down the stairs right in front of me, white T-shirt cut high above short black shorts, damp sheen on her stomach, sparkle from her navel. Otherwise it was dim inside the entrance hall. The place was hot, echoing and empty; each step creaked as she stepped on it. The overall effect was jarring. She pointed to the floor.

"You can just leave it there. I'll deliver it for you."

"Um, my friend Buddy said he'd get it delivered."

"I know, but he called and said he couldn't do it himself today. So I'll do it. I don't mind."

I set the box down and turned to go, but her image was already burned into my brain. I had to turn around and take one last look. She had large, dark eyes, black lashes, fair skin. Her eyes caught mine and immediately that sweet, hot current began to run down all through me. But she was looking at me expectantly, as if I had turned around to say something important. I couldn't think of anything to say at all.

"I don't mind," she repeated.

"Yeah," I managed to say. "Thanks." I stood there still, probably a little too long, boxed in below her in that hot little room.

"It's none of my business, but are you, like, a bodybuilder or something?" She made it seem like she was just curious, like she had no strong opinions on the subject of bodybuilding.

"A student."

A boy, she probably thought. And really, she was too old for me. Did they lose it even by then, by 25? You didn't see women out much at that age. Mostly married, or at least doing jobs and decorating apartments. Disappearing into the frou-frou. This house was empty though, not cluttered with cutesy junk, and solid, with old, beaten-up hardwood floors. So you could walk in and really stand there, be steady – not just balanced on the spongy padded carpet in some girlie apartment like a wary animal that everybody is afraid will throw up all over himself.

I tried to look only into her eyes, but my own eyes wouldn't follow my instructions, and they wandered downwards. "What?" I blurted out. "No tattoos?"

"You don't know that." She smiled like it was totally normal for me to check her out. "You can't see everywhere." She left that thought hanging. Sweat had plastered my own shirt to my body, and my diligently crafted muscles suddenly felt too big, overdeveloped. But she didn't seem to be grossed out or intimidated. She smiled again, a wide, pretty smile showing her perfect white teeth – but with a hint of wrinkles already at the corners of her eyes. It must really suck to get old.

Her eyes flashed down toward the box. She walked across the hall and crouched down next to it.

"I don't get it. This has a UPS label. It's already been delivered."

"Yeah. Delivered to me. I want it taken back to the person who sent it to me."

"What? Hey, this address is really close. Why do you need me to ...?" She saw me stiffen at her question and stopped. She quickly let go of the box like it was burning her hands.

I thought I needed to explain, at least a little. "I know it's close, but I really can't do it myself." I still didn't want to have to explain the whole story to her.

"Oh. Okay. No problem. I'll do it, like I said. What's in it?"

"I don't know."

"So why are you sending it back?"

"This was supposed to be like, just drop off the box two doors down the street at the house Buddy's parents own and he'll take it back for you, or there's this girl there and she'll take it back herself or some such crap."

She rose from her squatting position without taking her hands from her hips, quadriceps smoothly flexing as I watched.

"You don't have to yell at me."

"I just want to send it back and not have to think about it again."

"You're yelling again." She was right. I was acting like an idiot. I wished I could convince her that I was not normally this weird. But that would be hard to pull off now.

She crossed over and stopped right in front of me, leaning a hand on the bannister. "Sorry for prying. It's none of my business. I just had the idea you wouldn't mind telling me."

This house and this girl were solid. Why did I have the jitters? What instinct was telling me to run? The part of my brain that was sane was telling me exactly the opposite – that I'd be a fool not to stay there and talk to her. "I'd like to talk to you. I can't talk about that."

She looked like she might want to talk, but then her expression changed. "Right now, I have to get ready to go to a meeting. But I'm here for three more weeks."

I didn't know why she said that, so I went back to the subject of the box. "So, when will you actually take the box back?"

"I'll take it back this afternoon. Will you give me the two-minute version of the story of this box right now?"

"Do you need, like, money from me?"

"No, I owe a favor."

"Not to me."

"No, to Buddy. To his parents, really. They own this place."

"What's your relationship with Buddy?"

"What?" She stepped back.

"I'm sorry. It's none of my business. You're really nice to do this. I'm saying all the wrong things, I know. It's so hot in here."

Her eyes softened. "It's no big deal, really. I've never even met Buddy. His parents own this house. They know my aunt somehow. They're letting me stay here free until they rent it out."

I glanced at the rooms on either side of the hall.

"You don't have any furniture?"

"Bedroom furniture."

"So you just, what, arrived in this neighborhood from another planet or something?"

"I'm just housesitting for a month. I'm going to graduate school in September."

Oh shit. Smart, too. This was too much. This was just too right, like a beautiful package that's got to explode in your hands.

"Generally, for graduate school, it helps if you have a subject of study in mind."

"Why do you talk like that? You could just ask me what I'm studying."

Because you might explode in my hands.

"I'm sorry. Sorry."

She screwed up her mouth, the silliness of that expression exaggerated by her full lips. "I guess I should be glad you asked at all. Not many people do."

"What are you studying?" I said. "What's your name?"

"Eileen. I'm starting on my masters in psychology in upstate New York next month. Who are you?"

"I'm Tim. Did you just graduate this spring?"

"Yeah. I made it out in four years, even with a real slow start. My brother might have given me a bad example on that. He always told me the first two years of college were just for fun. Are you in college?"

"Yeah. Sort of. Badger Community College right up the street, actually. Not exactly graduate school. You starting graduate school – that's really cool." That was a lame comment, I knew. This girl made me wish I could find the middle ground between sarcasm and idiocy. I expected she'd just run up the stairs.

Instead, she sat down on the steps facing me. Those were definitely the most beautiful eyes that had ever looked into mine. I searched for imperfections and found only a very faint spray of freckles across her cheeks. "I barely got into the graduate program," she said. "I didn't exactly ace undergraduate school."

"So you didn't do that well in college? And that gave you the idea of going to graduate school?" I couldn't help taunting her. It helped keep the focus on her rather than me. I'd met her two minutes ago, she was gorgeous, and I already suspected she was out of my league and was just playing with me. Push her away before she pushes me. That's what I was doing. I had done it before. Okay, the results weren't that great. Some people thought I was a little strange. Mostly I hung around with my really old friends, but that was no way to get a girl either.

She gave me this look like she figured out that I couldn't talk straight to a girl, but she went on talking to me anyway.

"I know what I want now," she said. She paused like she would like me to ask her more. I guess I didn't pick up on that quickly enough. "What about you?" she added.

"I take eighteen credits at a time. I get all *A*s. I pick one course every semester and make myself learn more about it than the teacher knows. Right now it's *Coriolanus*, one of Shakespeare's plays. I'm a bike messenger for a living. And I lift weights."

"I can hardly remember some of the courses I took in my first two years of college. I used to party a lot, especially the first couple of years," she laughed. "I guess I don't regret it. Don't you have any time for fun?"

"I ... have some fun." Okay, it came out defensive. I do think you have to take some things seriously, but I knew she didn't want to be lectured. We were very different. I turned to go. But she got up and stood between me and the door.

"Come on. Tell me. Why are you sending this box back?"

"I'm sending it back to my father. I don't want to see him. I just want to send his package back."

"Oh! It's not like you were sent this box by mistake."

She was almost as tall as me, and she stood close, still flushed from her exercise upstairs. She pulled her hair up off her neck and I caught a faint smell of lilac. I felt pinned down by her eyes. I knew if she asked another question, she would extract another confession. Meanwhile she was sending that sweet current racing through my blood from my heart on down. I was stimulated to the point of distraction. In 30 seconds' conversation she had made me feel first like a boring nerd and now like a horny animal. I had to get out of there.

"Right. Not a mistake. Gotta go." I put my hand on the doorknob.

"So you're making like an ultra-cool insult to your father, sending his package back to him not even opened."

Shocks spread through the middle of my back, burned out like tiny intramuscular meteorites. If she touched me right then I would have fallen down. But she didn't. I was left kind of paralyzed, with my hand still on the doorknob. Don't get inside my head, I thought-begged her.

"What do you want?" I croaked.

"Isn't that kind of a rough way of making a point to your father."

"It's a rough life." I turned around.

She backed up a step. "When I was fourteen," she said, "my father took me out to lunch one day and introduced me to his mistress. Before that moment, I had no idea she even existed. I didn't speak to him for a whole year."

I stared at her.

"I'm not saying it's the worst thing that ever happened to anybody, but it really hurt at the time."

"I'm sorry."

"I got over it. I'm just saying, I know strange shit happens with fathers sometimes."

"The box is probably a birthday present."

"What birthday?"

"Twentieth."

"Oh, man," she said, "that's supposed to be a happy one."

"Who says it's not?"

She looked down at the box.

"I didn't want to take it back there myself, and run into him … or anybody. I mean his new wife. And I wanted to get rid of it, you know, right away."

"I'll take the box back today. But I'd really like to know why you're so intense about it."

"I don't like to talk about that."

"Just to me, or to anybody?"

"Especially not to you. You're too … mature, I guess, to understand. Sorry. Gotta go."

"Now I'm really interested. I'm going to personally deliver this box to your father. Any special message I should give to him?"

"Please don't. You know, never mind the whole thing. Just forget it." I reached for the box.

She put her hand on my arm. "All this drama. I was starting to think you liked me."

"Like" didn't seem like a strong enough word, since I had just experienced a mini-ejaculation the instant she touched my arm.

"I'm 23," she continued after a minute. I was still bent over, hiding my condition from her while reaching for the box, not able to respond. She went on, "No one ever told me I was too old for them before."

I gave up on grabbing for the box and stood up. Started to talk, but my voice came out strangled. Took a deep breath. She had a concerned look in her eyes like she was afraid I was having a seizure or something. "I'm fine," I said. My voice was back. "I didn't say you were old. I said mature, like you have your shit together."

"Oh."

"You seem really nice. It's just me. I can't get women right. Just give me the box and I'll go away."

"Oh no," she said, wrapping her arms around it. "I'm taking it back to your father just like I said I would. And I'm going to find out the story of this box."

Chapter 2

There was a phone message from my father's wife about the box. She wanted to make sure, she said, she had sent it to the right address. This was the game Anita played, always pretending there was some little scheduling problem or miscommunication foiling our arrangements to get together, instead of the fact that I always avoided the two of them for as long as I could. I was supposed to call her back to see what the problem with the package was. She knew I wouldn't call her back. I never called her back. No, that's not correct. Once in a great while I'd brainwash myself that it couldn't be that bad, and I'd call. Unfortunately, it had the same effect as intermittent reinforcement on laboratory pigeons.

I wondered how much Eileen would find out about my family situation when she delivered the box. Usually I skipped over that part of my life when I met new people. That was the part I couldn't do anything about. What matters is what you do with the part of your life that you can control. I aced all my courses. I made enough money not to be dependent on anyone. I sculpted my body with workouts. I spoke the truth to my friends. I didn't get too involved with women because once they get tangled in your life you can't always say what you mean even if you can figure it out.

I decided to call my father's office directly.

I usually hang up if his office puts me on hold, but I didn't this time. Some muffled sound, like his secretary was holding her hand over the receiver, held me up.

"Timmy?" His secretary was back on the line.

"Tim."

"Tim. I suggest you call your father at his house right now. Do you have the number right there?"

"Is this about the box?"

"I don't know anything about a box."

First there had been Anita's whiny, diminutive voice calling two weeks ago, asking me to call for no reason, then the call about the box, now this. I slammed the phone down and ran down to the basement and started pumping without counting, set after set until biceps and triceps were burning. Repeat while burning. The racing blood helped too, and the sucking in of air, and the concentration on the pain and the strength you can grow from that pain. If you keep going into that pain you can achieve maximum bodily perfection on a given frame. I think I read that phrase in some pamphlet that came with some of the weights.

"What'r ya'doin'?" Jeremy mumbled. He had just clumped down the creaky stairs to the Weights and Laundry Room next to where I sleep. Lazy, curly reddish-brown hair topped a chiseled face that would have been handsome but for the pudgy layer of randomly freckled skin. He had a devilish smile that made me think his mother had called him cute once too often. I'd known him all his life, and he was a little taller than average, but his body was pale and doughy. He squinted at the bare, gritty concrete floor illuminated by bleak fluorescent light, turned his head toward the shiny-white but little-used washer and dryer. He glanced over to the door to my bedroom in the corner.

"Man, it's harsh down here. Sparse and harsh."

"You've never come down here before? That means you never

wash your clothes."

There was a good little silence then. I believed in the power of silence. Jeremy had taken it hard when I told him I didn't have time to shoot the shit any more. But it was only because I found out he didn't know a thing. All he knew was the stuff that automatically sank into your head if you had your TV or YouTube on all your life and you eventually saw every part of every Discovery Channel show.

"Well, dear, Jeremy is a sophomore in college," my mother often reminded me in her sweet, insidious, coaxing voice. "He's getting it over with, jumping through all the hoops you have to jump through to get a degree."

She wouldn't say what she meant, which was that there was something wrong with me. Sometimes I challenged her: what exactly was wrong with six courses at a time, eighteen credits a semester, all *A*s? I knew more than you needed to know to ace Modern European History and Calculus I, and I've read practically everything that's ever been written about Shakespeare's *Coriolanus*.

"But a lot of people," my mother would say in her sweet, passive-aggressive way, "look upon college as a means to an end."

Jeremy walked over and picked up a fifteen-pound dumbbell and started some poor-posture, lazy-ass bicep curls. He takes pride in thinking he's too individualistic to be considered a normal college guy, but Jeremy is about as normal as they come. He has mastered the art of getting by while doing as little schoolwork as possible. He's really the definition of normal, even to the point of getting drunk in the pizza joint the other night and yelling "Fuck all this shit! All I want to do is get laid!" until they told him to leave. I had to step in front of the manager to keep him from physically throwing Jeremy out. I tried to explain to Jeremy later that it wasn't a good thing that we couldn't go in there again, and that his angst was so banal.

"Hey, Tim, this girl came by for you," he said now.

"What? Who?"

"She didn't say who she was."

"What'd she look like?"

"Dark hair. Long legs. Real low-cut shorts. Man, I could have taken that coming or going!"

"Confident – but with a sweet smile?"

"Yeah, I guess so."

"Did she have like, these beautiful dark eyes with long black lashes?"

"Definitely."

"High breasts that look like they might bust their way out of her T-shirt?"

Jeremy just nodded.

"Did she have those cut abs you can barely see, but you know you could feel them if you ran your fingertips across her skin down there?"

"Okay. Cut the shit. Who is she?"

"I have no idea."

He punched me on the shoulder. "She said she wanted to see where you lived. If I knew you were going to give me such a hard time about it, I'd have invited her in, tried my luck myself."

"She didn't say anything else?"

"She sure did. She asked me so many questions about you I thought you had applied for a job or something. And she said you should call your father."

I just nodded.

"I wish I could have seen the rest of that tattoo."

I didn't tell Jeremy she lived just two doors up the street. And I could count on the fact that he wouldn't follow me outside in the sweltering heat. I knocked on her door. She opened it wearing a two-piece exercise outfit, her face red and her skin damp. She had been working out on a machine in the bare room to the left with a fan blowing directly on her. She was trying to catch her breath. She walked back to the steps and pulled on a giant-sized, loose T-shirt. Less good stuff to see. Maybe that was better. She held up the hem of the shirt so the air from the fan could fill it up.

"It looks like you're wearing a giant pink balloon."

"It's gross, I know, but I'm so hot." She played with the hem in the wind. Now she looked like a triangular pink sail with the wind licking in just at the tops of those legs. "I wish you'd called first."

"You didn't give me your number."

"Oh, I'm sorry. You're right." She guided the sail into the wind. "You didn't ask for it."

"I was afraid to ask for it."

"Afraid of me? Right." She laughed. She let the hem go, and the shirt molded itself to her body. She kept pulling it away and letting it cling back against her as we talked.

"Why did you come to my house yesterday?" I said. But what I was really thinking was: I can call? That was the first sign of what she was doing to me. I was thinking one thing and saying another. The minute you start messing with women your mind gets hypocritical like that.

"I took the box back to your father. I talked to him."

"About me?"

"Yeah."

"Why?"

"I don't know. You come into my house looking strong enough to tear it down with your bare hands, but you freak out when you get a little present from your father. I was curious to see what he was like. Aren't you curious about what's in the box?"

"No." That wasn't exactly true. The truth was I just didn't want to talk about my father or the box. The truth was that Eileen was drawing me in toward her with a cosmic gravitational pull like the sun uses to suck on the planets. To keep talking to her in this conversational tone would be to deny the real physical truth that was rising up between us. Adrenaline jolted my heart. The itch flooded my body. My hands were shaking. But she stepped back.

"I really can call you?" It seemed like we had left off this part of the conversation an hour before.

She held her head a little to the side, her dark eyes focused on mine but with little detours back and forth to my hands.

"Sure. You know, your father seemed nice. That makes it even more of a mystery why you don't like him."

"Most women like him."

"I can see why. But I mean he talked about you."

She brushed past me and walked through the empty living room and through a doorway towards the back, her running shoes squeaking on the bare wood floor. My hands were left dangling in the air.

She didn't invite me, but I followed her back. I try not to be intimidated by women. It was a kitchen furnished with an old, chipped, steel-legged formica table and one torn chair. She was filling a glass of water at the sink. She wasn't surprised to see me follow her. She picked up another glass from the strainer near the sink and held it up with a question mark on her face. I shook my head no. She drank her whole glass in two or three little spasms. All of her skin was damp.

"There's only one chair." She offered it to me with a nod of her head.

I pulled it out and sat down, resting my arm on the tabletop, which was warm to the touch, like every other surface in that room.

"You talked to Jeremy when you came to my house?"

"Reddish brown hair, so high?" She held her hand up like she was indicating how tall a little kid had grown. I gathered she wasn't impressed with his height. I was glad I was two inches taller than he was.

"Yeah. That's Jeremy. He liked you."

"He was nice to me."

I couldn't help but compare in my head this comment to Jeremy's gross descriptions of what he'd like to do to her. "He tries to act all cool and above it all, but he's really very needy."

"You don't like him?"

"He's my best friend. Sometimes he gets on my nerves a little. It's not a big deal."

Even though we had just met a few days before, it seemed like we were continuing a conversation we had been having for years. We talked about college. She talked as if my school, Badger Community College, was the full equivalent of the real college she had just graduated from. She might have been 23, but her eyes still lit up when she described her uninhibited first year in college – drinking, cutting classes, tattoos, other activities that she left to my imagination.

"Wow, that sure is not me. I just live in my friend's basement and study. And work."

"I'm not like that any more," she insisted, her eyes drawing mine in. "I paid the price. Because I screwed around for the first couple of years, I barely made it into graduate school."

"They let you in, right? I'm sure you'll do okay." It crossed my mind that I actually had no reason to know how she'd do. But I still thought I knew.

"Jeremy said you're an *A*-plus student. He said you were super intense about everything."

"Why were you asking Jeremy about me?"

"I don't know. You seem like a nice guy, and I didn't get any information out of you the other day except those one-syllable answers."

"I was a little intimidated, walking in the door of this dumpy old house and suddenly there's this hot woman coming down the steps right in front of me."

I stood up and walked to a little window over the sink. It looked out over a narrow strip between her house and the next, a strip that consisted of a skinny, crumbling sidewalk barely visible between big clumps of burgundy and orange zinnias full of juice but withering at the edges under the blazing August sun. I could feel her own heat behind me, picture her dark eyes brighter, sharper than any half-dead flowers.

I was drawn back to that heat until my hands were flat on the table near the chair. She had taken the chair when I stood up. She met my gaze, then looked away at just the right instant. I kept staring. She was holding her hair off her neck in a way that emphasized her sculpted cheekbones. There was a noise, and I saw that I was vibrating the table against the wall.

"You should probably stop that."

"I should probably stop, period."

She broke eye contact, shifted in the chair, sat up straighter, still holding her hair up off her neck. She looked great. I didn't know what to do. I had always dreamed I would meet some sweet girl crazed by astrophysics or political science or Verlaine, and a tiny, invisible plasma flow would start between us and then gradually grow strong enough to alter the universe. But Eileen was nothing like those dreams. She was gorgeous, and not like me at all. She took off her giant shirt and started mopping her skin. Her white top was soaked at the bottom of each breast. She got up suddenly and walked away toward the window, and we stared together at those crazy lopsided zinnias in the alleyway, deepening in color as they died.

"Jeremy told me," she said, "that you turned down Princeton to go to community college."

"I would have had to take my father's money."

She raised an eyebrow. "Really? That would have been a problem? I would have taken my father's money in a minute."

"No, it works out better this way," I insisted. "I have a job that pays for everything. I can study any subject until I know everything there is to know about it. I have time to work out. I can keep my edge. I couldn't do that if I had to do all the other college crap."

"Some of that 'college crap' can be fun."

"I'm not sure it would have been fun for me."

I had last seen my father in the spring. He drove up and parked in front of my house without warning and called me from his cell phone and waited outside in his car until I showed.

"Nice." Riding in his car was like sitting on a leather sofa with an oriental rug on the floor while inhaling the faint odor from the waxed surface of a mahogany side table.

"I always wanted one of these Jags," he said. "Mechanically, they're pieces of crap. Won't last, but then either will I. When you get to be my age, you realize that you aren't getting too many more chances, and you have to go and take what you want."

"I thought you always did that."

He took his tie off and threw his suit coat in the back seat. Except for a pen in his pocket, there was no sign that he was supposedly a big local lawyer. At least I used to think he was someone important, until my own job as a legal messenger took me into his office once in a while. After I saw a lot of legal offices, I figured out that he was just a mid-level lawyer in this middle-sized suburban Pennsylvania town, but a mid-level lawyer with a faithful client base and a decent income, mostly due to a big smile, a good secretary and a deep bass voice. He drove me to a combination restaurant and bar in what you might call the higher-class end of the pizza district, one of those happy-hour places where office people start their weekends on Thursday afternoons. It had a large, U-shaped bar, a lot of small metal tables, and one wall of private booths covered in dark, fake leather. We sat down in one of the booths.

"You still like burgers?" he said. "I was wondering if you had become a vegetarian yet."

"What's that supposed to mean?"

"It would be another thing where you'd be different from me. That's what you want, isn't it?"

"I know I don't want to be led around by the nose by my Stepford Wife."

He ignored my reference to Anita. "And you want to be poor. And you want to be a bike messenger."

"And learn a lot about everything. And not pretend."

"And how would that would make you different from me?"

"You tell me."

"C'mon, Timmy." He called me Timmy because he liked to pretend I had been frozen at the age of ten. That's how old I was when he forgot I existed. I let it go this time. "I'm not perfect. I'm sorry I had to leave."

"It wasn't the leaving. It was the before. And the after."

He sat back. "How is your mother doing?"

Why was he now suddenly curious about the damage he had left behind?

He took a swig of his beer, swallowed it slowly, looked around like he was wishing there were other people in the bar who would come over and let him buy them beers too. His hands were restless, playing with his coaster. "I was drinking an awful lot back then."

"She didn't mind you drinking. She thought everything you did was great until you started chasing after Anita right in front of her face."

He didn't want to argue about my mother's qualities. "But tell me honestly what you think, about *me*."

"Okay. I remember you used to cry in front of me. You used to sit with me on the sofa on Saturdays when Mom was out of the room and tell me you loved me and cry for no reason. You would always whine in front of me. What was I supposed to do? And you're still whining every time I visit your house. 'Why has it been so long?' 'Why can't you stay longer?' Really, Dad: *boo-hoo*."

"I was crying because I was headed for the gutter. What you don't know is, Anita's the one who saved me. She's such a knockout, I never dreamed she was falling for me. It was months before she convinced me that she believed in me." I stared at him as he went on in a quavering voice. "I always knew there was something missing from my life, but until then I didn't even know what it was."

"What was it?"

He stared at me like I might be mocking him. "She believes in me. I can't live without that. I don't know how to say it any other way. I was half dead – turning black inside – until I met her."

"You still drink."

He held up his fingers. "Four beers a day. Two at lunch, two after dinner. Maybe six on weekends. Remember when I used to drink until I fell down?"

"No."

"You don't remember the time I got my face smashed up so bad I went to the emergency room and had to miss a week of work?"

"No."

"How could you not remember that? Oh. Your mother, of course. She must have covered up for me. Like always. Your mother is a saint." He shook his head in amazement, but the movement ended in a shiver, as if the memory of my mother sent a cold chill up his spine. "Anyway, I've been doing well at my job again for years. Got most of my clients back. Made up with my old friends at work. I'm at least halfway functional now. I owe all that to Anita."

"You made me lie for you."

He put his hands in the air out over the table, palms facing outward, then pushed them apart, like he was clearing away extraneous thoughts. "For just one minute can we focus on me?" he said. "I know you're seeing the bigger picture. But for me, the feeling is – Anita gave me my soul back. I couldn't function without her."

"Just you and her? Nobody else mattered?"

"Of course you mattered. I could see the big picture too. But the big picture was a smash-up either way. If I stayed, I would drink myself to death. If I left, I would destroy my family. There was no right way. My life was hit by a freight train. Destroyed no matter what I did. I pray to God that never happens to you."

"The only reason I ever come to see you is Mom makes me do it sometimes."

He took a couple of deep breaths.

"I hoped when you were grown up, we could at least go out together and have a conversation together like men. I guess we're having one now. Thank you for putting your cards on the table."

We drank another round in utter silence. Then he let out a loud sob that brought a few quick looks from the patrons at the bar. Luckily, they had turned back toward their beers before they could notice the tears that were streaming down his face. "Sorry. God, I hope none of my clients are in here and see me like this." He wiped his face on a napkin and blew his nose. It made a funny sound when he did that. We both looked anxiously around the bar, then saw each other looking around and laughed.

"That's not the only reason I come to your house," I corrected myself. "I would probably come even if Mom didn't make me. I just meant that it's hard for me to go there."

"Thank you." But then he started crying again, whispering to himself about something being late.

"What's late?"

He just cried more. I stood up to go, but his hand shot out and grabbed my arm. He motioned for me to sit down. "It's not you."

"What do you mean?"

"Something bad has happened. I can't tell you. I understand now that you don't want to see me crying. So let's just leave it at that." He searched in his wallet for bills to throw on the table. Then he stood up and walked out the door without meeting my eyes.

Our two-story, wooden house in the pizza district had once been somebody's cedar-shingled dream starter home. Now the shingles were curled and the front porch was rotting around the edges. On one side of the yard there was an eight-foot stockade fence separating us from the parking lots of the pizza district. On the other side of the street, there was a guy who sat on his wooden porch all day, talking to his mother who had died twenty years ago. A huge drooping tree screened us from the road most of the year, but the shade didn't keep the weeds from growing waist high, something that caused us to get cited by the county that summer. This was probably caused by the woman who lived next door, who was a cop. There was nothing she could arrest us for, but she didn't seem to like us.

My other housemate, Ben, was in a way of speaking our landlord. I had known him since he was nine. He owned the house we lived in – or maybe his father did. Anyway, he acted like it was his house, including taking on some of the responsibilities of an owner. In the past few months he had bugged the county until they got rid of two abandoned cars that had sat in front of our house for maybe two years. They wouldn't do it unless he cut the lawn first, and so he made us do that. Ben always wanted the rent paid in cash. My father told me years ago that people who deal only in cash are usually cheating on their taxes. I don't know why Ben did it. I would never cheat on my own taxes, but if Ben wanted cash, I was giving him cash.

The main street of the district was 50 steps away and on the other side of the stockade fence. It was a wide street, formerly the suburban community main street, and it used to have a movie theater, an appliance store, a hardware store, and a jewelry store. Now there were two gas stations, a motorcycle shop, a pool hall above a copy place, a vinyl record store, a used clothing store, a dollar store, a craft store, and a flower shop. There was plenty to eat and drink. There was a chain fast food restaurant, four or five little old-time restaurants with tiny tables and low ceilings and the same menus and the same people sitting there as ten years before. There were three or four bars, and five pizza places. No one else on this street had ever even heard of *Coriolanus*.

Eileen and I were still at the window when she turned to me, still holding her hair off her neck. The heat coming off of her skin was moist, unlike the stifling kitchen heat.

"I don't know anything about you," I said. "Where are you from?"

"Washington. The D.C. area anyway."

"Are your parents government people?" I asked.

"You could say that. My father's a lobbyist. My mother has had a couple of jobs in agencies. My brother's in the army now."

"I don't know anybody in the government, or in the army," I said. "And I don't even have any brothers or sisters."

"I have a step-sister too. She's sixteen. She's smart, and funny too. My father lived with her mother for seven years but just got married a few months ago."

One reason it was so stifling in there, I realized, was that she hadn't opened any of the windows. I tried to push the kitchen window open, but it wouldn't budge. She asked me to stop before I broke the frame. I saw the windows were painted shut, like most of the windows in our own house.

"Your parents are divorced too?" I said.

"Oh yeah. Now I have two families. I guess that's kind of normal these days." Her eyes were seeking my agreement, but I never feel qualified to say what's normal. She changed the subject. "Who do you hang around with?"

"My friends. Jeremy. You met him. And Ben, my other roommate. That's about it. We've known each other our whole lives, went to high school together three miles away from here. Do you get along with both your mother and your father?"

"I don't send my father's presents back unopened, if that's what you mean." I could tell she thought she might have said the wrong thing. So she touched my arm as if to make up for that. "I don't mean to make fun of you. Families can put people in weird situations."

I nodded. She took her hand off. There was no polite way to ask her to put it back. My hand went out to touch her waist, but it seemed to be moving so slowly it would never get there.

"Ouch!" She had backed into the hot metal edge of the table. "Can we go for a run?" Immediately she started fastening her hair back into a long ponytail with one of those elastic bands that all girls seem to have on them at all times.

I followed her outside. We settled into a jog too fast to talk, too fast for the heat of the day. The more we ran up the hill away from the pizza district, the less funky the neighborhood got. This was where the people who were still functioning in the economic system lived. The sidewalks were not all broken up by tree roots like they were in front of our houses. Small cottages were scattered like tugboats tending to the big foursquare houses. We ran by the elementary school with three overcrowded basketball courts where Jeremy and

I sometimes played after midnight by flashlight. Then there was one of the first suburban developments of brick row houses. Every one of them was meticulously kept up, every postage-stamp front yard perfect, everybody busy and no one in sight.

The sky was a blinding white. I let her set the pace. I stayed ten steps behind her. Her long runner's ponytail poked out from the back of her baseball cap and twitched from side to side with each stride. I heard the rhythm of her running shoes grinding into the thin gravel strip next to the road. Then the gravel strip disappeared and the asphalt was too sticky to run on, so we ran on tiptoes on the edges of people's private yards. Finally there were some high trees and shade, then a tiny, white, nineteenth-century clapboard church, with its old cemetery on a green rise behind a wrought iron fence. The graveyard was a deep green, with colorful dots of impressionist flowers glowing at the bases of the tiny headstones. This was the quietest place I knew, but you couldn't tell how much longer the tranquility of the departed would last. The woods past the graveyard were fenced off now, and there were bulldozers parked there as if the land were being prepared for transformation into something much more profitable and profane.

We came to the top of a long hill past the cemetery and turned onto Ribbon Road, a winding two-lane country road now turned commuter artery that ran along next to a golf course. We ran for another mile, past the thirteenth, fourteenth, fifteenth and sixteenth holes. Then into the entrance of the community college. This was where I went to school but, like most students, I had never gone there on foot. We climbed the long, hilly entrance road, circled the loop road around the administration building, crossed a couple of mostly empty parking lots and went through an opening in a chain link fence and down the long concrete steps to the campus track.

Four laps and she was done. Beads of sweat tracked down into her shirt. She walked over and grabbed the chain link fence, stretching both arms high and suspending herself against it. A nice, girly body. Hips, nice shoulders and, when she turned around, breasts just bold enough to never let you forget they were there. I pulled myself off the fence and staggered around the track for another hot lap. Then I hung with her against the fence, baking in the sun, sucking in the humid air.

"That was ... pretty rough." Exhaustion was keeping my sentences short.

"Maybe we went too fast in this heat," she admitted. "Sorry."

"I didn't know you were such an athlete."

She laughed. "I'm not an athlete. I was never on any teams or anything. I took up running a couple of years ago. Just to, you know, get something off my mind."

We let go of the fence, reached the stairs and climbed the long set of concrete steps back toward the entrance to the track.

"I'm a bike courier for a downtown law firm," I said. "Absolutely everything is a super rush. You have to ride between the lanes of traffic. There's no brakes on my bike. That job can really get stuff off your mind." We came out of the track enclosure and began walking down the winding campus drive.

"Would you go out with me sometime?" I asked, finally getting to the main point I had been thinking about since the instant I met her.

"Sure." She smiled to herself. "I thought I was being pretty obvious about that."

"But then you ran away from me in the house."

"I just can't start a relationship with you by making out while being backed up against a hot kitchen table."

"I get that a lot."

There were some tall trees giving us shade along the campus entrance road, and even more on Ribbon Road. She made a point of walking alongside of me. She seemed interested in my courier job. She said she had never run across anybody with a job like that. I told her the legal business ran in our family. Then she said she couldn't understand why I wanted to be an expert on *Coriolanus*. I said I couldn't explain that one, except maybe I was trying to be a smarty-pants. She laughed at the word. Neither of us was a chatterer, though, and we went for a long while without saying anything.

We were almost home and were approaching the old white clapboard church before she spoke again. "It's really none of my business."

"What?"

"What's wrong with your father?"

"How much time do you have?"

"No. I mean physically. He's sick, right?"

"I have no idea."

"You don't?"

"Let's just run."

Chapter 3

I could hear someone crashing down the creaky steps to the basement. I knew it was Jeremy because he started bellowing my name halfway down.

"Stop studying, for God's sake!" he screamed.

I closed the door on him and locked it. But I could hear him light a cigarette, and I knew what was next. Soon he was blowing the smoke through the keyhole.

"Jeremy!"

"What are we doing Thursday night?" He grinned as the door swung open. He had already put the cigarette out and was holding a dumbbell in one hand, working it with about the amount of energy you might use to play with a yo-yo.

"We're doing something Thursday night? What, is YouTube offline that night?"

"No, smartass. And I don't want to hear another word about *Coriolanus*." He sat down uninvited on my bed, bouncing the dumbbell on the mattress. He picked up my heavy Shakespeare book, flopped it open, and turned to the marked-up pages at the back. "What's it about, anyway?"

"This Roman general. He has a chance to become ruler of the empire, but he refuses to go through all the phony political bullshit required."

"Good for him. I never heard of it before. Why'd you pick such an obscure play?"

"Because in six weeks I can know more about it than anybody at Badger."

Jeremy threw the book aside. "But let's fast-forward 500 years to today. Let's talk about what we're doing Thursday night. No, let's talk first about last night."

I knew from his shit-eating grin exactly what it was. "You met some girl?" I asked. "Is she in one of your classes?"

"No, not one of those. No, she's a real estate chick, sells houses or something."

"And?"

"Her name is Dory. Really cute. Tall, super-skinny, super-blonde."

I looked at him intently without saying anything. Sometimes I do this for fun, just to torture him. He wanted to tell me so badly I knew I didn't really have to ask.

"I like her," he went on. "She talks like a real person. Natural, no attitude. You know what I mean?"

"You mean she's bland?"

"No, Tim, I don't mean she's bland. I mean like when she's talking, she's actually talking *to me*. She's not all trying to make me think she's special."

"Maybe she's not special."

"Oh you are so wrong, Tim." But suddenly he didn't look so elated. "We went out last night, and it was cool and all. She's really fun. More important, I thought she liked me. But – we didn't touch. I mean, nothing. Not a handshake. Just a very nice goodbye, and she gets out of the car and walks away to her house. So I was having this great time for a while and, believe me, getting all excited, but I end up feeling more frustrated than ever. What kind of bullshit date is that?"

"If only Shakespeare were here to tell this tragic story."

"You read all those books, but you don't really know anything, Tim. That's your problem."

The door at the top of the stairs opened again and Ben came down halfway. Ben was built like a fireplug, and the steps creaked louder under his weight. Ben couldn't be more different from Jeremy, but they'd been friends for years. Jeremy needed you to like him and was pretty sure you did. Ben didn't seem to care whether you liked him or not.

"Tim, the phone's for you," he called. There was some annoyance in his voice. I was the only one in the house who didn't have a cell phone, and so almost all of the landline calls were for me. Ben would never criticize me, though, for not having the money to pay for a cell phone. Besides being sort of our landlord, he worked at an auto parts store at the edge of the pizza district, making not much more than the minimum wage. He understood that if you can't afford something, you don't buy it.

The call was from Anita, my father's wife. Anita never openly demanded anything from me, but I knew her now. Behind that high-pitched, seemingly hesitant voice that asked for nothing, there was a will that wanted everything.

"Tim, do you think you could make it over to our house to see your father tomorrow?"

"I don't know."

"Your father is asking for you. He's, um, sick."

"Sick?" I said, as if I hadn't heard a word about it. A different woman, a different situation, a different tangle of anxieties, and now a half-truth if not an outright lie.

I started to tell Anita I had to work, but that would have been another half-truth. I was scheduled to work, but they seemed to like me at work and I was sure I'd have no trouble getting the morning off. I told Anita I'd come.

Ten o'clock the next morning, Anita met me at the door to their house. She had dark brown eyes, high, curved eyebrows, hair perfectly styled but thin, dark, dyed. She was almost as tall as me when she stood in her heels and looked me in the eyes. Her clothes seemed a little overdone, or maybe just over-clean, over-pressed, like she was wearing one of those old-fashioned hospital nurse uniforms – only with an elaborate brown blouse with ruffles and a high collar and lots of jewelry and makeup. Her eyes were red around the edges, but she had obviously pulled herself together for the occasion.

"He's asleep. But he can only sleep for a few minutes at a time. He'll be awake soon. I'm sorry to bother you like this. I know you had to take off work."

"It's not a bother." Another lie. "Wouldn't he really rather just stay asleep and skip talking with me?"

"You must be hungry. Why don't I fix you a sandwich?"

"What's wrong with him?"

"Maybe a glass of water?"

I walked behind her into the kitchen. Everything was stainless steel, dark glass and granite. I sat on a barstool-type thing. She put ice in the glass, then a sprig of mint, like she needed to find some way to fancy up even a glass of water. She sat down facing me, drumming her meticulously painted long fingernails lightly on a brown cork coaster. She really must love him. She knew before she married him that he was a mess in so many ways.

I looked down at the countertop. Something was missing. "You're not smoking?"

"I quit." She lifted her chin. "I quit, and I made your father quit, a month ago. Cold turkey."

"That would make anybody feel sick."

"Tim, he is really sick. I've been staying home, trying to take care of him."

I tried to figure out the look in her eyes. She didn't seem as depressed and beaten-down as you would expect in a woman ministering all day to a really sick husband. She had a look of determination on her face, but that was nothing new. She seemed committed to nursing my father, but her intensity was annoying because there was an undertone of joy in her manner, like she was an acolyte of many years' service who had finally been granted the privilege of wiping the Buddha's ass.

"You know, Anita, he's always had one sickness or another. A lot of it is psychosomatic. Sometimes it's alcohol withdrawal."

"Tim, he has cancer."

"Oh."

I wanted to punch her. She had already ruined almost half my life. Now she was announcing in her matter-of-fact voice that he was probably dying. The half of a father I had already gotten was all that I would ever get. Thanks a lot, Anita, I thought. It didn't seem fair that I still had to be civil to her. I stared at her until she jerked her head at a sound upstairs.

"He's awake," she whispered. When I said nothing, she added, as if it made any difference now, "He'll be so glad to see you, Tim."

My father was propped up in bed. His lion's mane of wavy grey hair was completely gone. He was now a bald, bulbous-headed gnome with scabs all over his face and scalp. He had lost a lot of weight. There was a small plastic pan by the bed, full of green vomit. I thought I would gag from the stench. But I resolved that if Anita wasn't going to crack, I wasn't going to hurl.

"It's the chemo," my father said in a new, high, weak voice. "I'm puking out my own insides, it feels like." Anita apologized, I don't know for what, and scurried between us and whisked that pan away.

With a sudden jerk, my father reached out, clawed at the back of my leg, and pulled me toward the bed. He used to put his hand softly on the back of my neck and steer me through crowds when I was eight or nine. His bony grip was desperate now. I had never seen anybody that sick before. I let that arm pull me toward the bed. The smell was awful, his teeth were protruding, his skin a greenish-grey.

"Oh God, this is miserable! I feel so hot."

He obviously had a fever. The red scabs on his face were almost glowing.

"I feel like I'm burning up, Timmy," he whined. "Feel my forehead."

He was always like this: look at me, look at my pain. He'd get me alone as a kid and open his mouth and say look at my cavity. There was always a lot of talk about me and what a fine boy I was, but at the center of everything were his cavities, his colitis, his hangovers, his nervous breakdowns.

He now forced me to touch him. The skin on his head was hot, and dry like paper. He had one hand taped down so he couldn't move it and dislodge the IV dripping into his arm. His other hand clawed at me, but it didn't hurt.

"You're really sick," I said.

"I tried to tell you before, in the bar, but I couldn't."

So, he had been crying about himself in the bar. About his diagnosis. I had thought he was crying about why he had left me and Mom – his uncontrollable passion for Anita, the freight train that destroyed his life, and all that. He didn't normally cry in public. He normally cried only in front of the people he'd done harm to. In the bar, he had never gotten to the point of telling me he was crying about something new, something real that wasn't his fault and that anybody would feel sorry about. He had talked mostly about the power of that freight train that destroyed his life.

He grimaced and tightened his lips, fighting against something that was trying to come up from his stomach. The small plastic pan was gone. I cupped my hands next to his face and waited. He squeezed his eyes shut with effort.

You never want to see your father like this. In a minute the crisis seemed to pass, and he opened his eyes. We looked at each other, smiling in mutual relief. He started breathing more easily. I started to pull away, but he suddenly retched and threw up green vomit that poured right through my bent fingers and all over the sheets and pillows and down to the carpet. The green stuff was pooling down there. I was reflexively still holding my palms together, uselessly. The pattern of my life repeated itself. I couldn't cure my father's sickness, or even contain the collateral damage.

Anita grabbed a towel and cleaned off my hands first. Then I took another and started cleaning up by working on the rug, as far away from my father as I could get. I made motions like I would help her clean up the mess on his face and neck too.

"Get out." He forced the words out in a high squeak. "Please. I don't want you to see me like this."

I stepped out of the room but watched from the doorway as Anita ministered to him. His body was so limp she pushed him around easily as she cleaned. His IV had become dislodged. She started to call the nurse from the home care service who had put the IV in, but he forced her to hang up. He instructed her how to do it herself. "I've seen it done so many times. Christ, I feel like a pin cushion." Then she gathered up the dirty bedclothes. I took them from her and asked her where the washing machine was. She met me coming back upstairs. She said he was already asleep.

"Tim," she said, her voice strangely deep, "this is bad, but it's not as bad as it looks. They took the cancer out. They think they got it all. This is just the side effects of the chemo, the doctor says. They warned us that the side effects would be minimal at first, then they would get worse, then they would peak."

"Yeah," my father's faint voice carried all the way down the stairs, "God, I hope this is the peak!"

She was wringing her hands as she let me out the door. She looked like she had put herself together for the occasion but the pieces weren't exactly fitting any more. Just at the end she looked up at me with some question in her large, red-rimmed eyes, but I had no idea what she wanted.

Jeremy had talked Ben and me into going out to Larry's, and we went there a few days later on Thursday night. Larry's was a little bar where they accepted our fake I.D. cards. Although we were underage, we went there so often we were almost regulars. Sitting in a bar was not the cool adult experience for me that it was for Jeremy or Ben. My father used to take me to bars when I was a little kid. He'd sit me down in a booth on the side and order me a soda. Of course, when you're a kid, it doesn't strike you as strange that your father is spending Saturday afternoon in a bar with you.

There was a long bar on one side and a lot of tables everywhere else, small wooden squares, each with thousands of scratches deep enough to feel with your fingertips. We sat in the back, way back next to the dart board, so as not to be obvious.

As the Pirates game blared out from the TV across the room, Ben and I allowed the dart game to hypnotize us through the smoky haze. Because of all the other noise, we had to just imagine the quiet *thunk* each dart made as it hit the target. We slowly gorged ourselves on thick sandwiches and mouthfuls of beer. Ben had a round face and small, dark eyes. He was not great looking or especially glib, and it was a rare occasion when he had a date. But he was smarter than most people thought at first. And you could always count on him.

If they hadn't been friends their whole lives, he and Jeremy probably wouldn't have been able to stand each other. Ben was not amused by Jeremy's constant attempts to draw attention to himself. Jeremy was always saying that hanging around with him was like having a rock for a friend. Jeremy's insults didn't seem to bother Ben at all. Ben would just flick his eyes to the side and go about his business. We all knew he wasn't really fat, just stocky. We also knew that there's something to be said for having a rock for a friend. Part of the stress between the two of them was Ben's job of keeping the house together financially – which pretty much meant trying to get Jeremy to pay his rent on time. Jeremy seemed to think that the rules would usually be stretched just for him. Jeremy talked so much that I sometimes preferred to let him go on while I sat and stared at the dartboard together with Ben.

"You know," Jeremy started again, "I'm halfway through college. And I still can't picture myself, you know, like sitting in an office, anesthetized, obedient, doing some kind of crap over and over again in order to make somebody else rich. I'm just …."

"How about to make yourself rich?" Ben interrupted.

Jeremy stared incredulously at Ben. "You know me, Ben. That's not me. I don't care about money. I don't need money."

"You don't need money as long as your father buys you a new car every time the last one breaks down."

"Used cars. He buys me used cars. And anyway, the only reason you're collecting rent from us is your father bought this house for you."

"The down payment," Ben shook his head disgustedly at Jeremy. "He gave me the down payment. I'm responsible for the mortgage payments. I use the rent to pay the mortgage payments. You don't even know how it works when you buy a house, do you?"

"I never watch the real estate channel."

Ben shook his head and took a gulp of his beer. Jeremy smiled his usual Jeremy smile, the smile of a guy who knows that, no matter what you are saying to him, it doesn't matter because he knows you really, really like him anyway. "I know, Ben. I gotta learn things like that. It's just ... I know I don't want to be a landlord or a real estate person, like you. I just don't know what I want to do."

Ben put his mug on the table. "I don't like collecting rent any more than you like paying it. It's not fun. It's a way of getting by. Somebody has to do it." He glared at Jeremy, but his aggravation soon melted away, as it always did.

"Yeah, well, I couldn't stand doing it."

"I guess you're lucky Ben can stand it," I said.

"Guys? Guys? It's me, Jeremy. You have met the enemy, and it is not me. Besides, we've got more important things to figure out, such as whether I will ever get Dory into bed." Jeremy's talk about his lack of a sex life was the background theme song of our lives. We hardly noticed it any more. But just when you tuned him out, Jeremy could shift gears. "See that table over there? The four guys and two girls?"

They were probably just a few years older than us. An after-work drinking crowd. Two guys in neckties, two others in jeans, one of each with a shaved head. One girl a little chubby and way too loud, the other blonde and cool, tossing back her hair. The conversation, which included imitations of somebody at work who they all thought was a dork, got louder and louder. They were laughing so much they were spilling their drinks.

"Here's my prediction," I said. "All within a year. The guy with the shaved head and the necktie will hit somebody driving home and get a DWI. The fat one will get fired when the boss gets tired of seeing her hung-over face lying flat on the desk every morning."

Before I could finish my scenario, Ben took it up. "The blonde who thinks she's so hot won't get fired because her boss will still dream of getting into her pants. But she'll get a divorce when her husband gets tired of waiting around every night for her to come home, stinking."

"Those will be the lucky ones," Jeremy chimed in. "The ones that nothing happens to – those are the ones I feel sorry for the most. They'll just slowly get fat and ugly and alcoholic and wrinkled and have red noses and tiny red veins that break out all over their faces."

"But when that happens," I said, "will we still be here watching them?"

Jeremy stopped talking and put his mug down on the table like he was never going to touch it again. Ben looked down at his hands. Usually I could count on these guys to save me from dwelling on my harshest predictions, but this one might have hit too close to home. I racked my brain for something to say. "Jeremy, what about that girl? What's her name – Dumby or something? You went out with her again, right? Did you get anywhere this time?"

"Oh." Jeremy jerked his head up. A little smile crept onto his face. He reached for his mug and took a sip before answering. "Her name is Dory. Oh, yes. Went out with her again last night. She is so nice. So ultra-cool. Not like a student at all, but so smart."

"When you're talking about this girl, you start talking *like* a girl yourself," Ben said.

"And you only answered half of the question anyway," I said. "The important part is, did you get anywhere with her?"

A blush reddened Jeremy's face. The longer we stared, the deeper it got. "I don't want to say," he mumbled into his beer. "Okay, maybe

I'm still not to first base yet."

"What? How many dates?"

"Two."

"Are you sure this super-skinny chick isn't really a guy?"

"Hey, guys! Come on. She's cool." Jeremy's face was still red, but he had an additional, funny look there. There was definitely a little smile he was trying really hard not to show. You wouldn't have even recognized it if you hadn't known him all his life.

Jeremy was trying to eat his burger and plead Dory's case at the same time. It didn't work, and he went into a coughing fit. By the time he got himself together, half the people in the bar were looking at him. He seemed to think that talking extra loud would keep it from happening again. "But let's talk about you, Tim. You know that hot girl with the hair that you chased all the way up to the Badger campus without getting any?"

"Yeah. Everybody in the bar doesn't have to hear about this, Jeremy."

"I thought you had a date with her for this weekend."

"So did I," I admitted. I spoke softly so only the two of them could hear. "I know what you're going to say. She's gone. The house is empty."

"That gorgeous honey puts her shortest running shorts on and twitches her ass in front of you for four miles in the baking sun and then stands you up and leaves town. What is wrong with you?"

"She didn't owe me anything," I shrugged, hoping to stop the conversation right there.

"You have no idea how to deal with girls, Tim. I think you might need our help. *Your abilities are too infant-like for doing much alone.*"

"Where the hell did you get that from?'

"*Coriolanus*, of course. You're not the only one who can read, Tim."

"Can you guys just leave me alone on this one?"

"But you owe us one. We just found out that she lived two doors away – and you never told us." Jeremy wasn't going to drop it.

"Okay. I admit it. I wanted her just for myself. Now you're making fun of me. I accept my humiliation as punishment for not telling you guys. I deserve to be made fun of. Ha ha. Can we just drop it now?"

"You might not want us to drop it completely. Because, Tim, unlike you, *we* talked to Eileen when she left."

"You talked with her? Really?"

"There is such a thing as text messaging, but since you are stuck five centuries back in *Coriolanus*, you don't have a cell phone."

"Did she come over and talk to you guys?"

"Yeah, she did. She came over to apologize to you. She had to leave right away to take some kind of make-up course before graduate school starts. She hopes you'll call her."

I couldn't stop myself from grinning. "Thanks, guys."

"And she left you this note." He threw a small yellow envelope on the table. When I reached for it though, he quickly pulled it back. "But in order to prevent any further concealment of critical Eileen-related information on your part, we are requiring that you open it right now. And read it out loud."

Chapter 4

"I don't see why you haven't called her," Ben said bluntly. "That note was pretty nice."

"It was. But it's hard for me to believe ...." I stopped. It was excruciating for me to discuss my love life in front of my mother, but Ben just sat there silently and forced me into it. "It's hard for me to believe that this 23-year-old woman actually wants to go out with me. I think she just wrote that to be polite."

I was at my mother's house, my old house, for a dinner on a Sunday, and I had invited Ben along. I hadn't asked Ben's opinion about whether I should drive to upstate New York to chase after Eileen. He just blurted it out at the dinner table. Though I wouldn't have minded hearing his opinion in a bar, his confronting me here really annoyed me.

"I like Ben," my mother had told me privately, in the kitchen. "He doesn't have an education, but you can tell he has a lot of common sense. I bet he'll do fine." She of course had not known then that Ben had opinions. And strong opinions, unless couched in the most delicate language, were not welcome in this house.

"You talk like you like everything about her," Ben persisted. My mother looked down at her plate like she also was embarrassed by any talk dealing in any way with romance. "What are you afraid of?"

"I'm not afraid." It came out a little too loud. And it was only half true. There was a reason we didn't talk about romance in this house. And we didn't talk about the reason either.

"You don't have to yell, Tim," my mother interjected, her own voice soft and tentative. Her head was slightly bowed, as if it were her duty as the hostess to let Ben speak, and we should just endure his questions. "But, Ben, there can be a lot of reasons why Tim might not want to pursue this particular relationship." She had no idea, of course, what relationship we were talking about. The important thing to her was to defend me – without offending Ben.

My mother was like this. Smoothing things over. Making everyone feel good in the process. Ben didn't press his point. My nervousness about seeing Eileen was based on common sense after all. She was obviously out of my league. And she was really nice too. And that would just make things worse in the end. Why torture myself?

My mother loved to chat up any new person who came to her house. Soft-spoken and gracious, she allowed them to believe they were interesting, the things they were doing (or even thinking of doing) fascinating. She talked about books, current events, politics. You could tell she had strong opinions, but she would never explicitly say what they were. Nothing could ever be said in her house that might possibly offend anyone. You could talk to her for an hour – or a lifetime – and still not have a clear picture of what she really liked, what she really regretted, what she really feared.

After dinner we sat in her living room with its beautiful dark cherry floors, Persian carpets, French Provincial furniture. The late afternoon sun shone brightly through the wide windows. What the hell were Ben and my mother talking about now? Did she really care about the real estate course he was taking? About his opinions of the proposed zoning changes around the pizza district? She made you believe there were many paths you could follow to make the world a better place, and you would find one if you tried. There was always an aura of care and high expectations generated by the woman behind the curtain. She was bursting with enthusiasm for everyone besides herself.

I lost track of the conversation. I stared at the August afternoon sunlight refracted through the crystal decanter onto the marble-topped table and across the wooden floors, listened to my mother sympathize and connect with Ben as if she had no problems of her own, smelled the fabric of the old wool rug warmed by the sun. Nothing had changed in ten years.

After Ben left, she made an extra cup of coffee for the two of us. Suddenly she put down her spoon. "Oh, Tim, there's a box here. Anita had it sent over. It's definitely for you – I think from your father."

"Yeah. It's a birthday present. I don't want it."

"What is it?"

"I don't know, but whatever it is, I don't want it. I don't want to have anything to do with him."

She looked down at her cup as she stirred her coffee for a long time. "You never go see him?"

"Actually, I saw him a couple of weeks ago. He has cancer."

She folded her hands in her lap, which was about as close to an angry gesture as she could manage. "You didn't tell me?"

"This isn't your problem, Mom. You shouldn't have to worry about it."

She took a long breath in very slowly, like she was figuring out how she felt. No. She was figuring out which way she *should* feel that would be best for me. "He's still your father."

"I told you, I did go see him." I knew I was taking credit for doing something I would never have done if his secretary and Anita hadn't practically forced me to go. "The doctors took the cancer out, but now he's on chemotherapy."

"Well, how is he doing?"

"It was a week ago when I saw him. He was really in bad shape, mostly from the chemotherapy. Now they say he's already a lot better. But that was Anita talking, and you can't go by that. She can't see straight where he's concerned." Why was I going on about Anita? "Anyway," I went on, "you don't have to care. Mom, you're totally entitled to put him out of your mind. You should."

"I can't think of him like a total stranger, Tim."

"You're divorced, Mom. For years he was all over your back, then after he left he strung you along when he had no intention of coming back. Now you want me to pretend nothing bad ever happened between us and him. I won't do it. Can't something in this house be real?"

When my father left, it wasn't exactly a clean break. He moved into an apartment of his own. He wouldn't call our house, but he picked me up after school a couple of times. There was hardly anything in his apartment. He didn't have anything to drink there except water and beer. Then he'd meet me instead at odd times at a burger or a pizza place. My mother would ask me what he said. He said he was getting his head clear, that he'd be back by the time of my eleventh birthday. Then my twelfth. I believed him, and I think my mother did too. I believed him until he took me to Anita's house for dinner. He said he wasn't living there, but even I could figure out he was lying. After he had taken me there a couple of times – to soften me up, I guess – he said he was now living there, but I shouldn't tell my mother because he missed me so much and telling her would mess up his chances of coming back one day.

I didn't tell my mother. I kept on letting her believe he was coming back. But once when she asked about him when I was almost twelve, it hit a nerve in me that had never been hit before. I couldn't just say the usual two words, "He's fine." All of a sudden I couldn't stand the suffocation in the little cocoon of denial we lived in. "He moved in with Anita. He's been living there for six months. He's not ever coming back." Her face crumpled up and she walked out of the room, and things were never exactly the same between us after that. That was when I first realized there could be such a harsh penalty for speaking the plain truth to a woman.

To go see Eileen, I would have to cut out on my job again. The people at my job had just let it go when I took off that one day without prior notice to see my father. It turned out that word of my father's illness had spread through the local legal grapevine, and our company, being a law firm, was a big branch of that vine. But I was the only courier at the firm who normally would do the downtown route, and so they asked me not to skip out again.

My father had gotten me the job. When there were no courier runs to be made, I photocopied, put together folders, whatever. They seemed ridiculously grateful just to have somebody who could show up every day, deliver a document to the correct address, and put "Attachment A" on the document that was Attachment A and "Attachment B" on the document that was Attachment B without getting the two of them mixed up. After I delivered five packages to different destinations in two hours one sweltering July afternoon, they even gave me a raise without my asking. I arrived back at the office multiple times a day in my shorts, T-shirt and backpack, usually covered with sweat from my urgent bike ride cutting through traffic to deliver a document that (always) had not been prepared until the last minute. I clearly didn't fit in with the formally dressed lawyers and secretaries. I didn't want to be one of them – or to have to wear those clothes – but everyone there had always been kind to me. When you're good at schoolwork, you might get nice written comments on the edges of your papers and good marks at the end of the term; but you don't get what you get at work, which is people actually smiling just to see your face.

I called Eileen one night, but she told me she was too busy for me to come up that weekend. I would have made a point of telling Ben "I told you so," but I was too humiliated by her rejection to mention it. I resolved not to call her again, certain that her note had been just a polite way of saying goodbye. So, I was really surprised when she called one Wednesday in early September and asked me to come up the next day and go for a run. "If you can make it then," she said. "It's unbelievably hot up here now, but it's the only free afternoon I have."

For a second time I broke the unwritten code at work, the one that said that Tim was paid extra because he was always on time, was always the fastest, was never absent or late. When I called them up and said I wouldn't be in, I couldn't keep my voice from coming out flat and dead from guilt. My boss, Robert, kept asking what was wrong. This made me feel even worse, and I had to get off the line. I needed that job. Halfway up to State my little Nissan started losing power on the hills, but all I could do was press the gas pedal down harder. I kept wondering if Eileen and I were going on a date or not.

She opened the door to her dorm room wearing a grey T-shirt, thin jacket and silky green running shorts. I had forgotten how gorgeous she was, forgotten those smooth muscles under the perfect skin of those legs. I shouldn't have gone up there without a firm commitment that this was a date. I had been pretending that just seeing her in person, talking to her, would calm me down; but the opposite was happening. Sometimes I come up with theories about women that are just dead wrong.

We ran on the country roads near her college town. It was hot, the air thick with humidity. The university was on top of a huge, broad hill that sloped down a long, leafy, mile-long drop to the town. Big old wooden houses of all kinds lined one side of the road that went down that hill. The other side was still a forest. On the houses side of the road, students came in and out of doors, climbed in and out of cars, sat on porches drinking, reading, talking.

We started down that hill, then turned onto a bridge that crossed a deep ravine and then ran up an even bigger hill that towered over both the college and the town. The road stretched up through a few residential blocks, then through patches of woods, then orchards and farms with scattered country houses and barns. I pulled ahead of her as we climbed above the town. As we pushed higher past the wooded area, the canopy of foliage overhead separated and then disappeared, and we ran under a clear blue sky scattered with puffs of white clouds.

I fell behind on purpose, just so I could watch her legs and her long runner's ponytail. Further up the hill, the sky spread out wider on both sides, the setting sun turned the edges of the clouds pink. I was used to running this far, but the steep hill was making my lungs burn. There was a huge fallen tree trunk in an open field near the top of the hill, its silvery wood bleached and bare and smooth. She pointed towards it, I gasped a yes, and we stumbled over towards it.

The tree was too hot to sit on. She stood, feet apart, put her hands against it, then walked her hands down, bending her back, then her knees, working her way down until her hands were on the grass. Then she lay down in the grass. Her shirt was soaked, her face red, her chest heaving, her shorts riding up. I turned away to look at the sky, looked back at her. She sat up and leaned back against the tree, her legs folded against her chest, looking down toward the town below.

"So," she suddenly turned to me, dark eyebrows raised, "I see you didn't feel the need to run farther than me today, like you did that day we ran on the community college track."

"You remembered that? Oh, of course, every instant of that momentous day must be etched into your memory. It must be dull up here by comparison."

She grinned. "I admit it – nobody up here has backed me into a hot kitchen table yet. But seriously, I didn't mean to leave town so fast. I had to. Anything exciting happening in the pizza district?"

"Um. Jeremy found a girl he likes. And my mother's taken an interest in Ben – trying to encourage his interest in real estate. She needs some young guy to tell her his ambitions, since I haven't got any she can understand."

"You should come to school up here," she said.

"The pizza district isn't so bad."

"But there's so much more here. You like learning so much. I think you would really like it here."

Layers of clouds, first white, then gold, then red, were sliding over the mountains on the other side of town. Way down below, the little town was in shadow, and tiny little lights were already popping on. Her hair, normally so dark, was tinted orange in the sunset. She stared across the valley, her face flushed even more by the setting sun. Her dark eyes were squinting against it. I didn't understand how she could have such classic beauty and be so unique at the same time.

"About me coming up and going to school here? I've been kind of afraid of going into debt."

"Why don't you just take the money from your father for college? You said he offered to pay."

I told her about his cancer and his chemo and his recovery.

"I'm sorry. Maybe you should talk to him more now. And maybe take that box from him. I'm sure it would mean a lot to him."

As we watched the western sky, I stole a glance at her profile. I was definitely under her spell – but that didn't mean I bought all of her opinions.

"I was thinking about what I told you back in the pizza district," she started. "That I was so wild in college." She had my attention. "I think I was bragging a little, probably because you seemed so uptight. I wasn't really that bad. When I first started college, I was probably imitating the way my older brother acted in his first two years of college."

"How much older is he?"

"Six years. He's the one who took over, took me to school things, took me to friends' houses on weekends when my father dropped the parenting ball."

"Did you have a lot of boyfriends in college?"

She looked down at the town for a minute like she wasn't going to answer. "Okay. I had one for a while in freshman year, kind of left over from high school. A couple in sophomore year. There was a lot of drinking. I ended up thinking the party scene was not the place to find true love."

The sunset deepened towards purple. The clouds bunched together and now formed violet mountains that rose up at the horizon and dwarfed the hills surrounding the town. More lights came on, pinpoint by pinpoint, in the little town below.

"I risked losing my job by coming up here today."

"I have 200 quizzes to correct by tomorrow."

We jogged down the hill to the town, the descent easier on our lungs but very tough on our ankles and knees. By the time we reached the main street, people were abandoning the sidewalk chairs and tables and retreating into the pubs. There were a lot of people walking around, almost all of them close to my age. The town seemed to be missing two whole classes of people you saw in my hometown: the old, worn out, beaten-down semi-alcoholics parked on the same bar stool or restaurant seat for the last ten years; and the frenetic commuters on their way home, sprint-shopping for take-out while double parked with half their families in the car. In this town, young people were everywhere, on the street, in the bars, the restaurants, the electronic stores, the bookstores, the vegan food stores, the used clothing stores, the ratty old vinyl record stores, the trendy clothing stores – even in jewelry stores. We spent half an hour in a non-profit store that sold only household objects and beautiful artwork bought directly from craftsmen in Central America. We both said we wished we needed something they were selling.

"This sure beats the pizza district," I had to admit.

We sat down at a wobbly table in a combination bar and restaurant. At this time of day it was more bar than restaurant, with people, mostly students, standing two deep at the bar and encroaching on the table area. She ordered a beer and took a sip. My fake ID was good enough for Larry's in the pizza district, but it didn't pass muster in this place, so I was drinking soda.

"I've never gotten away from my town, away from my old friends," I said. She smiled and reached out and touched me on the arm. The tables were now filling up too.

"You can see from this bar that going away to college itself is no big deal," she said, looking around. "Just normal stuff in a different place."

"Did you have a serious boyfriend?" I persisted. "I mean in your last two years."

She stared down at the table, holding her beer mug tightly, then held my eyes with hers. "Okay. In my junior year, there was this professor. He's the one who first got me interested in psychology. He helped me make sense of my life. He took me seriously, which was a really big deal for me at that point."

"What happened?"

She hesitated, broke eye contact as she spoke. "I knew he was married. I still couldn't think about anything but him. I thought it was just me, going crazy on my own. Then one day in his office we both sat there for a long time, kind of bewildered, and then he said he loved me. He said it was a good thing and we could help each other, as long as we never touched."

"That doesn't sound so bad."

"I know I was a better person for a while. I got better grades in everything. I had more patience with my mother. I became good friends with my roommate at the time, Miriam. She's in California now, but she's still my best friend."

"A platonic relationship. I could never do that. But it sounds like it worked for you."

She sighed. "We used that word a lot. We didn't touch, not even to shake hands. Then late one Friday afternoon in his office, when I was going out toward the door, he put his hand on my shoulder. That's all it took. My whole body went weak and … honestly, Tim, it was only that one time."

"You got hurt bad?"

"As I walked back to my room that night I could feel thrills so deep inside it seemed like they were infiltrating into my soul. But the more I thought about what I had done, the more it changed to a queasy feeling. I felt like I had turned into something awful."

I started to reach across the table to hold her hand but chickened out.

"I knew I needed to call my mother," she went on, "but I was too ashamed. I sat staring at the phone for an hour. Then it rang. It was my mother. She was so upset already she didn't notice how bad off I was. 'We just found out,' she said, 'Brittany has been running around on your brother for over two years. Mike is devastated.' I said 'okay, okay,' but I couldn't really talk to her. I didn't feel like I had the right to tell her right then. I never told her. I've never told this to anybody else, except Miriam."

"You were his student. You were the victim. You were just a kid."

"I was twenty. Your age now. I get it – I'm not the only person in the world who ever made a mistake. But I'm sorry I did." We stared at the boisterous bar crowd for a few minutes. "But life sure goes on, doesn't it?" She smiled.

I knew she wanted to talk about something else besides the professor. "Did your brother take it hard, with his wife cheating on him, I mean?"

"You might say that. He joined the army the next day. It wasn't one of those 911 patriotic things. It was like how people used to join the French Foreign Legion – he thought it was the only way he could get Brittany out of his mind."

"Are you close to him?"

"We e-mail each other all the time." She didn't say anything more about her brother, or the professor, and after a minute she turned to me. "What's the deal with your father? I'm not that close to my father either, but I'm glad he hasn't forgotten me."

I took a sip of my drink, feeling so juvenile to be the only one in the bar drinking soda. "My father and I used to be really close. Now he wants to get close – not to me, but to the ten-year-old I used to be. He still even calls me 'Timmy.' It makes me cringe every time I hear it."

"Ugh. Can't you just tell him to stop?"

"I do. He can only remember for a minute or two. I wish he'd stop trying to send me that box."

"Oh well. We're both on our own now. It's a beautiful day. Let's play some game other than 'parents suck.'" She wasn't the kind of person to go down in the dumps and stay there.

She smiled, then looked over my shoulder around the room, her tongue playing around inside her cheek. Some guy a few tables down yelled out as he hit his head on the hanging light, sending wavering white halos around the walls. She caught the eye of the young, clean-cut bartender, and he immediately brought her another beer. This brought a chorus of "oh, my, aren't we special" talk from the crowd of mostly guys. She dove her lips into the foam, smiled at herself, wiped her mouth. There was something natural and girlish about her, and you could see it fighting against the sophisticated professional she was trying to become.

When I returned a few minutes later from the men's room, she was sitting a little back from the table, her mug hand clenched near her chest, watching as a big guy holding a beer stein in one hand leaned over and mopped something off our table with the other. She looked at him intently and did not seem amused.

"Oops! Got a little foam on your shirt there too," he boomed. His powerful baritone voice was freed by alcohol from the normal indoor restraints. "Need me to wipe that off for you?"

When he saw me approaching he jerked back, spilling even more beer on our table. I wasn't afraid to fight anyone, but I believed that, generally, the best thing to do was to walk away. Not if your date's being harassed, of course. Was she my date? And she didn't seem the least bit intimidated by this guy. I stood silently across the table from him, my arms crossed, the only one of us embarrassed.

"Oh, you're with a date," he boomed. "Sorry." But he couldn't let it go at that. "When I saw that soda sitting there, I thought you must be out having dinner with your grandmother." He nudged his buddy who was now standing next to him.

She stared at him. "He can't drink," she said. "It's a condition of his parole."

His buddy spoke in his ear and tugged at his arm.

"My bad. We didn't know she was with you." He started to move away, but the crowd was so dense it pushed him against our table, and he spilled more beer.

"No big deal," she said. "But would you mind cleaning that up too?"

"Oh. Gladly, Ma'am."

"Come on!" she said. "*Ma'am*? How old are you?"

Kyle and his friend Billy were both 22. In fact, it was Kyle's birthday. "Happy birthday," she said.

They looked uncomfortable, but then she started to draw them out. Kyle and Billy were both seniors, both communication majors. They were skipping class to celebrate Kyle's birthday. She asked them if they had girlfriends, and they both admitted they didn't – and neither had had a date for weeks. She asked them what they were going to do when they graduated and they just looked at each other and laughed, toasting each other yet again.

"So, what are you," Kyle asked Eileen, who was the subject most immediately on his mind, "some kind of parole officer or something?"

"A graduate student in psychology."

"Whoa! Billy, watch out! She's going to analyze our relationship with our mothers."

"Speak for yourself. I deny having a relationship with my mother."

Eileen egged them on like she was their combination den mother-drinking buddy. They kept performing their lost boys act for us. They had a few more beers before I admitted I wasn't on parole. That meant they could kid me too. Which they did. At the end, we promised each other we'd meet there again some night, though nobody took down last names or phone contacts.

Outside again, the sky was dark and tumultuous, without stars. The scene was lit only artificially, mostly by the bar lights. The street was teeming with moving shadows. The sidewalk was tricky, changing surfaces every few steps. The way was filled with other travelers and obstructed by chairs and tables and awnings and other useful objects.

"You were amazing in there. You had those guys eating out of your hand," I said.

"I grew up with a big brother. I can handle guys like that."

As we turned the corner and slowed, Eileen answered the question about our relationship that I had been afraid to ask by suddenly grabbing my hand. I held it strongly in mine as we walked straight ahead, hoping it was not just the rush she got from flirting with three guys all afternoon. I had no idea whether you were supposed to turn and kiss a 23-year-old woman who does that to you. So I went with the default of just holding on, walking straight ahead, pretending there wasn't a heat storm rising in my blood.

From town, we had to walk up to the bridge across the ravine to get back to the college. Welcome gusts of cooler air swept through the streets behind us. We reached the bridge over the ravine. We could hear the sound of the wind above picking up, and the air was suddenly fifteen degrees cooler. There were few people left out on foot, and all of them were scurrying along to get out of the way of the approaching storm. Just then, the wind, which had been mostly just blowing the clouds around in the sky, swooped down low and spattered us with cold raindrops. By the time we got to the other side of the bridge the wind was pelting us sideways with big, fat, cold, separate drops of rain. We didn't have the option of taking our time.

"God! It's going to pour." She unhooked our hands and led the way, turning the corner and running up the hill toward the college. The road was dark, rising in a narrow corridor, one side a high wall of trees hissing in the wind. Sheets of rain lashed at us with sudden cold shocks, the water penetrating immediately through our thin clothes. Stroboscopic flashes of silent lightning lit up the way. The road leveled off a little, but the rain came down harder, slanting right into our faces. I was blindly following her footsteps as she splashed through sheets of water that were sliding down the road. Jagged lightning started crackling in the distance as we reached the very edge of the campus. We sprinted up the mall and through a shallow pool forming on the lawn between two massive buildings just as a sharp clap of thunder echoed between their walls. She pulled open a huge white wooden door.

"This isn't your dorm."

"Engineering Building. We can cut through."

We sloshed down one corridor, ran up a flight of stairs, pushed through a few swinging doors. We dashed out the back door of the Engineering Building and splashed through another flooded walkway to her dorm. I followed her to a side door to the dorm, but we couldn't jerk it open because it was locked.

"Come on!" she screamed, bolting down the footpath and around the corner of the building.

"What's the rush? We can't get any wetter."

"Lightning."

We went in the front entrance to the dorm, ran up the stairs to the fourth floor, and dripped into her room, breathing hard. She started scrambling through her dresser and her closet. "I've got nothing that will fit you. Oh wait. Here." She handed me her giant pink T-shirt. "I'm going to take a shower down the hall," she said through chattering teeth. "You can come. It's a girls' shower, but I can cover for you."

"That's okay. The T-shirt's fine. I'll just put it on here. Go take a warm shower."

She gave me a towel, then disappeared down the hall. I dropped my running clothes in a pile and dried myself off quickly and put on the giant T-shirt. The window wasn't all the way closed. A dense curtain of rain pounded the glass and spit into the room through the crack. Then the rain started coming straight down and I opened the window all the way and knelt down to watch the lightning flashes illuminate the campus.

"What are you doing?" She was back in the room and had come up next to me.

"Just watching the storm. Have you ever felt anything this powerful?"

She knelt down with her hands on the window sill. She was wearing a soft white robe with her hair wrapped up in a yellow towel that she wore like a turban. The outfit made her dark eyes even more dramatic. Staccato flashes of lightning illuminated her features, impressed them on my retina, on my brain. I normally don't let women into my life, but I knew I'd never again have a chance to be with someone that beautiful.

She leaned close but didn't touch, probably because I'd been too timid when she took my hand earlier in the town. When she started at a close clap of thunder I put my arm around her, and she turned and pressed her lips softly to mine. I pulled the turban off. Her hair was half-dry and astonishingly full, and a bit wild. With the power of the thunder at my back I pushed open the front of her robe and touched her. I could hear her suck in air. She leaned into me.

"Let's close the window and get into bed," she said then.

"I can't let go of you." I stood and helped her up. We stumbled backwards together. Just then, lightning exploded close to the building. The impact tore through trees, pushed into the room and knocked her little desk lamp over. The bulb gave out one last super-bright flash of light before it died. She pushed away from me to try to pick it up, and then the other lamp blew over but stayed lit. It rolled on the floor, sending arcs of light back and forth across the ceiling. She was crawling around, holding her robe closed with one hand while trying to retrieve both lamps in the wavering light. The wind was coming in the window now and whipping her hair across her face.

I chased after her on the floor. "Stop it. Please," I cried through the sound of the wind. She answered my kiss, let me touch her, let me lay her down on her open robe on the floor. She asked me to close the window and I did, but I left it open a crack. It was only the storm that was giving me the nerve to take her. She seemed overpowered by the moment too. She was stroking me, grabbing my hair as I explored with my fingers and my tongue. Her crystal belly button stud was sparking in unison with the lightning outside. The wind was shrieking through the crack in the window, backed now by a continuous low roll of thunder. She stared at me, her mouth open, nodding yes as I moved on top of her, and then she opened her legs. I was shuddering with anticipation, but the joy struck too soon – way before I was in her, and I came half on her and half on her robe.

I was grateful for the racket the storm was making outside. She looked at me, still breathing heavily as I moved off of her. Her legs were twisted together and she was squirming a little. She put my hand on her belly. I tried to slide my hand further down, but she resisted, twisting away. She trapped my hand in hers, sliding it back and forth across her belly.

"Will you get in bed with me? And close the window all the way?" she said.

I did as commanded. I climbed into bed with her, smoothed down her hair over and over, tried to think of something to say besides how beautiful she was. She was not taking out her frustration on me, nor was she going ahead without me. The glaze of passion in her eyes was fading, and I wondered if we would end up being just friends, after all. But that just didn't seem right. I started kissing her again. She ran her hand up and down my back, over my chest, like she still wanted me. "Give me your hand," she said.

She began sucking on my finger, in and out, in and out. She worked it sweetly while looking in my eyes. Soon she got me going again, as much from the fact that she still wanted me as from what she was doing. I didn't have a free hand to touch her and so I told her how much I had thought about her since she left. She took her time, sucked my other fingers, slowly deflowering each one with her lips until she could see the need in my eyes.

"This time," she said, "do you think you could use a condom?"

"I'm sorry," I said. "I was carried away before. Overpowered. I …."

"Can we stop talking?"

She wrapped her legs around one of mine, holding me against her down there. Meanwhile, she teased me with the tip of her tongue.

"Now?" she asked, and I did as commanded. It was what she wanted, normal. She cried out a little at each touch inside. I didn't have quite the edge as before, but now I could slow down and feel her response, and that was the most exciting thing I had ever felt.

Afterward we lay together, exhausted, cuddling under the warm sheets. Her eyes were closing.

"This was a great day," I said.

She roused herself and touched my face. "Who says it's over? Aren't you going to spend the night?"

I felt compelled to hide the fact that spending the night would also be one of the biggest thrills of my life. I needed to get back to school and work, but I wanted to stay. Every idea she'd had was better than mine – the bed instead of the floor, the window closed against the storm, the condom. Now, staying the night. She was either really sure of herself or really sleepy, because she fell asleep before I even answered. Of course I was going to stay. I was already possessed by her.

I woke in the middle of the night while the rain was still pouring down. The one fallen lamp was still lying in the corner, casting only the most indirect light. I smoothed her hair away from her face without waking her. I fell asleep and woke again, and this time the storm was gone. The sky was clear and the moon was out. I went to the window and saw broken branches everywhere on the ground. A lot were only halfway ripped off their trunks and were hanging quietly in the new stillness. A truck was shining its lights on a tree that had fallen across the road in the distance. There was no sound but the faintest whisper of cars on the freeway, and the faraway whistle of a freight train.

I woke up in the morning to see her coming back into the room from the hallway, wearing the giant pink shirt she had given me the night before. She had washed and towel-dried her hair, and she was trying to hold it out of her eyes and gather it together with her hands.

"You look beautiful."

"Right. Um, would you mind turning around so I can put something on?"

"Really? After last night?"

"Please?" A moment later she was dressed in jeans and a T-shirt and was getting ready to blow-dry her hair. "I know what you're thinking," she said. "But I only have two hours to dry my hair, get dressed and correct those 200 quizzes."

"A hundred quizzes each. I'll do half."

"How could you possibly …?"

"It's on Chapters 1 and 2, right? I read the first eight chapters of the Psych 101 book the night before last."

"Why would you do that?"

"Because you were teaching it."

It was just a little introductory quiz. The main point of it was to see if the students had even opened the book. It was very simple and easy to correct. When we finished, she came over behind my chair, put her chin on my shoulder and put her arms around me from behind.

"Mmm. Last night was really, really great," she said.

"We do have fifteen minutes right now."

"We do."

~ *Chapter 5* ~

Five hours later I was back at the law firm. A lot of the secretaries and administrators were getting ready to leave, but most of the lawyers were still working at their desks. I realized as I walked in at 4:20 that there would be no documents to be delivered by courier. If something had to go by courier, it had to get to its destination by 4:30 that same day, and so it had to be put in the hands of the courier by 4:00 at the latest. I started going around to the lawyers' offices, asking if they needed any copying or collating or mailing to be done, when Robert interrupted me.

"Tim, you're not supposed to be working here."

I stopped. "You mean, *today*, right?"

"What? When you called in, you said you were taking off yesterday and today, right?"

No. Robert was confused. Because of his generous and trusting nature, Robert had decided, when I hadn't actually come in at my normal arrival time of 1:00 that day, that I must have told him I'd be out for two days.

"I got back a little early from my errands," I said, avoiding answering his question. "I thought I'd just come in and check on things."

"We're fine, Tim. Go home. We'll pay you for an hour for showing up."

"You don't have to do that."

He smiled at me. "Take it."

I had also missed a whole day of school. This wouldn't matter if you weren't obsessed with getting all *A*s, including in Calculus II. I had gotten an *A* in Calculus I, but always had the feeling I was just skimming over the surface. Now that I was in Calculus II and trying to figure out partial functions and techniques of integration, I knew I was lost. I hoped if I did an extra hour a day I could catch up. I was going to do that first extra hour right after I got home from talking to Robert at the law firm, but Ben jumped up from the sofa as soon as I opened the front door.

The first floor of our house consists of one, open, L-shaped room. The front room was on the short side of the L and had a door that opened directly onto the front porch. Ben and Jeremy spent a lot of time in there on the sofa across from the giant flat screen TV. The long side of the L ran down the side of the house. The kitchen was in the back of that part. Ben's hours had been cut back, and he was home an hour earlier than usual watching television when I came in. "Want to get something to eat?" He jumped up as soon as I walked in, punching his fist loosely into the palm of his hand.

"Pizza?"

"Sick of pizza. Something else," he said. "Subs! I'll call them in."

"Sure." There was nothing unusual about this, except that Ben seemed anxious to talk.

"You know, the walls in this place are plaster, pretty thick," he started. We had come back from the sub shop and were sitting on the sofa unwrapping our subs. "But some of the doors upstairs don't even close all the way."

"What?"

"Jeremy. He got that girl, Dory, to come home with him last night."

"Wow. Is she nice?"

"Really nice. She's into real estate. She told me a little about it. But the thing is, my room's right next to Jeremy's. She spent the night. You can hear everything through those cracks. And Tim, she's a real screamer."

We ate our subs silently. Poor Ben. At the same time, I was mostly thinking about whether you would describe Eileen as a screamer.

Not only did Dory sleep with Jeremy, but it looked like she was moving in with him. With us. I figured this when I came down into the kitchen on a Tuesday before school. She was sitting on a stool at the kitchen table, where she had cleared off a little place for herself. She was wearing jeans and a blue-green T-shirt so tight and thin you could see the outlines of her nipples. Dory was tall and skinny, with blonde hair that hung down her back in two long plaits. She would have looked like one of those Norwegian ice queens except for her round face and friendly smile.

"Hey."

"Hey," she answered. "Since you guys don't know what a refrigerator is for, I went out and bought some milk and some eggs and some cereal."

"We know what a refrigerator is for." I opened the door. "To keep stuff cold. Like this bottle of tequila. Feel it. It's plenty cold."

"Jeremy said you were kind of nuts." Sitting up straight on the stool, folding her arms, she raised one eyebrow and looked at me. Her tight shirt revealed that she didn't have that much in the way of a chest. Then she relaxed, put her hands against the wall behind her, and rocked back on the stool like she was an old pal or a little sister who didn't care what kind of impression she was making.

"So what do you do, Dory? Do you, like, have a job or something?" I know it's impolite to ask someone you just met what their job is, or if they're going to school. You're not supposed to measure people like that. Better to ask what drugs they are into. But now even that is frowned upon as an opening line. Anyway, I already knew what her job was.

"Oh, I'm in real estate. I mean, I'm not an agent or anything yet. I enter stuff on the computer, hammer in signs, sit in open houses and wait for the wives to drag in their husbands before I call in the actual agents. I'm going to get Jeremy up. This is my day off and he hasn't entertained me at all yet!"

The next day I saw Jeremy alone in the morning darkness just before I left for my run.

"Is she moving in?"

"I think so. I'm pretty sure. She could always go back to her apartment, but," he smiled, "I don't think she will. She likes me."

"I hate to tell you this, Jeremy, but she doesn't approve of the way we keep our refrigerator."

"No, no, you're wrong. She doesn't care. She thinks it's fun, the way we live."

"Jeremy, you always said you were looking for some weird, passionate but unemployable chick whose only goal in life was to compulsively fuck you silly."

"That's kinda what she is!" He grinned until he did look silly. "Except she has a job. And you'll really like her. She's a good girl."

Why not a smoother transition?

My father recovered to the point where he could make it to the bar. I walked right by his booth at first because I didn't recognize him.

"Timmy," he called out. I gritted my teeth. "Tim." I stopped.

He tapped me on the arm, "God, you're looking at me funny! Here." He reached up and pulled his thick mane of curly grey hair right off. "It's a wig! Anita bought it for me. Two thousand dollars. She said I deserved it." He flopped it back and forth in his hands like he wasn't sure whether he liked it or not. "My real hair's coming in too. Just a little fuzz, like baby hair. It's like I'm starting all over again. Here, feel it."

He grabbed my hand, pulled it onto his head.

"Go with the wig," I said.

"It probably has been hell living with me the last three months. Anita's been a saint. She couldn't have been kinder to me. I'm back to work, part-time, starting tomorrow."

"You look much better."

"I've got to tell you something about these doctors. Yesterday he comes in with a big smile and says, 'I have good news for you.' He just keeps smiling, and I say 'So I'm cured?' And then, Timmy, then that fucker says – I can't believe the fucker looks so happy when he says this – 'You have a 50 percent chance it hasn't spread.'"

"Fifty percent!" my father repeated. "I went through all that, four weeks of vomiting up my stomach lining, day and night, all the time, six weeks of radiation. All that I went through, and I have only a 50 percent chance!"

"What do you want, Dad?"

"I'm your father, and I'm telling you I have a 50 percent chance of dying."

"Everybody has a 100 percent chance of dying."

"I'm your father."

"Fifty percent my father, if you're counting by years."

But I knew you shouldn't count by years. One night when I was a kid, there were fifteen minutes at the kitchen table that will last to eternity in my mind. I had just cleaned my plate. The dinner table was utterly silent, as usual. I heard my father's silverware crash down hard on his plate. His face had suddenly changed. Hard lines of anger were drawn down from the corners of his mouth.

"What is it, David?" my mother asked.

"DO YOU CALL THIS FOOD?" My father's new voice was tight, pinched. He was squinting, his lips curled in disgust. "DO YOU CALL THIS DRIED-UP MESS COOKING?"

"David, it was ready an hour and a half ago. If you had come home …."

Up to that instant, I had thought of our flexible dinner schedule as a point of pride. Sometimes we ate at six, sometimes at seven, sometimes eight-thirty, depending on when he got home from his job. We weren't tied down to a rigid schedule like most of my friends.

"DON'T TELL ME WHEN TO COME HOME."

"I'm not telling you when to come home, David. I'm just …"

"… MAKING EXCUSES. YOU'RE FULL OF EXCUSES FOR EVERYTHING, AREN'T YOU?" Then he went into a long, whiny harangue, berating my mother for everything she did for the family – poor cooking, poor housekeeping, financial incompetence, obstinacy, not taking him seriously, and especially for making decisions behind his back when he wasn't there. But even when I was ten years old I knew that he was hardly ever there. It seemed like his harangue went on for days, though it probably wasn't more than fifteen minutes by the clock. She wasn't allowed to say a word. He got so carried away he knocked over his own beer glass. I jumped to clean it up. He looked at me.

"Thank you, Timmy. I'm glad there's somebody here who cares about this goddam mess of a house."

"No," he said now. "No. I'm 100 percent your father. My old life was destroyed. Hit by a freight train. I had no choice about that."

"That's your excuse, anyway."

He looked defeated. "You returned that box I sent you for your birthday. Did you do that on purpose?"

"Yeah," I admitted. "I don't want to pretend our relationship is normal." Just then I figured out why. "I'm afraid of being sucked down along with you."

But I wasn't afraid of talking to my father while I sat across from him at a table in a bar. The only thing better would be if one of us were in prison and we could talk to each other only through thick plate glass. Then he couldn't make me feel his hair, or pat me on the arm like I was still ten years old.

Eileen's best friend and old roommate Miriam was coming to visit her at State the next weekend. "Won't you come?" she pleaded on the phone. "You'd really like her, I think."

I explained I had to work all day Saturday to make up for the time I had missed.

"Sunday?"

I told her I had promised my father I'd eat dinner with him and Anita on Sunday, to celebrate his surviving chemotherapy.

"Oh, that's great! I think it's good that you're getting to know him again. Tell him I said congratulations too, if he remembers me. I'll tell Miriam you'll meet her next time. You know, she helped me a lot when I got mixed up with that professor."

"You must have had it pretty bad for that guy."

"I did, but she's the one who showed me that I wasn't just in love with him, that I really loved psychology itself. And I could do it without him. I owe her a lot."

"You're not still in love with him, are you?"

"No. Absolutely not. Listen. Miriam also did some snooping around campus. She found out he does it every year. Picks a new female psychology student. I was just one in the long line of his dupes."

If I couldn't see Eileen, at least there was no lack of entertainment in the pizza district. I enjoyed watching the sweet, simple ways of Dory, her long plaited hair, her round scrubbed face. She wanted Jeremy to move out with her and get an apartment together.

"I'm a real estate person. I get places for couples all the time," she confided to me one morning when we were both at the kitchen table. "Wouldn't you think he would want us to get our own place?"

"I think he's afraid of the money, that big fat rent bill coming every month for the rest of his life."

"Why are guys so afraid of that?"

"You gotta admit. It's kind of the beginning of the end. The bills pile up and pile up and pile up, and pretty soon all you're living for is to pay them off."

"But at least you'd be living a life. What's so great about this falling-down house with torn wallpaper and empty pizza boxes all over the floors and mold in the refrigerator?" She pulled a can of her special carrot juice out of the refrigerator and pulled off the foil tab so hard it made a loud, ridiculous "swoouuck" noise.

"What makes this place so great," I said, holding out my glass for a shot of her juice. "What makes this place so great is all the possibilities."

"I know what it really is." She sat stiff and straight, her elbows tight against her sides, her nipples, for once, not showing through her thin T-shirt. "He just doesn't like me that much. Getting an apartment is too much of a commitment."

"You're wrong. He likes you a lot."

"So what are Jeremy's possibilities? Am I keeping him from becoming a great scientist or astronaut or something?" She looked suddenly contrite. "I mean, I think he's great. He's going to college. I'll never be a college person. I just never liked school."

Besides working that Saturday, I started doing office work for the law firm for a couple of extra hours two mornings a week. I wanted to obliterate any memory in that office of me missing two days in a row. But working extra hours in the law office didn't help me in Calculus II. I put out a notice to see if anybody wanted to form a study group. Only two people were interested. One, a Korean guy named Kim, was an absolute whiz at calculus. I think what he really wanted was a chance to practice English with me and the other member of the group, also named Kim. The second Kim was a regular girl about my age, creamy skin, round face, nice eyes behind black-rimmed glasses, pretty enough to get your attention but not so ravishing that you forgot why you were there.

I had hated Calculus I, and so it had made no sense to sign up for Calculus II. Now I was stuck. If I dropped it, I would drop below eighteen credits, and if I didn't bear down harder I would get less than an *A*. But bearing down harder was something I was good at. For some reason he could not explain to me, Korean Kim was also taking a class in Shakespeare. He'd been in the country only three months. To help him in that subject I would have to first translate Shakespeare into modern English, then translate that into something he could understand. His English was almost as hard for me to understand as Shakespeare's. It was limited to about 300 words, spoken in a heavy Korean accent, and without any rhythm at all. He corrected all my calculus problems in the first few minutes of the very first study group. I told him to draw a red line at the point where I went wrong, and let me figure out the rest from there. All the lines were right near the beginning of the problem.

"Easy. I show. Easy."

"No. Do not show me. Show me only the right part and the wrong part. I want to do the problems myself."

"No. Calculus easy. I show," he insisted. "English hard."

"Calculus is hard. English is easy. I wouldn't have taken calculus had I known the teacher would have required knowledge of partial fractions."

He stared at me blankly. I realized I had proven his point. By the second meeting, the American Kim and I had figured out that calculus itself had its own language and there wasn't any point in trying to get Korean Kim to translate it into English. He did give us the final answers to every problem, and that helped a little.

I ran into Dory in the kitchen every once in a while. She had a regular full-time job that she had to be at by eight, while Jeremy slept until ten, two days a week. Jeremy admitted after a few weeks that he was wrong about her – Dory would never adapt to our lifestyle. Two weeks after moving in, Dory demanded that Jeremy clean the refrigerator out with bleach.

"What is it, Dory?" I asked her one morning. "You got a set idea somewhere in your brain? There's only one way the inside of a refrigerator is supposed to look?" I put both my hands on the table and leaned down over it to confront her.

"What good is it, Tim, if it's full of moldy old crap?"

"You're here voluntarily, but you don't like anything about this place. You take a sponge and clean off your own little spot on our table before you even sit down. You think we're all untouchable."

"I'm not afraid of you, Muscle Nerd." Her soft eyes belied the challenge in her voice. I had to drag my eyes up from where they had wandered toward the tight contours of her T-shirt.

I leaned down and licked a big X right through her clean spot on the table.

Yes, it bothered me, hearing her crying out in Jeremy's room all night as they eagerly exchanged bodily fluids, then seeing her in the morning cleaning off anything in the kitchen that I might have touched.

She put her bowl of granola down right at the center of the X. "I try not to bother you, Tim, really."

My schedule was complicated even more by problems with my car. The clutch was slipping and it was losing power to the point where you couldn't start off going up a hill. I asked Ben about getting the parts to fix it. He came down to my room one afternoon and told me he could get Nissan parts at a 40 percent discount. "But who's going to put the new clutch in?" he asked.

"Me, of course."

"You don't know anything about cars."

"I'm a fast learner."

Ben stood there, his wide body blocking the entire doorway. "No," he said, shaking his head. "No. You don't have time. Get some sense of proportion, man."

I stopped driving my car to work and started riding my bike there and back. To make up for that lost half hour, I got up earlier to do my weights. The light in our laundry and exercise room was harsh, but it was dead quiet there in the early morning except for the buzzing of the fluorescent lights. The concrete floor was bare but scoured clean in the ten-foot space where I did my squats and curls. You do each rep until you reach muscle failure, then repeat. The quicker you repeat, the more muscle fiber you build. The more muscle you build, the less vulnerable you will be.

My father's recovery pushed him safely behind the prison glass. Once I had done the Sunday dinner, I figured I could ignore Anita's calls again for a while. I wanted to go up to see Eileen the next weekend, but she told me on the phone she had a project that was due on Monday and she had to go to two faculty receptions over the weekend that were mandatory. We talked on the phone almost every night. She talked about Miriam, but mostly she asked me a lot about the new courses I was taking, my job at the law firm, and anybody new I had met. She was especially interested in American Kim. "Okay, I'm jealous," she admitted. "You're 300 miles away, you're smart, you're great looking, you're interested in everything. And definitely heterosexual. I don't want you to get distracted."

After that I tried to focus on other things besides women, though Eileen crept into my dreams a little. I could predict that I was going to get my *A* in Calculus II with the help of my friends, the two Kims. Jeremy was deliriously happy, and Ben seemed to be getting used to Dory. Except for her pickiness about food, Dory started to seem like just one of the guys. She even stopped disinfecting her place at the kitchen table.

Chapter 6

At seven one morning, when I arrived at the law firm for my early office duties, Robert rushed out of his office and handed me a slip of paper.

"Call your father's wife," he said. "She says it's urgent."

Anita said my father wasn't feeling well and they were taking him in for tests.

"Why?"

"He's having some kind of relapse, Tim. He feels really weak, but they say it might just be a little setback."

"I thought he was over the chemo problems."

"All they say is he's weak. I could have told them that."

"You never told me what kind of cancer it was anyway."

"I thought you would ask him."

I pictured him in his silly wig sitting with me in the bar just a few weeks before. A gift from Anita for surviving the cancer and chemo. Surviving the cancer and chemo and being given exactly a 50 percent chance of living seemed to have made him a little easier to talk to.

"I can see it every time," he had said in the bar. "Your face hardens and your eyes squint up whenever I mention Anita's name. But she's been good to me. Not that your mother wasn't always very kind too." He had said that last thing, I knew, just to mollify me; but it worked.

Of course, I had known Anita over the years, watched her laugh at every one of his jokes, endured her cajoling me to come over and visit him on holidays. And I knew she had lately been taking him to the doctor and bringing his computer and his work papers home to him when he was sick. And nagging me to come see him. I had always thought of her as nothing but a mindless dingbat, but I knew now how much work she put into babying him.

"Good women. Let's drink to the both of them." He had raised his glass with a sudden, guilty smile. Without really thinking, I went along with it. He had smiled broadly, finished his glass and set it down. "I'm not supposed to be drinking any alcohol."

Now Anita was telling me on the phone that he'd already been hospitalized again.

"Anita, I don't think they hospitalize people just because they're a little weak."

"I don't know, Tim. The doctors are being very vague about everything. He asked me to ask you to get an answer out of them."

A few days later, my mother left a message at my house for me to call her. "Why don't you come for dinner?" she said when she picked up. "I have something I want to talk to you about."

We hugged at the door.

"Oh, my. Tim, you're so strong," she said, as always. She almost stumbled on something in the hallway. "Oh, this box is still here. Why don't you take it?"

"I don't want it. I'll send it back. You know Dad's sick again, right?"

"No, I didn't." Her voice was thin.

"I didn't want you to be bothered. You shouldn't have to worry about him any more."

"Did the cancer come back?"

"They thought they got it all. He was pretty happy. But he's having some kind of complications. He's back in the hospital again."

"You didn't tell me right away?"

"Is that what I'm supposed to do now? Carry messages between Dad's new wife and his old one?"

"I loved him. I lived with him for twenty years."

"You shouldn't have to live through it now. He's Anita's problem now."

"Why are you so judgmental?"

"Why are you so not?"

"Tim, I'm asking you to do just one thing. Let me know what's going on with your father's cancer. And tell Anita that I will help her if she needs anything done."

It wasn't until we were finished dinner, and dessert, and coffee, and after-dinner drinks in the living room, that it struck me.

"Mom, you never said what you wanted to talk about."

She sat up tall and took a breath, brushing her skirt straight.

"What is it? You're not sick?"

"This is a little embarrassing, coming from someone my age. Tim, I've met someone."

"What?"

"I met him at a conference. Alan is a widower who has two grown children."

"Are you sure of his background, Mom? You are the kind of person it would be so easy to take advantage of."

"I am being careful, Tim. And I want you to know I would not do anything, ever, to jeopardize anything that is due to you from me."

"Stop it, Mom! Nothing is due from you to me. That's not what I mean at all. I just don't want you to be taken advantage of."

She stiffened as she brought her drink to her lips. She was still good-looking. The gentle and intelligent glow on her face made her look wise and kind, not old and weak.

"I've thought about this, Tim. I've decided he's worth the risk."

"Who is this guy? What's he like?"

"His name is Alan. He's a widower. I really enjoy talking to him. You know, living alone, you have a lot of time for crazy thoughts to run around in your head. It's good to have somebody to talk to. Anyway, he worked for a property developer for years, in human resources. Now he's a social worker. I think you would like him."

She lifted her eyes to mine. "You might be surprised. He's really, really different from your father."

I tried to call the doctor many times, between classes and when I was in the office at work. When I finally got him, I didn't get any better answer than Anita had gotten. I made it to the hospital once, but my father was completely out of it. He was asleep or unconscious, looking like a small figure sunken down into the white sheets. My mother really wanted me to meet her new boyfriend, but she said of course that it should wait until my father's situation was cleared up. Everything seemed like more of a rat race this semester. We were doing *Othello* in Shakespeare. It was such a well-known play there was not any hope of reading even one percent of all that had been written about it, much less becoming an expert as I had with *Coriolanus*.

For a third weekend in a row, Eileen and I couldn't get together. Then she sent me a card, in the mail. I left it unopened on the kitchen table where Ben had thrown it.

Dory picked up the envelope one morning. "Why don't you open it?"

I lowered my voice. "I'm afraid."

She whispered back. "Of what?"

"She's up there with 8,000 men. A lot of professors and graduate students. She's already finished college. Last week, there was some reason she couldn't go out. I'm just waiting for the axe to fall."

"How can you know if you don't read it?"

She had me there. But I still couldn't bear to read it. I slid it across the table.

"Here, Dory. You read it. Don't tell me what it says. Just give me a thumbs-up or thumbs-down."

"Oh, no. This is really personal."

I lit the one working gas burner on our stove. "You read it or I'm burning it up right now." I reached for the envelope.

She held it close to her chest. When I backed off, she carefully opened the envelope. "You have some kind of a problem, Tim."

And this was before she even read it!

She blushed as she read the card.

"Well, what's the gist of it?"

"She misses you. You should call her. Soon."

"Man, I can't believe it! I just can't believe it!" Jeremy had never raised his voice in anger before in our house.

"Dory's sleeping here, using our bathroom, eating our food." Ben's voice was very firm. "You gotta pay 30 percent extra rent for her. She has a job, anyway. She could pay it herself."

"She just sleeps in my room. And none of us even cooked food before she got here!"

"I didn't say she wasn't nice. But you gotta pay rent for her, that's all."

"I thought we were all friends. Man, you're like some kind of greedy capitalist or something. Ben, you got to think about what you're turning into."

"She can afford it. She's got a real job."

"She's saving up for a security deposit on a real place."

"This is a real place, Jeremy."

Dory was a much-needed breath of fresh air in our grungy old house. You had to work around her bathroom schedule a little, but it was worth it. Before she came, Jeremy's room smelled so bad it stunk up the hallway. She made him clean it up. And she was pretty nice to look at. But all of her other charms and powers were nothing compared to the real miracle she accomplished with Jeremy. She stopped him from whining.

But now he was whining about her paying rent.

“Ben’s right,” I said. “Dory’s using the house like everybody else.”

“Why are you taking his side?” Jeremy sat in a chair, head down, not really looking at me.

“It’s just real, man. She’s using the house. She’s cool, she’s very nice, she’s your dream girl, but she’s still gotta pay the rent. That’s real too.”

I would be sorry if Dory left. At first there had been too many mind-flashes of her stretched out on a mattress with that blonde hair unpinned and those long creamy legs going up and up and up. But I was getting used to her being there, the screaming at night in bed, the whole thing. The main thing was, it seemed like she was becoming my friend, and a different kind of friend than I’d ever had before. But all the other friends had to pay rent. She shouldn’t get a pass from paying rent just because Jeremy was pumping his joie de vivre into her every night.

“But she’s living in my room,” Jeremy whined.

“She uses the house. I agree with Ben. It’s two to one, Jeremy. You have to pay up.”

“This is no two-to-one shit,” Ben glared at me. “It’s my house.”

I ran into Dory again at breakfast again the next week. She was mixing oatmeal and honey and nuts and God knows what else in a big bowl. When she saw me she scooped up a lot of it into a smaller bowl and plunked it down in front of me.

“Looks kind of heavy.”

“Try it. Twenty grams of fiber. Omega oils. Protein.”

“So, Dory, do you really need to diet?”

She hesitated only a millisecond. “I’m too skinny, you mean.” She dipped into her spoonful of congealed glop.

“You’re thin, but a good thin.”

She just ignored my comment.

“It’s not a diet. It’s good for you. When I eat this for breakfast I don’t get the munchies at work.” I glanced down at my bowl. “Go ahead and try it," she said. I gulped a huge spoonful.

"Well?" she said.

"Um .... Yeah, it's, um .... Somebody might like it."

Jeremy came down the stairs quietly in bare feet and walked into the kitchen in just his underpants.

"Oh, gross," Dory mumbled.

"What's the problem? It's not like you haven't seen me naked all night."

"But this is breakfast. It's the start of the actual work day, and other people are here."

"Hi, Tim." Jeremy waved to me like we were casual acquaintances running into each other at somebody else's party. He glanced at the oatmeal glop, then grabbed some bread and put two slices in the toaster. He opened the refrigerator and leaned over real far to look at the bottom shelves, sticking his ass out at us way too far, and for way too long.

Dory ate a little bit more, looked at her sleek plastic watch and stood up to go. She pushed her chair in, stood there a second until she caught my eye, kicked him in the ass with one of her plastic platform sandals and ran out the front door.

"Ow." Jeremy still didn't pull his head out of the refrigerator until long after the front door had slammed. "She's kinda different from what I first expected."

"Do you still like her?"

"Oh. Oh, yeah. But, Tim, do you want to know what the funny thing is? The more I like her, the more she bugs me. You know what she's doing now? She's looking around for what she calls a 'real apartment.'"

"She's a real estate person. I guess that's what they do."

"Anyway, I asked her what was wrong with this place. She said it's fine for a bunch of guys but she wants air conditioning, clean carpets, and a pool."

The smell of burnt toast suddenly filled the room. Our toaster never pops up by itself. Jeremy pulled each piece out with his fingers, yelping each time he was burnt, and dropped the blackened pieces on the little table next to the toaster. He opened and then slammed the cabinet doors for a while until he proved to himself that there was no other bread. Then he laid out the two crispy black pieces on a plate and ground a pile of grape jelly into each with a knife.

"Different things are important to different people, Jeremy."

"I know. It's not crazy to want a better apartment. What bothers me is the reason that she wants it. The only reason she wants it is because all her girlfriends are getting apartments like that."

"She wants to civilize you. Did you hear that comment about your underwear?"

"Is this apartment just the beginning? Do we have to do everything her girlfriends do, buy everything they buy, forever? You know what I mean? Is there, like, a big, long list of mandatories, invisible to the naked eye, that I'm buying into?"

My father couldn't pick up the phone in his room, and Anita and I played phone tag for a few days.

"Jesus, Tim, if there's anybody who needs a cell phone, it's you," Jeremy pointed out. "Why don't you just go get one?"

"The clutch in my car is going up. I've been saving up $85 a week so I can get it fixed. A cell phone would wipe out half of what I've saved."

I skipped our calculus study session and drove over to Anita's house after school that day. She opened the door, squinching up her shoulders with the effort of trying not to hug me. She asked me if I needed anything to drink, or if she could fix me a snack. I didn't, but I also didn't want to hug her, so I said that would be great.

"You're dressed up," I said. "Did you just get back from the hospital?"

"Oh. No, no, I haven't been anywhere." She made me a couple of mini-sandwiches, tuna salad on whole wheat bread, with the crust cut off. "Hope you like it. Whole wheat is much better for you. I'm the only one who usually eats it here. Your father says it's an abomination."

"Yeah, we have a health nut living in our house right now. Some of the stuff she eats – I would call it an abomination too." She sat across the granite counter from me. It wasn't appropriate to laugh or even smile. Her eyes, lips, hands were even more perfectly controlled than normal. "How is he?"

"Not good." Tears moistened her eyes but did not run out over her eyeliner or makeup. "I think they're telling me his cancer came back, but it sounds like they're not going to take it out."

"Why? What do they say?"

"Nothing. The nurses will never say anything, and the doctors are never there, and when I do get them on the phone, they just … won't say anything."

My father's face was livid, the grey shade of his scalp almost blending into his new frizzy hair. His arm, the one that was not strapped to the hospital bed rail, was shaking.

"They won't operate. Goddam cancer comes back and they won't take it out!" He moved his head from side to side. "They say I'm too weak for the operation."

"What's the alternative?" I asked. "What are they saying?"

"They're not saying anything. They're afraid." He sighed, but then he seemed to get some of his edge back. His new tone was bitter. "I know how these things go. They'd rather have me die of cancer – natural causes – than die from their surgery."

"Don't say that." Anita was upset. "They're not going to let you die of anything."

He turned to me like I was the only one who would understand. "Will you talk to them, Tim? Tell them I demand the second operation. Tell them they'd better do it, if they know what's good for them."

~ Chapter 7 ~

Eileen called me and asked me to come up, but I couldn't make it until late Saturday night.

By the time I got there, it was too dark to run on those country roads near the campus, so she showed me the fitness center. It was a huge place. One room must have had 50 treadmills and 50 other exercise machines. We worked out on treadmills next to each other for an hour, running too fast to talk. It was after nine o'clock and the room was almost empty by the time we ran ourselves out of breath. No one could look good, red-faced and sweating in that harsh fluorescent light, sitting on a bench press in a room full of steel machinery and wires and weights and silent flat screen TVs. But she did.

I told her then about my father's relapse. "He asked me to get the doctors to change their minds and operate."

"Isn't it his choice?"

"That's what I thought."

"The whole thing's so sad. He's such a nice man. If there's anything I can do, you'll let me know, won't you?"

She showed me the rest of the fitness center. We ended up at a large walled-in indoor pool.

"Wow, a skylight," I said. "That must be great in the daytime. I wonder if at night you can see …."

"You can. Wait here a minute."

She walked out and I was alone in this big pool room. Then the ceiling lights went out. The green glow of the underwater lights, undulating up and down the walls, was all that was left. I looked for the stars through the skylight. She took a long time to return because she had changed into a bathing suit, a modest black one-piece. If that was supposed to be a signal that we should cool things off, it didn't work for me. The door closed behind her with a deep, echoing click.

"We're breaking all the rules of this pool," she said.

We weren't supposed to go into the pool after running without showering first. We weren't supposed to turn the lights out. We weren't even supposed to be there at all, because the center was officially closed.

"If we had a pitcher of beer, this would be perfect," I said.

"We'll have to settle, then," she laughed. Then she pushed me into the pool.

She was the better swimmer. Long after I gave up and leaned back against the side in the chest-deep water, she continued to swim laps, her long hair streaming behind like a shimmery black flag, the sound of her breath echoing off the walls and up to the skylight. But soon I could hear from the rasping sound of those breaths that she was getting tired, and I asked her to come over by me.

She faced away from the water, resting her palms on the edge of the pool while she caught her breath, then turned to face me. The reflections from the water grew still. In the dim light she looked exotic, her skin flawless, her eyelashes long and black and wet, her hair dark and sleek. Then she was floating a foot away from me in the tepid water.

"I've been thinking, all the time," I said, "wondering about that night in your room, in the storm, if that was just a one-night stand."

"Tim, I …."

"I have to tell you this. I finally decided, even if that's all it was, that night was the best night of my life."

She put her hand on my side and floated herself towards me until we touched belly to belly under the water. We kissed, our mouths hungry for each other, my hands pressing her body hard against mine while our faces bobbed at the water line. She helped me along as I pulled her out of the pool and laid her down on a towel on the smooth tiled surface. She eagerly helped me take her suit off. She did have a tattoo, a small yin and yang on her lower left hip. I touched it, kissed it, pretending it was the secret button that would open her heart. At least it opened her legs. She wasn't a screamer, but her little cries echoed off the walls, driving me insane. Afterwards we lay down facing each other.

"Tim, I don't think either of us are one-night-stand kind of people."

Later we sat at a little sidewalk table outside of a restaurant downtown, eating brownies and drinking rum and cokes by starlight. She'd put on a dark blue, silky blouse and a black skirt, the fanciest clothes I had ever seen her wear. The blouse was split at the top but pinned together with a gold pin. She had square shoulders and sat naturally tall and straight.

"What's graduate school like?"

"It's harder than I thought. I'm taking this course in cognitive neuroscience. We're studying what kinds of brain dysfunction are caused by different kinds of brain damage."

"That sounds interesting."

"It does. It sounds cool. That's why I signed up for it. That's why I took a whole year of statistics in my senior year, to qualify for taking it. It sounds exciting, but once you get into it, it's more like math than anything else. I hate it."

"Can you drop it?"

She looked at me. "I don't drop. Did you drop Calculus II?"

"Do you like the rest of your courses? I'm loving *Othello*, Western Civ."

"I never took Shakespeare. I feel like I missed something." The tables were small, but the restaurant had boldly put out so many, and so haphazardly, that they were halfway blocking the sidewalk. Some people stepped into the street to get around us, others squeezed by the back of my chair. "What I do love is cognitive psychology. How do people solve problems? What parameters affect their decisions? Right here, if you knew enough of the parameters, you could predict who would walk around us into the street and who would stay on the sidewalk and squeeze by behind you."

"Yeah, but why would you want to do that?"

Suddenly she looked over my shoulder with a surprised look on her face, her eyes wide with recognition. A skinny little guy with disheveled hair crashed right into my shoulder. "Oh! Sorry. Sorry," he repeated, bumbling past, bouncing off my other shoulder in the process.

"What was that all about?" I pulled my chair in a little.

"I thought at first he was one of my students. But look, I think we've discovered a parameter here." Looking past me, she put on the same wide-eyed, surprised look of recognition when the next guy passed by. I got hit again, again on both shoulders.

"Very funny. Okay, stop it. But it's just you. We could switch sides and I could smile at these strangers all day and not one would come any closer."

"That would be a different parameter."

There was a middle-aged couple at the table next to us. The woman caught Eileen's eye. "We were saying, you two might do better if you switched sides." They both smiled at us. You could almost be certain they had kids our age. The man was a short, grey-haired guy with silver-framed glasses. He wore a blue shirt and a tie. His wife also wore blue. Her short brown hair had undoubtedly looked sculpted and smooth that morning, but it had been a long day.

"Are you visiting here for parents' weekend?" Eileen asked them.

"Yes," the woman said right away, turning to her. "We're visiting our son Holden. He's a sophomore, a business major. We're taking him and his roommate out to a late dinner – if they ever show up."

"Oh, they'll show up for free food," Eileen suggested.

The man chuckled, but he wanted to say more. “Holden told us he wants us to see where he lives and, you know, understand his life up here. We’re so happy that he wants us here. And we’ve met one of his friends. Are your parents here?”

“I don’t go to school here,” I said. “I’m actually just visiting her.”

“Yeah,” Eileen said, “and he’s definitely not my parent.”

They laughed. We talked until they got a call from Holden, who wanted to meet them somewhere else. “I wish you two could meet Holden,” the father said as they stood up. “But I understand. This is such a big place you’d probably never run into him again anyway. I wish you both good luck with your studies … with your lives.” The mother patted Eileen on the arm before she turned to go.

After they left, Eileen didn’t want to talk. She just stared for a while in silence at the people passing in the street. Normally, she’d be looking around at the crowd, listening in on different couples’ conversations, speculating with me about what was really going on. But she didn’t seem to be having a good time any longer.

“Are you okay?”

“Oh. I was lost there for a minute. That couple, those parents – they were so nice. I was thinking, Holden is so lucky.”

“Yeah. Are you tired now? Do you want me to walk you back?”

“No! We hardly ever get to see each other. The night’s not over yet, is it? Do I embarrass you by jabbering with people, and messing with people passing by on the sidewalk?”

“Are you kidding? It’s like a revelation to me – strangers will talk to us! I could never do that on my own.”

“When I’m out with you, sometimes I get a little over-excited.”

“There’s a lot of that going around.”

I asked her about all the faculty affairs she’d been going to.

“I had never heard of this until I got here, but the school prides itself on its cohesive faculty. They really stressed that in orientation. First there was a big reception for the entire Humanities faculty. Then they got smaller and smaller. The older professors seemed to drop out first. Now there’s little groups of five or six. Like I said, everybody is really nice. But it's mostly the younger unmarried professors and the grad students now. I was with this group at a professor's home the other night, and everything's very civilized – but, you know, more and more personal. And I suddenly had this feeling, like I was auditioning for the role of faculty wife."

"Hope you don't get that part. At least you have people to talk to. You seemed kind of lonely, the last time I was here."

"It's much better now," she said. "Because I've made a friend! Jen. She's a new psych grad student like me. We're both wondering what's going on with all these faculty receptions and dinners and things."

"Do you really have to go to all of them?"

"I'm trying real hard not to offend anyone. I've been slowly phasing them out. I mean, I should be allowed to have my own personal life."

We stayed until the restaurant closed. Then we meandered around the shuttered bar and restaurant district with our arms around each other's waists, stopping to kiss in every other alcove or doorway, watching the town close down, imagining out loud to each other the story of each straggler who passed by on the way home. She showed me the lake on the other side of the town, and we sat on the docks and stared at the starlit water, our conversation punctuated by the listless pinging of the wires against the sailboats' aluminum masts. We walked back through town and across the bridge over the ravine. She asked me to spend the night.

She had a bottle of rum in her room. Another broken rule, because it was part of her job to be a sort of mother hen to the undergraduate students on her floor of the dorm. She said she couldn't be too strict with them or she'd feel like a hypocrite. We didn't drink much of the rum before we started making out, and then one thing led to another.

"Can you come up next Friday night?" We were on her mattress on the floor, and she was sitting up, sliding on her bra right in front of me. I wasn't used to seeing that. When she saw me looking, though, she turned away shyly. She spoke with her back turned. "I want to show you off to Jen."

"What have you told Jen about me?"

"Oh, the usual." She stood up. Since she knew I'd be watching, she turned to the side and slid on her panties as fast as she could. "Handsome. Fit. Smart. Expert on Shakespeare. Scared of women – except for me for some reason."

I stood up, hugged her hard. "You should have told her – *more* scared of you than of anybody."

She allowed her body to melt into mine. "You'll come up Friday, right? It'll be fun."

On the way home I worried about her auditioning all next week in front of God knows how many guys for the role of faculty wife. I couldn't blame those guys. I'd just have to have faith. And I certainly wasn't going to start whining about it.

The clutch started slipping going up the long, steep hills, the engine was revving too high, and the car was using a lot of gas. Could I bend my principles just a little and borrow the money to fix it? I tried to focus on ways to keep Eileen interested. Maybe a 23-year-old woman wanted something more sophisticated than running, drinking and screwing. Maybe I could take her to a play. I wondered if anyone in the U.S. had ever put on *Coriolanus*. It wasn't that great a play. I admired Coriolanus because he refused to fake it, but the point seemed to be that you have to pay at least a little attention to what other people want.

All I knew about doctors was you waited for half an hour in an empty room, naked except for a paper gown, until he rushed in, touched you for a second, mumbled something quickly, and then rushed out the door, pointing to another door that led you to the receptionist who handed you a bill. Apparently my father's doctor's rule was, if you wanted to talk to him, you made an appointment, even if it was life or death. Anita and my father had been following this rule but hadn't even managed to get an appointment to talk with the surgeon.

Dr. Gerard's office staff said he had no time to see me within the next week. I thought he was avoiding me. They told me I could call him after his surgeries – but there was no telling when that would be because he also handled emergency surgeries for the hospital. I asked for his home address but they wouldn't give it to me. I asked what days he was at that hospital and they wouldn't tell me. Finally I figured out his schedule from the internet and went to find him at the hospital. I waited at the nursing station, where a lot of nurses stood staring intently at computer monitors or rolling around carts full of bottles and syringes and stuff, all in a deliberate, heads-down pace. They were cramped already and there was no place to stand, so I backed up against a wall and made myself as inconspicuous as possible. A few visitors wandered through from time to time, looking as lost as I was. Dr. Gerard was on the ward and would not be available for an indeterminate amount of time, I was told.

I didn't have any argument prepared. When he showed up, he shook my hand like he was performing an important but unpleasant duty. Then he asked me how my father was doing. I just blurted out that my father wanted an operation to take the new tumor out.

Dr. Gerard nodded thoughtfully. "It's not the new tumor we found that's making him weak. It's the last operation, and the chemotherapy, and his compromised liver function, and his compromised immune function – those are the things that are making him weak. He's not a candidate for further surgery."

"But that tumor is going to spread fast if he doesn't get surgery, right?"

"It's a very malignant type of tumor. There's not much else we can do about it. Maybe radiation would slow it down, when he's strong enough for that."

"You're saying he's going to die from this tumor, unless you take it out."

"He's not a candidate for surgery. Do you understand? The surgery itself could kill him."

"But he'll have a chance if you operate. All he wants is a chance."

"He would never get medical clearance for surgery. He's not a candidate for surgery."

"He's my *father*, Dr. Gerard. He wasn't a perfect father. He's done nothing about his problems but whine about them his whole life. But now he's finally fighting, for his last chance to live. I want him to have that chance. Tell me you're going to give him that chance. If you won't, send us to a surgeon who will."

A nurse approached us, a red phone in her hand, her eyes on Dr. Gerard's face, her finger poised over a button. "Security?"

I talk too loud sometimes and it scares people.

"That won't be necessary," he said to her. Then he turned to me. "I'll check on him tonight before I leave. Call my office early in the morning."

Dr. Gerard did the second operation and took the new tumor out. The surgery went well and was over quickly, and my father looked no worse when he came out than when he went in. The further he got from the day of surgery, the less chance there would be of "complications," as Dr. Gerard put it. By "complications," he means death, I told Anita. She just stared back at me with those large eyes outlined in black. Once he got out of the recovery room I got back to my schedule of study, work, weights, run, study, work. I didn't go back to the hospital for a few days. I'd lost another day of work and I needed that money for the clutch. And I didn't want to hear my father whining again as he got stronger.

"You didn't even tell me about this second surgery." My mother's disappointment in me could be heard in the tone of her voice, even over the phone line.

"He's not your problem, Mom. How did you even find out?"

"You're a grown man. I can't force you to do what you should . . . ."

"Okay. Okay."

I cut another Western Civ class and urged my car over to the hospital, trying not to stop at all so it wouldn't lose its momentum. I knew my father would buy me a new clutch in a minute if I asked him, but I didn't want to owe him anything. But I did promise myself I would ask my mother for the money that night.

The biggest shock I got at the hospital was that my mother was there. She was in the tiny waiting room, standing with her back to the window above the parking lot, looking back toward the hospital corridor as if she were expecting me.

"Mom! What?"

"Tim, I'm so glad you came."

"Why are you here?" I kept my voice low.

"I thought and thought about this, and I eventually realized I don't have to have a reason. I loved your Dad for almost 25 years and I think I need to see him when he's …"

"... dying."

"He's not dying! Why do you say that? He's sick. But he'll be fine."

"Sorry. Did you and Anita arrange to be here at different times or something?"

She looked at me. "Something."

"Oh. I get it. I was part of the plan too. You and Anita arranged it so you and I would be here at the same time."

"That was very kind of her," was all my mother would say. "Would you go in there with me now?"

He didn't really look that bad. It was just a regular hospital room. Some reality show about hoarders was blaring on his roommate's TV. He had only one IV in his arm, and his face had some of its normal pink color back. There was only one small monitor hooked up to him. His new hair was actually growing out a little more.

"Hi, Honey," he said to Mom. Force of habit, I guessed.

"Hello, David," she said. Her voice was strained but calm. "Anita knows I'm here. I just came to wish you luck."

"I thought I had it beat."

"One more step, I guess."

"It's been a lot of steps."

"Tim's with me." I had to step up into his line of sight.

My father made the effort to speak up so I could hear him. "They were going to let me die before you talked to the doctor. What the hell did you say to them?"

"I promised them you would fight, if they would give you the chance."

"That's great. We can beat this, Tim."

There was a really awkward silence then. I felt like my mother wanted me to go, but my father wanted me to stay. I knew he would be afraid of being alone with her. She would definitely be nice to him when they were alone, but I knew from personal experience that her aura of total niceness would make him feel even worse about everything that he had ever done that was wrong.

He had done wrong. Nobody but my mother would have put up with his flare-ups, which happened more and more often in the year before he left. I was there for all of the harangues at the dinner table. I always sat mute, not knowing what to do. I cringed each time he singled me out as the good one, the one who didn't share all my mother's numerous vices. I felt like it was lying not to say anything, but I didn't say anything. My mother would sit there and take it, blank-faced, and afterwards apologize to me for my having to hear it. One time he broke all the dinner dishes, cracking each one dramatically over the edge of the sink in a demonstration of how sick he was of my mother's leftovers. She stood up but didn't have the nerve to try to stop him. I stood behind her. I knew right then I should stop him, but I was afraid.

You would have thought that was the last dinner he ever had with us. He did stay away for the next two or three, but then he came back as if nothing had happened. My mother went on as if nothing had happened. There were months more of dinners, though we couldn't always count on him showing up. There were more harangues, but mostly he wouldn't talk to my mother at all: "Timmy, ask your mother to pass me the salt."

. . .

I was walking across the waiting room when a thin, middle-aged man suddenly jumped up and put out his hand to me.

"You must be Tim." I had no idea who he was. "I'm Alan. Nice to meet you. I came here to support your mother."

"Oh."

"Maybe she hasn't told you …."

"No. Oh, Alan! She told me. Sure." I shook his hand. "I just didn't expect you to be here with her now."

He was much shorter than my father. His curly hair, mostly brown, was receding fast. He wasn't particularly handsome, but his blue eyes seemed to radiate warmth. I knew he had previously been in business but was now a social worker.

"I'm very happy to meet you," he said again. "Not the ideal circumstances, of course." The late afternoon sunlight was blazing into the small and sad waiting room.

"To be honest," I said, "I never thought my mother would …."

He smiled shyly. "Yeah, I got lucky. Oh. I didn't …. I didn't mean …. That didn't sound right. I meant I'm the one who was lucky enough to meet her."

"I got it."

"This has got to be tough on you, your father being so ill."

I turned away and looked at the window. The parking lot on ground level was already in the shade, the spectacular sunset wasted over the barren concrete rectangle. I kept reminding myself that he was a social worker and these were the kinds of things he said for a living.

"Don't analyze me, please."

My mother wanted me to go to dinner with her and Alan. She chose a nearby restaurant that was just one notch above the restaurants in the pizza district. This was not her type of restaurant, but I knew why she chose it. Later she confirmed that Alan had offered to pay for us all, and she didn't want to make it really expensive for him.

One difference I noticed about Alan right away. While my father was always elaborately polite, almost courtly, Alan barged ahead right out of the elevator door as soon as it opened. He walked right up to the restaurant hostess and stood a little too close to her and got us a table for three. He gave me the impression that he was carried away with a quiet enthusiasm for our little plan. We sat down and the waitress came over and we engaged in a lot of unnecessary talk about three glasses of water. Then we all fell silent.

"Your father said that the doctors were giving up – and only you could get the surgeon to agree to operate," my mother finally said.

"He asked me to. He wanted it. He fought for it himself."

I glared at Alan, daring him to try to get into the conversation. I didn't understand at first why she had chosen to bring him around at just this point. Then she told me.

"Alan gave me the courage. I didn't want to be the pitiful, abandoned ex-wife, too damaged to pay my respects to the man I'd been friends with for 25 years."

Chapter 8

Pump until muscle failure occurs. Rest. Pump to muscle failure again. Rest. Repeat. The shorter the rests, the more the muscle bulks up. Work with one weight until the rests are five seconds or less, then increase the weight. Then decrease the rests. I started lifting weights right after high school, when I realized I wasn't going to go to any special college, and wasn't going anywhere else. I lifted alone, first in my mother's basement and then in my basement room in the pizza district. I had no money to go to a gym, and I assumed most of the other lifters there would be knuckleheads anyway. I didn't have a girlfriend, or a career track like my father wanted for me, and burying myself in books all day left me at night with a raging energy that I channeled into bicep curls and power lifts and dead lifts. Eventually I grew strong enough that I was no longer afraid. Then I bulked up more until no one asked me why.

Eileen had never mentioned my muscles after the first time we met. I had always pretended to myself that they weren't supposed to be obvious, but when she totally ignored them I was surprised. The more time you rest between occurrences of muscle failure, the less the muscles bulk up, but the more you increase your actual strength, and your endurance. I started to do the longer rest periods.

I needed to talk to my father alone. It was going to be difficult to arrange because Anita was there in his room, holding his hand, almost every visiting hour of every day. The one time I had managed to avoid her, my mother and Alan had decided to visit. Anita called me on Saturday afternoon. "He's getting weaker. You really should try to see him today." I cancelled my date with Eileen.

"Your mother was here."

"Yeah, Dad, that was yesterday. I was with her. Don't you remember?"

"Yeah. Yeah. That's right. It's all confusing. There's no day and night here. They're waking me up and taking me for so many goddam tests all the time. They won't tell me anything. I think they're so pissed that I made them go through with this operation."

"Look, I brought you some real food, a burger from Bennie's."

"I can only use one hand. Thanks. Oh God, that's good! Oh, man, if I only had a Heineken."

"You do."

"One hand."

"And one of mine. Say when."

He held the bottle and I held the burger, feeding it to him one bite at a time like he was a little baby – only a little baby who took a swig of Heineken after each bite.

"I guess I don't have any right to ask for more salt." He caught my eye, and I knew what he was talking about. Another incident in the past with my mother at the dinner table. He had taken great offense at the fact that the salt shaker was empty. My mother, for once, didn't oblige him. She just sat there and sighed. I stood up and reached for the salt shaker myself, but he jumped up, knocking his chair over behind him, grabbing the shaker and reaching into the cupboard for the big salt container. Hands trembling in anger, he screwed the top off the shaker and tried to pour the salt into it, but he kept missing and pouring salt over the table instead. Then he flew into a frenzy and stood up and spun around in a circle, spraying the salt all over the table, the floor, the counters, the sink, jumping up and down like a maniac to make sure every surface in the kitchen was defiled – but stopping six inches short of my mother's folded hands.

"Please don't judge my whole life by my worst moments," he asked now.

I gave him some salt. He wasn't even hoping for a smile, but he got one. When he finished the burger he chugged the last of the beer. Visiting hours were over, but he wanted me to look at all the bruises on his wrist where they had put so many IVs in. "The doctor told me since you made it through the operation, you have a 60-40 chance."

"Sixty-forty? That beats 50-50 like they told me a month ago."

"You gotta think they really don't know. I think they're giving you 60-40 just because you're fighting."

"I didn't realize ...." He had to stop while he endured a long coughing jag, his face reddening with the effort. "I didn't realize this doctor business is as much bullshit as the lawyer business." His laughter made him cough again. By the time this second bout of coughing was over, he was exhausted and he drifted off to sleep. But I wasn't ready to leave yet.

I kept an eye on the waiting room and the corridor to make sure there wasn't anyone around. There was a soft October dusk settling in outside the waiting room windows, but you couldn't see it from his room.

"Why did you make me lie?" I confronted him as soon as he woke up and turned his eyes to me. "After you left, why did you make me tell Mom you were still living by yourself in an apartment? That you might come back?"

"I never told you to lie, just not to tell her that I had moved in with Anita."

"Don't talk like a lawyer. You know what I mean."

He looked straight ahead without moving until I thought he might have fallen asleep again. "I was lying to myself too," he said finally, still looking straight ahead. "Waiting for a miracle to happen so I could split in two and be both places at once. That's the kind of fantasy a weak man dreams up so he doesn't have to face what he's really doing." He turned to me. "I'm sorry."

"You said it hit you like a freight train."

His head collapsed on the pillow. "It smashed me up good, didn't it?"

I wished that I could put him in the wheelchair and take him out to the waiting room and show him that lavender sunset. But he was still tied to the IV under those fluorescent lights, and he started coughing again. I waited through that, and through his next nap, because there was one more thing I wanted to tell him. But when he woke up, he started first.

"I'm glad your mother finally found somebody. He sounds like a good man. Better than me. God, I wonder if I even make the top 50 percent." He laughed so hard at himself the coughing started again. This time he didn't fall asleep.

"Dad, do you remember last summer, you sent me that box, and I sent it back. And this girl delivered it back to you? Do you remember that girl?"

"Couldn't forget that one. And she was real kind, when she saw I was sick."

"Yeah. I'm dating her now." I wished she could have been there right then.

"That's good." Of course, he couldn't have known how proud I was of risking my own personal freight train just for her. I put my hand on the arm that was strapped to the IV lines. He opened his eyes and smiled at me. It was probably just my imagination, but it seemed like a real smile, for me – the real me, twenty-year-old Tim. There was probably more to the man than I had given him credit for. I had blown every chance to find out. I knew I hadn't been the bravest person in the past ten years, waiting until he was that weak to talk to him frankly. But maybe that was the best I could do. Maybe I just barely made it into the top 50 percent myself. He fell into a deeper sleep and his hand lost its grip on the Heineken bottle. It clinked against the steel bars of his bed and hit the floor with a hollow sound and rolled to my feet. I picked it up and put it in my knapsack and took it away.

Dory breezed down to the breakfast table every morning like a kid stepping up to the counter for a Happy Meal. Ben finally stopped grumping about her when she started paying rent. Then he started showing up in the kitchen every morning to talk carbs and calories and antioxidants with her. Their talks about nutrition, all of which they learned on the internet or from the numerous health magazines they subscribed to, were so serious you would have thought they were biblical scholars studying the eschatological visions of Saint Bernard.

Each week Dory told us how much money she had saved up for her security deposit, and she described in excruciating detail the features of the apartments she had looked at. Ben's eyes grew wide when they talked about square footage and heating costs and grades of carpet.

Dory and I were alone over a breakfast of yogurt and granola about six one morning. The thin pink sky had just started filtering through the drooping trees outside. I turned to her.

"We like you, Dory. Why don't you and Jeremy just stay here with us?"

"Oh, gross. Hey, there's this model house I've been sitting in? Furnished really nice with that, you know, smaller furniture they use? Faux Chippendale. Refrigerator, dishwasher, stove, microwave, everything new."

"Yeah, yeah. You're not mistaking me for Ben, are you? I'm just not interested in real estate, Dory."

"No. What I'm saying is, I got the key. For the weekend. Let's do a party."

"I don't think you want to do that, Dory. You'll get fired if you get caught."

"Uh-uh. My boss, Cameron, is really cool. He said we could do it on one condition – that we invite him too."

Jeremy accused me the next day of going after Dory.

"What? You're crazy."

"You're not interested in her little real estate job, but you talk to her like you are. I heard you the other morning telling her that she had a good body."

"I just said she doesn't need to be any thinner. She does have a good body, if you like them really thin."

"I bet you fantasize about her when you hear her in my room at night."

"I usually can't hear her from the basement."

"I hear you in the morning talking to her. I know you like her. I know you have to be fantasizing about her sometimes."

I shrugged. We looked each other in the eye. He laughed. We had known each other too long to deny the basic facts of life.

"You never talk about Eileen," he said.

"I don't want to jinx it. You know, too good to be true."

"So you're going to sabotage things with Eileen, like you always do with girls, huh? You're a regular one-date wonder, you with your head games." He broke eye contact. "Do what you want with Eileen. All I care about is Dory. You'd better not be working on Dory as an insurance policy."

"Listen, Jeremy, you got a cool girlfriend. She's nothing like those skanks you used to chase after in high school. Everybody likes her. Get used to it."

Dory had a lot of friends, and they all seemed to be at her party by the time I got there the following Friday night. I had been going back and forth between school and work since six that morning, and I was really tired. The law firm was getting its money's worth out of me. The security guards at the courthouses all knew me and stepped aside while I walked in carrying my bike in one hand and my filings in the other. If the bike wasn't moving on the road or being carried on your arm, you were wasting time. Even though my mother promised to pay for my clutch, I was in a race against time to get it fixed before my car totally died. I got a low *A* on my first *Othello* paper and I wasn't happy about that. I felt too tired and tense for a party, but Dory would take offense if I didn't show up.

She was feeling good by the time I got there. "This is my friend Tim," Dory put her hand on the small of my back like I was her favorite brother as she introduced me to a couple of her girlfriends. Her braids were pinned up around her head like some kind of ropy blonde crown. Her legs looked even longer in her tight white pants. I put my arm around her waist and she swayed into me, willowy and casual.

"Dory is great," I told her girlfriends. "Our whole house is going to miss her when she leaves."

I was surprised to see that one of her girlfriends was Kim, one of the two Kims in my calculus study group. The American Kim.

"Hi! Hey, how do you fit in at this party?" I asked her. "Most of Dory's friends I've heard about aren't in school. They all have jobs."

"I have a job," she said, offended. "I work for Cameron's company too, part time. I do closings."

Dory's friends, the girls with jobs, weren't mixing well with Jeremy's college friends, who were acting so stoned and cool you couldn't really tell if they knew each other at all. Dory's friends were a little younger and a lot better dressed. Kim pulled away from the group and spoke to me.

"Your face is so red!"

"Just got off work. Bicycle messenger. Sorry about these clothes. I didn't have time to change."

This apology would be considered completely unnecessary and weird on the other side of the room. But I could see that how you dressed did matter to the real estate girls on this side. And it was their party.

"And your clothes are soaked through. You're a real mess tonight."

"Thanks for the compliment." I looked for a feature of hers to insult. She had good skin, full lips, and a smart look behind rectangular, horn-rimmed glasses. It was the kind of look you would want to see on someone who was counting your money at the bank. We got drinks together and stood there and talked about the other Kim in our study group, Korean Kim. That guy was just too far advanced to understand the basic problems we had with calculus.

"He's more than just the stereotypical Asian smart math person," she said now. "He's picking up English faster than you would believe. I think he might be an actual genius." Then she lowered her voice. "But have you ever talked to him about his life? He told me he lives with his uncle, and it sounds like his uncle treats him like dirt."

Kim had just moved out from her parents' house herself and was living in an apartment with Tracey, another girl who was also at the party. Kim's party clothes were different from what she wore at school. She had on a silky, purple ribbed thing that didn't even come close to meeting the waistline of her dark pants, and a slim gold chain with a blue stone pendant that just tickled the tops of her breasts. I liked these real estate girls who just showed you what they were and told you what they wanted. The two of us kept chatting away until, after downing a couple of beers and a half dozen of Dory's special anti-oxidant-enriched zucchini brownies, I suddenly needed to sit down on the sofa. Kim wandered away.

"Ben showed up! I want you to see!" Dory grabbed my hand and dragged me up off the sofa and into the kitchen area. There, she pulled my head down and talked into my ear. "It's pretty bad. Ben's acting strange. He's freaking everybody out. You have to talk to him."

Ben was sitting on the smooth granite counter top in the kitchenette, leaning back against the cabinets and staring off at nothing in particular. There was a tiny smile on his face. He nodded his head to the beat of the rap that someone was playing in the living room. Short and stocky, with wide shoulders and a big, squarish head, and not being much of a talker, Ben never got the girls' attention. At first I thought Dory was just pissed that he was sitting right on the counter, right next to all the elaborate food that Dory and her friends had prepared and set out.

"We were talking about, you know, houses and all, and all of a sudden he starts this really weird stuff, and now he's not saying anything at all. Ben, wake up!"

I stood in front of him but he just looked right through me. His eyes were way dilated. "What's up, Ben?"

"Oh man! Oh wow! I can like see the music."

He wasn't looking at me at all. He was staring across the room, but there was nothing to see there but blue wallpaper overlaid with some kind of an abstract white domino pattern. I stared at it for a while myself.

"Ben, are you okay?"

"I'm great. I don't know where I am, but it's great. Isn't it?" Then he fell asleep and started to slide off the counter. Dory let out a quiet yelp. I caught him and lifted him up and carried him into one of the bedrooms, where I laid him down carefully on one of the miniaturized beds. His body filled it up completely.

"I'm so glad you're here," Dory said. "I guess those muscles are good for something."

A short guy in a beige sport coat and black turtleneck walked in the front door without knocking and looked around with steady eyes and a bobbing swagger. He didn't seem to notice he was ten years older than anybody else. Everybody waited so see if he was a cop, or the owner.

"Dory's party, right?"

"This is Cameron, my boss, everyone," Dory shouted from the rear. "Hey, Cameron! Come over here!"

"Dory! Tracey! Kim! Brought my own bottle of Jack!" People parted as he passed by like goldfish avoiding a finger in a bowl. He was soon talking with Dory and her friend Tracey, jabbing his finger to make his points. Cameron was maybe a little over 30, short, with thick brown curls just brushing his collar. He was showing Dory and Tracey and Kim a necklace he had bought for his wife. Tracey tried it on, posing and batting her eyes. Dory edged back toward Jeremy.

The party rolled on, but the two groups, the students and the real estate people, didn't mix that well. Cameron tried to put his hands on the shoulders of all the girls who worked for him. When he tried to do it to her, Dory left the group. When he came after her a minute later, she let out a loud whoop like she was really drunk and suddenly jumped on Jeremy's back, wrapping those long legs around his waist from behind. Jeremy tried to keep talking and swaying casually to the beat, as if he was used to having a blonde goddess riding on his back. I had been forced for years to listen to Jeremy's various sexual fantasies, and this came real close to some of them. When I caught his eye a minute later, though, he was listing to the side under her weight, and they both fell sideways into the wall of the model living room before she managed to slide off.

Later Cameron was in the kitchen with Dory and Kim. He had gotten an arm around each of them and was smoking pot and drinking whiskey. Kim had a death grip on his bottle of Jack Daniels, and Dory was drinking from it too. It sounded like the three of them were making fun of the president of their parent company. Jeremy was nearby, leaning back with both hands behind him on the counter, squinting at Cameron, who mumbled into the ears of his two young employees until they laughed. Kim moved away, taking the bottle of Jack Daniels with her. Dory noticed Kim's escape with the bottle and laughed so hard her Jack and Coke ran out of her nose.

My stomach suddenly turned over and I ran outside. Jeremy followed close behind me. I knelt down on the sidewalk. He brought me a sweatshirt from his car. I put it on over top of my wet T-shirt.

"Something just hit me all of a sudden. My stomach doesn't feel good."

"I'll wait with you." He sat next to me, waiting for me to throw up. When nothing happened right away, he started talking. "I gotta admit, Tim, what you said about Dory is true. She's so great, everybody likes her."

"Yeah, we all like her. Ben and I will just have to learn to live with her nighttime sounds. It's just Dory. That's just the way she is."

"Maybe I can ask her not to make so much noise."

I had to laugh. "Oh man, that would be a terrible mistake! That would be like trying to shut down one of the wonders of nature. God would punish you for that."

I convinced Jeremy to go back inside and try to pry Dory out of Cameron's arms without getting Dory fired. I knew I couldn't go inside without throwing up all over everything. There was nothing to do but wait it out outside. Across the street was vacant land being cleared for new houses. Beyond that, far below, I could see the tiny dots of the red tail lights of the commuters on the beltway streaming home from work in the twilight. I used to think all the nine-to-fivers followed each other like mindless drones because they were too weak to blaze their own paths. I thought the most important thing was never to be weak like that. The whole triple line of cars rounded a curve far below, the red dots of their taillights sparking in unison. I knew now that I knew nothing about the lives of the people in those cars. They were probably working people, caught in a routine, but that didn't mean their work meant nothing to them. When they were young, they might have gone to parties like this one, searching for lovers, or to get high, or to meet people doing something interesting or something that mattered. Most of them had made a decision at a certain point to put their faith in someone.

Then I found myself on all fours on the concrete steps where the front walk descended to the public sidewalk, throwing up between two clumps of chrysanthemums that had just been planted in front of the model home. Kim came out and sat down next to me.

"I didn't think you drank that much. Do you need a ride home?"

"Maybe I ate too many of Dory's anti-oxidant brownies."

She smiled. "I never eat any of Dory's special health food." The conversation died as we both waited for my breathing to even out. "I hear you guys have a cheap place," she said. "A lot of people our age spend almost all of their salary on rent."

"You know about our house?"

"Dory told me all about it. In the pizza district, right?"

"Is it really called the pizza district, I mean in the real estate business?"

"Oh, yeah. Any house within a 150 feet of a pizza place, and you deduct $30,000."

"Then I guess we're worth about zero."

I asked her if she wanted to take Jeremy's room in our house if Dory and Jeremy moved out. She looked at me like I was crazy.

"I'm kind of a neat freak," she explained.

"I feel a lot better now. I think it was just a one-time throwup."

"You're shivering! Wait right here." She ran inside and came back in a minute with a towel. "Take off that sweatshirt. Your shirt underneath is soaked is the problem."

"Yeah, yeah, good idea."

I started to dry myself off.

"I'll get your back," she offered.

"That's okay. I got it."

"It would be my pleasure." She did a very thorough job. The sweatshirt was plenty warm enough once the wet T-shirt was gone. She smiled, showing her perfect white teeth following the line of that square jaw. "Why didn't you bring your girlfriend here?"

I liked her approach. Direct.

"She's a graduate student up at State, five hours away, and having a hard time of it right now."

Despite my efforts to chemically defoliate the chrysanthemums, they looked like they would make it. Their puffy blooms glowed pink and white in the faint streetlight and still gave off their sweet, musty scent. Kim stayed there with me. It seemed like women were attracted to me now that I had a girlfriend.

"Your friend Dory is nice," I said. "She talks to me all the time. It's almost like she's my sister or something."

"She told me you're nice. But I already knew that from the way you treat Korean Kim."

Dory came running out.

"Tim, you'd better come inside. It's Ben. He woke up, and he's in some kind of argument with Cameron. And Jeremy's acting like he's going to fight Cameron."

Ben was still sitting in the same position on the bed as when I left. Cameron was sitting in a chair facing him, laughing, sipping on his whiskey bottle, which he must have retrieved from Kim.

"Your short fat friend is flying!"

"He's all right."

Cameron's curls were wet with sweat and flattened against his forehead. He was enjoying harassing Ben.

"Hey, wake up! Wake up, man! Why the hell are you nodding off with all this young pussy around?"

"Leave him alone," I said.

"Hey, I want to show you something, man." He stretched out his leg and kicked the bottom of Ben's shoes. Ben's eyes popped open. "Man, he doesn't even know who did that! Oh man, he must be on some wild kind of trip! Tell me, man, can you even tell me what century it is?"

Ben moved his feet out of the way. Cameron laughed and shook his head like he'd never seen such an amusing thing. Dory had already pushed Jeremy out of the room to keep him from fighting with Cameron.

"Leave him alone," I said.

"Go fuck yourself! What are you going to do, beat me up? You're one of those steroid freaks, I can tell. Pathetic. Burning your brain down to the size of pea to grow those freakish muscles. You're a disgusting freak, man."

I ignored him. "You okay, Ben?"

"I'm just really tired now. Will you take me home?"

"You might as well cart him off," Cameron interjected. "Mr. Acid Head here is not adding anything to this party."

"Shut up, Cameron." Dory stood in the doorway, looking really tense.

Ben didn't even notice that he had been insulted. "Great. Great. I'm just going to close my eyes now."

Cameron had barely enough balance to stand up. "The both of

you just get out of here! It's my company's house. Just go. Nobody's going to miss either of you."

Jeremy appeared just behind Dory, but she bumped him back so he couldn't get in the room.

"Come on, Cameron," Dory said, "you don't know what you're saying. You're just drunk. This isn't like he usually is." She looked at me and then back at Jeremy. "Usually he's really nice. Cameron, do you want to lie down in the other bedroom and take a nap? I'll sit with you for a while. Or I'll drive you home."

"No you won't." Jeremy's voice was strong for someone who looked so unfocused.

Dory clamped her lips tightly together.

"Sweet little Dory," Cameron started, "if you trust yourself alone in a car with me right now, you're more naive than I thought."

"She's not driving you home," Jeremy put his arm around Dory from behind.

"I'll drive you home," I said.

Cameron's gaze was hostile. "Just what I need, Mr. Steroid Upchuck tossing it all over my BMW."

"It's that or call your wife."

Dory stepped up real fast and put one hand on the bottle that he still had in his hand. "Your eyes look terrible, Cameron. You'd better stop." She pulled the bottle out of his hands. "You're the only one in the office tomorrow."

I drove him home in his own car. Cameron's hostility shrunk down to whining threats the whole time that if I scratched his car, he'd sue me. Kim followed us in her car and drove me back.

"You know, we're going to have to do this for Jeremy and Dory too."

Jeremy had gotten sick on the bedroom rug while we were gone. Dory came up to us. "I can't believe it. Jeremy too? He wasn't drinking that much."

I caught Kim's eye and she mouthed the word "brownies." I pulled Jeremy out of the room while Kim began to help Dory clean up the mess.

"Dory." I popped my head back into the room. "I'll finish. And I'll make Jeremy come back tomorrow after it's dried and deodorize it or whatever it takes. I promise you won't get in trouble on account of this."

"I'm trying to tell you," she said, "it's no big deal. Things happen all the time in model houses. We had somebody die in one once. There's a clean-up crew coming in tomorrow anyway."

Jeremy recovered fast, just like I had, but Dory was still worried that he was too drunk or high to drive, and we had to get Ben out of there too, so I took them all home while Kim followed me in Dory's car. Then I took Kim home. She was shorter than Eileen but had a nice figure.

"Do people think I take steroids?"

"To be honest, Korean Kim and I had a conversation about that after the last study group."

"Oh, man, I would never do that. I'm just trying to be strong."

"Yeah. I told him I didn't really think you would take steroids."

"You don't like muscles, do you?"

"Not generally. But maybe they're okay on some guys."

I drove into the parking lot of her apartment complex. She touched my arm before she turned away.

"I don't think that girl up at State is your girlfriend."

Chapter 9

When I got back to the house from taking Kim home, Dory was the only one downstairs.

"We put Ben to bed. He's okay now. Jeremy's the one who's really not feeling good."

"Is he still throwing up?" Since I had also eaten Dory's antioxidant brownies, I was wondering about my own prognosis.

"No, that stopped," she said. "Just like yours did. I wonder what that was all about. He didn't drink that much. I don't think he knows how to drink."

"Hmm."

She sat down next to me on the sofa, the ripped and stained and dribbled-on sofa that normally she refused even to touch. "I'm sorry about the way Cameron talked to you. I've never seen him like that."

"He was just drunk."

"Thanks for taking care of Ben, and Cameron. This thing would have been a total disaster without you." She unfastened her braids and pushed them to one side and actually relaxed back until her silky lavender blouse was touching the untouchable fabric of our sofa. "You were the most mature person there."

"Were you trying to set me up with Kim?"

She got a funny look on her face. "We talked about you one day a while back. You seem like a good guy and, I don't know, it seemed like you were being sort of … wasted."

"I have a girlfriend."

"I know. I don't like her already."

"You would like her. You have to meet her. You would love her."

She had a cooler of stuff from the party, and we sat there and each drank a soda without saying very much of anything. There were no sounds from upstairs.

"I think I'll drive up to State."

"Did you call her?" Dory said.

"Yeah. Left a message. I think she's busy. If she's there, she's there. If not, I'll just go drinking or something. They have great bars and places to eat in that town."

It was pitch dark, and all the commuter traffic was gone. I'd finally gotten my car fixed the day before. When I had asked her to help, my mother had been so pleased to pull out her checkbook it seemed like I was doing her a favor. And then Alan, who was sitting right there, recognized that I'd need the cash right away and handed me the money in bills. Ben asked his friends at the auto parts store to recommend a shop, and that shop had the car ready to go in two days.

I wound my way around some back roads until I hit the interstate headed north. The concrete zipped by under my headlights. I liked driving in the dark where there was no color or shape to the other cars, just abstract white and red lights, binary colors – and in just two categories, either this-could-hit-you or don't-worry. Dory was my friend, like the sister I never had. I could sit next to her on the sofa and not say anything to her if I didn't feel like it. Before I left, she changed her mind and said if I liked Eileen that much, she was sure she would like her too.

I drove through a long flat stretch of forest where my mind wandered from regressions to *Coriolanus* to *Othello* to visions of Eileen lying naked on that pool deck. Less than an hour north of town the road started climbing through rolling countryside, then huge hills. Soon the moon appeared with Venus hanging below it like its dangling earring. Soft mountains rose up on both sides of the road. I pulled off at an exit that had gas signs raised 70 feet in the air, pumped the tank full and went inside the attached convenience store and bought a couple of bags of nuts. After a lot of persistent questioning and searching, I found a pay phone and called her.

"Hey, I got you on the phone live! You're sitting in your dorm room at ten o'clock on a Friday night?"

"Actually, I'm on a sailboat on the lake."

"Auditioning?"

"Um, yes, definitely. I could kill Jen. I'll tell you about it later."

"I'm coming up."

I stood outside of the gas station, leaning against my car, watching the stars hanging there millions of miles deep in the sky. Just as bright, and moving across the constellations in a straight line, was one of ours, a satellite. One of ours, made by us humans, traveling for a purpose. I ate a whole bag of walnuts and watched that tiny satellite spark its planned, certain, human-determined path through the cold universe of random stars. A steady wind was funneled down this moonlit road by the mountains on each side. There was no sound but the faint whining of tires and the slow ticking of the Nissan's engine as it cooled.

Eileen told me to come to her dorm and she would get somebody to let me in. I got there and stood in the glare of a floodlight in front of the locked dorm door. A woman approached me. Square face, medium-length blonde hair that hadn't been washed, glasses, grim smile.

"You're Tim? Jen. I'm a mess, I know. Eileen is so pissed at me for backing out of the sailboat ride at the last minute. She called and made me get my ass out of the lab to let you in." She opened the heavy front door. "I have cards to get you in the main door and into her room, but once you're in there I can't leave the cards with you. If you go out after that, you'll be locked out."

"So you're Jen. Weren't the three of us supposed to go out a few weeks back?"

"She wanted me to meet you. She told me all about you. I can't do anything tonight. Can't even talk. I'm sorry. I have to get back to the lab."

I didn't want to look at Eileen's computer, or her papers, or her clothes. I didn't want to lie in her bed without her there, but the place had such good memories it felt like home. She had printed out a picture of me she had taken with her cell phone.

She came in an hour later wearing faded jeans and a big floppy hat. "Protective gear," she said.

"Who were you with?"

"Dr. Kelly, a professor in the sociology department. This is it. I'm never doing this again."

"Auditioning?"

"Worse. It was supposed to be four people, and then it was only three. And then Jen dropped out at the last minute. So it was a date, an involuntary date."

"Did he, like, go after you?"

"No, nothing like that. But he's a single, 30-something guy, and he couldn't wipe the smile off his face when he found out that Jen wasn't coming. I mean, I hope he finds somebody, but I told him he's just wasting his time on me."

"Was the whole thing awful?"

"It was a beautiful ride. It was so quiet on the water, and the lake was just sparkling in the moonlight. We've got to do that sometime." She stopped, threw off her hat. "I'm so glad you came."

I had never talked with a woman in bed before. "I miss you," she said. "Why don't you transfer up here? You would love it here. I found out they have eight different Shakespeare courses. There are courses in everything. And we could run. And downtown is fun. And now there's the lake. We've definitely got to do the lake."

We decided to do the bar scene downtown for what was left of Friday night. Even before I took the first sip of beer, I was high on the idea of transferring up there. I wondered out loud if I could take enough credits to catch up to her.

"Why?" She looked at me.

"I guess to be on the same level that you're on."

"But that's the good thing about you and me, right? There are no levels."

In all the ways that really mattered, Eileen was much smarter than me. But she still liked me, so I guessed there weren't any levels to that either. We drank silently as she looked around. She pointed out one of the girls at a table near us. "Tim, don't be obvious, but see if you can get a look at that little blonde over there. She couldn't be more than sixteen, could she? I wonder what kind of fast talking she did to get served in here, even with a fake ID."

"You want to find out?" The girl was coming towards us on her way to the bathroom. She had to pass through a narrow aisle between our table and the wall. I leaned back, tipping my chair all the way to the wall, blocking her passage. It was an encounter Eileen would have engineered with much more finesse. When the aisle was suddenly blocked, the girl stopped, confused, blushing a deep red, desperate not to draw attention to herself. I moved my chair back immediately. I was suddenly just as embarrassed as she was. I just didn't have the panache to pull off this kind of stunt.

"Don't mind my brother." Eileen called over to her. I waited for her to rescue me. "He's a little … slow." She looked around the bar, then spoke in a lower voice. "But he's not dangerous. Really, he'll do anything I say." She turned to me. "Timboy, let her go. Come on now, pull your chair all the way in and let the nice girl go."

But the girl stood there even after I pulled the chair completely in. I thought she might be too flustered to keep going, but that wasn't it. The embarrassment faded from her face and her eyes suddenly lit up with interest. She talked over my head to Eileen. "But he looks so ... fit. He must work out a lot."

"Oh, yeah, the body's good. But that's pretty much all there is, if you know what I mean."

But if Eileen thought this would scare this girl away, it wasn't working. Instead of leaving, she leaned down and put her hand on my shoulder.

"He seems really nice."

"Well, he's very difficult to talk to."

"Do you mind if I try?" Before Eileen could say anything, the girl turned to me. "Timboy, how are you? Do you go out often with your sister?"

"Bwa bwa bwa."

She tried an easier question. "Is this your sister, sitting right here?" Pointing to Eileen.

Following where she was pointing, I looked at Eileen with the blankest possible expression on my face. Eileen clenched her jaw to keep a straight face. I knew she was really sorry she had started this. She kicked me under the table.

"Do you take him out a lot? That's really nice."

"He lives in a nice house with three friends his own age. I take him out whenever I can. It's a little bit hard on my academic life, but I think it's important that he doesn't forget who I am."

"I know what you mean. I have a brother too. I mean he's not exactly the same, but he has neurological problems. We had to put him in a home just last week."

Eileen was completely mortified. Her face turned red. I gave her a little nudge with my foot under the table. She squirmed, then tried to recover. "Timboy is very well-behaved usually, but he has trouble with, you know, boundaries. He's not too good at handling his, you know, sexual urges. Maybe you shouldn't stand so close to him."

"Bwa bwa bwa."

She kicked me hard.

"I thought you'd never let it go!" We had just made it outside the door. Eileen was trying to be angry.

"You got yourself into that."

She punched at me between laughs. A couple hugging and laughing together is not such an unusual sight out on the streets of this town at night.

"You know I'll be kicked out of the School of Social Sciences if they ever hear about this stunt."

"You just picked the wrong person to play games with."

"The wrong two people."

We leaned back together against the brick wall of the bar just outside the entrance canopy. Two faux Grecian urns held huge balls of chrysanthemums long past their prime. A couple of guys pushed past us on their way into the bar. She muffled her laugh against my neck. I could smell beer and her skin and her scented hair while she pressed her body, heated by shame, hard against mine.

"Oh God, what if she comes out now and sees us like this?"

We watched people move towards us from down the street. They seemed like insignificant little dots at first, moving randomly like tiny nobodies under the weak streetlights. Then each one would grow, and just for a second, as they passed in front of us through the colored lights thrown by the bars and restaurants at street level, each one came alive for us, as a human. You could see that each was one of us, each had a purpose. You could feel the little grain of certainty in each of their lives. Then they passed by and faded again, scraps of their laughter or conversation trailing behind them like a download of incoherent sound bites. Eileen was quiet then, her arm around my waist under my coat, her head on my shoulder. There were no levels. The little dots kept coming down the street, lighting up and morphing into humans as they passed. I had no desire to be anywhere else. I could feel the certainties flowing around us, sparking like satellites.

~ Chapter 10 ~

The intensive care room was dim and quiet except for the blinking monitors and chirping alarms. Anita was there, her body rigid, her eyes flickering back and forth in search of hope. His veins were collapsing and they had to search for a new place for an IV each time. His wrists were tied to the bed rails with gauze tape so he couldn't rip anything out.

"Don't call them," he rasped when Anita saw the bloodstain oozing around one of his IVs. "God knows where they're going to stick me next." Suddenly he managed to free one hand and waved it around nervously. Then he reached up and grabbed at the air.

"Damn if I didn't just see a bottle of Heineken there."

"It's just the drugs," Anita murmured to me. "And his voice, that's just from the tubes they had down his throat."

"For a while they came around every morning at the crack of dawn to pump different crap into me. The last batch – Jesus God! – burning up everything inside me like hell. I made them triple my dose of morphine."

"I thought they would wait until you were stronger before starting chemotherapy again."

"They talked me into it. Then they stopped it. Didn't tell me why. I figured out how they work it here. When they don't have a clue, they just stop coming around."

Anita was now spending twelve hours a day in the hospital. Her face was drawn, but her expression always optimistic. She really did love him. I thought I should stop treating her like dirt.

Jeremy was still refusing to get an apartment with Dory.

"I can't see why we always have to do what she wants," he complained to me in the kitchen one morning. "I mean, she's the greatest girl in the world, but does that mean I have to do absolutely everything she wants?"

"She's good for you, Jeremy." I explained how many times she had physically restrained him from attacking her boss, Cameron, at the party.

"He was acting like an ass."

"Yeah, and he's her boss, but she had him under control until you started trying to get in his face."

"I don't remember that."

"That's another problem."

Dory came down into the kitchen then. She had some print-out in her hand, probably of apartments for rent, but she put it face-down on the table when she saw we were both there.

"I can't afford it," he said, assuming that she had been listening to our conversation. He was taking only twelve credits. If you got his password and got onto his X-box, I was sure you could see what activity, besides fucking Dory, he spent the most time on each day. But Dory didn't need a password to know that. She looked at him, then down at her yogurt. I was getting worried that Jeremy really was a slacker under the guise of being cool. Dory had every reason to call him out on it. I stood up and left quickly so as not to be there when that happened.

Whenever I ate breakfast alone with Dory, I would tell her that Eileen might really be too good to be true. Dory's opinion was that if I didn't see Eileen at least once a week, it wouldn't work out. I told myself that Dory was just a citizen of the pizza district who didn't understand anything beyond its borders. The weekend after Eileen and I messed around with that little blonde in the bar, she had to drive to Chicago to meet her friend Miriam. And I knew she was leaving to visit her father in Washington, D.C., over Thanksgiving. Things seemed to be getting worse, until they got better. She called me.

"We can never seem to get together enough. And in a few weeks I'm going home for Thanksgiving. I was wondering if you'd want to do this. Assuming your father is out of the woods by then, what do you think of going with me to visit my father's family in D.C. over Thanksgiving?"

"His new family?"

"It's not really new. A few months ago he finally married Robin, the woman he's been living with for seven years. She's really not that bad. And I have a step-sister, Kit, who's sixteen. You would like her. My brother's not due home for another month, though, so he won't be there. I'm talking fast, aren't I?"

"Um . . ."

"You should come. It's not high pressure. I'm not the favored child. Usually I just show up and hang around the edges of the conversation."

She had me at "talking fast." I had never before had the power to fix anything that was worrying her.

"What will we say about who I am?"

"My boyfriend, of course."

"Can we sleep together?"

"I don't think we should. I don't want to push things. They're thinking about Kit. She's only sixteen."

"It's okay. We can do the platonic thing for a night or two."

"I don't like that word. But I'll try to set it up that way. If you think you can keep your hands off me."

You go to the intensive care unit one day and things look pretty bad, but it is the intensive care unit after all, and you assume that care will be given and everything will be okay in the end. But the next day you come back and he's still in the intensive care unit and the monitors are blinking in the shadows and now he's got a needle in his groin and you can tell that things have gotten worse. You come back a third day and his body is white and withered with dark IV splotches up and down both legs and arms and everything is mechanical and routine and he gets one more symptom and they pump in one more drug and you confront his doctor and you can see there really isn't a plan and they are just keeping him alive as long as they have a chemical that will stretch it out.

Anita is there twelve hours a day, and I'm the only other one visiting. Anita is so blind she cannot see the obvious fact that he is dying. She is always hoping that she will be able to see the doctor tomorrow and he will give her some hope and she will find some way she can help. Maybe twice a day he will open his eyes and flutter his free fingers toward her. When that happens, she leans over and whispers to him frantically, asking him whether he wants water, or morphine, or telling him his kidney function is two percent better or some other pathetic little meaningless factoid.

I told my roommates I wasn't going back to the hospital.

"I got mid-terms. I got to go to work too."

"No," was all Ben said.

He called American Kim and Korean Kim, and told them I had to get my calculus mid-terms postponed.

"I have Shakespeare too."

I got a call back from Korean Kim. "I set it all up. Just call the teachers."

"Oh thank you. And thank American Kim too. But I have other exams. You don't even know …."

"All. I postponed all."

My friends probably had no idea how boring it could be, sitting in the vinyl-covered waiting room chairs looking at all the other people waiting, trotting in to see my father's eyes slit open and closed, open and closed, sitting next to Anita with nothing to say while waiting for the next chance to jump up and go into his room. When we went in, he was mostly out of it.

My father had always made fun of himself. He was always ready with a self-deprecating joke about his inability to stop drinking. But I think he saw his drinking as a means of defiance also, defiance against conformity and the dull office routines that weren't really compatible with his hyper-emotional nature. Now one of the main things screwing up his recovery from the surgery was the hardening of his liver, which was barely functioning and was screwing up his metabolism. This was entirely due to alcohol, his doctor told him. When my father mentioned that to me a few days before, he didn't express any regret at all. In fact, he seemed almost proud that it wasn't really the cancer, or even the surgery, but his own chosen lifestyle that was doing him in.

Back at the house, just as I was going up the steps to the porch, Jeremy came up behind me in the twilight, panting, and collapsed dramatically in front of me.

"Dammit, Tim! Could you get a harder job?"

"What ...?"

He had done my courier job. I would've gotten fired. I had forgotten to call in that afternoon.

"You pretended you were me?"

"You're not as unique as you think, Tim. I convinced them all I was you. Even at security. Everywhere. 'Yes, sir, that's my picture.' Could've been Osama Bin Laden. All in the attitude."

It was Friday and Ben was having a little party, just pizza and beer. He made sure that Dory invited Kim and Tracey and any other friends she had. It was a make-up party for him; he wanted to be awake for this one. Ben had discovered that he had one strong quality that appealed to these girls, his interest in real estate. It was the first time I had ever seen any girls going out of their way to talk to him. They knew more than he did about the business; he was mostly just asking questions. But he seemed to emanate an aura of calm competence that lowered the anxiety level around him. I could see instantly where he was going with his life, and that he wouldn't be going alone.

Jeremy moaned and groaned about how hard my courier job was while wringing out his T-shirt theatrically in the sink. American Kim came over to me.

"How is Miss State University doing?"

"Don't be like that. I'm meeting her family at Thanksgiving."

We had a few beers, and Dory lit her little pipe. The smell of pot and beer and pizza was everywhere. I pulled Dory aside.

"I'm sure it's tonight," I told her. "My father's going to die tonight."

"Oh, I'm sorry, Tim." She touched me gently. "You should be there, not here."

"The people in this room saved my ass today." I told her what Jeremy and Ben and the two Kims had done. "And they're normally such assholes, except the Kims."

She put her lips to my ear. "You have good friends. That says a lot about you." Her breath was on my neck as I stared across the room at Jeremy. Then the phone rang.

"Tim, I don't understand you." My mother's distraught voice cut through all the noise in the room. She was yelling at me. That was a first. "Why didn't you call me? Don't you think I'd want to know?"

"I ... I don't know."

"Don't you think I deserve for you to tell me that the man I was married to for twenty years might die tonight? Do I need to hear it from Anita?"

It wasn't the yelling or the sarcasm that was the most shocking. The most shocking thing was hearing my mother say she deserved something.

"He's in bad shape."

"You should go over there right now."

"I've been there all day. They kicked me out."

"You can make them let you in."

Dory ran down the porch steps after me. "I'll drive."

"You're as stoned as I am drunk."

"I can drive very well stoned. You're not yourself. I can tell."

Dory went in with me to the hospital. When they asked if she was immediate family, she said yes, she was my sister. After over an hour's wait, they let me into his room for five minutes.

"I'll go in with you," she said.

"No. Not this time. Let me see how it is." When I came back out I shook my head at her. "No."

Anita had been there since nine in the morning. Even she was nodding off in the waiting room. Of course she had on her high heels and jewelry, but the whole kit seemed to be dragging her down by this point. When she got the chance, she asked me very timidly who Dory was. "Oh. I didn't think she looked like the one who brought back the box. I'm a little confused now. Really tired. Thanks for coming back, Tim."

The person I didn't expect was Alan, my mother's boyfriend. "Your mother sent me to help you. In case you wanted to talk, or I could go out and get some food, or just get lost, or anything."

"How did you get in?"

"Well, officially, just for today, I'm your father's brother. I suspect you don't really need me, with that beautiful young blonde here to keep you company."

"Just a friend."

"Whew! I never had friends like that when I was young."

He stayed behind and talked with Dory each time Anita and I went into the intensive care room. My father didn't open his eyes, and he looked the same every time. They had run out of chemicals and tubes to put into him, and everyone was just hoping he had enough life left to fight his way out of it himself. Then, when the sky was just turning light outside, a new doctor came in and moved him to another room. They let us see him after a while, through a window. It was like watching your father in close-up on a giant, flat screen TV while a big hose taped to his mouth mechanically pumped his chest full of air. Anita didn't seem to understand what was happening.

The third time in, I realized it was up to me.

"You know what they're trying to tell us." I cornered her in the waiting room when we were back out. "He's got no kidney function. He can't breathe on his own. His blood sugar is completely out of control. His brain isn't responsive. He's just being kept alive by the machine."

"He's so young. I keep hoping."

I stayed out the next time. Dory and Alan were both out cold, stretched uncomfortably across the plastic sofas. Anita, I thought, needed to see him alone, for herself. She came back out, but this time she just sat across the room, and for the first time she cried. I put my arm around her and she cried into my shoulder – just for a minute, and then she pulled herself together. The doctor came and said the respirator was very rough on his lungs and his labs were getting worse. The doctor was staring at her with almost puppy-dog eyes. We walked in together and took one last glance while he was still technically alive.

Instead of details, a big scene w/ emotions would be nice!

~ Chapter 11 ~

Neither Anita nor I watched for more than 30 seconds after they pulled the plug.

Five minutes later, a hospital person dressed in a suit came in the waiting room and sat next to Anita and started asking questions about what to do with the body. Anita jerked herself up even stiffer and straighter than usual. Her arms were frozen at her side. Tears were streaking through her makeup. She stared straight ahead without responding to him at all.

He turned to me. "You're the son, right? Can you tell me at least if the family has a pre-arranged funeral contract?"

"Of course not. Why don't you just get out of here and leave us alone?"

Alan, his face still creased from sleeping on the waiting room sofa, jumped into the conversation, asking that the four of us be allowed to have a moment alone. "I've done this before," he said, speaking directly to Anita "when my wife died. The hardest part is admitting to yourself that it's over. You get to do that yourself, on your own time. What they're asking you now is to make decisions on the mechanics of it all. That part is not important. There is no such thing as a wrong decision now. Just talk with me for a minute and I'll go out and deal with everything."

And he did. When he came back, Anita thanked him profusely.

He gave her what turned out to be a very awkward hug. The instant my father died, the only relationship I had with Anita was over. But she had no one else there, and so we hesitated to leave. Luckily, her sister arrived just at that moment. Anita formally introduced all of us before she went into a corner with her sister, bent her head stiffly, and cried on her shoulder. The rest of us left.

I was angry that my father had gone so suddenly downhill and I had not had a chance to find out where his head had been for the last ten years. He said he might not be even in the top 50 percent. He always told me I was the best, but what was the point of anybody rating anybody when we're all going to die in the end?

Alan got us in his car and refused to take us home before treating us to breakfast. He ushered us into a restaurant and encouraged us to eat. He asked us about our lives and schools and jobs – all as if he were the luckiest person in the world to be in the company of such young, good-looking and accomplished people. He encouraged us to order dessert and extra coffee. "Take it easy today," he advised. "You've been through a lot. You don't owe anybody anything today."

After we got out of the car, Dory turned to me. "Is your mother's new boyfriend great, or what?"

I borrowed Dory's cell again so I could call Eileen from my bedroom, but I just got her voice mail. It didn't seem right to leave a message that my father died on voice mail. I fell asleep with the phone in my hand before I could figure out what to do.

Dory's knock on my open bedroom door woke me up. The casement window was just letting in the last of the day's light.

"You should eat something or you'll wake up hungry in the middle of the night. I brought you some food."

"Food?" I thought about those brownies.

"Here." She put it on my bed. It was big, a fourteen-inch, pepperoni and mushroom pizza. I must have looked surprised. "It's not all for you." She sat down on the bed, forcing me to make room for her.

"Did you call Eileen?" Dory usually called her "that girl" or "that woman up at State." I was getting all kinds of concessions today because my father just died. I handed Dory back her cell phone, which was dead. "Alan called you on the house phone," she said, "but you were sound asleep. Anyway, the funeral's the day after tomorrow."

"What do I have to do?"

"Um, Anita called to say you don't have to do anything."

"Good."

"Um, I don't think she really meant that. I said you would call her."

"I thought I was finally rid of her."

"I think she wishes you would do a walk-through at the funeral home tomorrow."

I could tell that Dory really thought I should do it, and so I said I would.

We started to eat the pizza. She sat straight up on the bed with her legs folded under like only girls can do. She told me Jeremy couldn't do my courier job again that day, and so he had called the law firm and told them they'd just have to wait. I asked her if Jeremy had relented and would move out to an apartment with her.

"No. It's just .... No."

"Just give him an ultimatum."

"You don't understand how people do things, Tim. My mother says give him a little more time."

"You talked to your *mother* about Jeremy?" I laughed. "Oh wait, let me guess. You also talked to Tracey, and to Kim, and to all your other friends at work, including even Cameron, and ...."

She hit me. "... and *you too*!"

"Oh. Oh yeah. Me." I laughed again, at myself this time. It was embarrassing. I had thought I was so special I was the only one Dory was confiding in. I guessed they did talk about romance in Dory's mother's house. "I'm just an idiot, Dory. Hit me again."

Anita held a little wake after the funeral. I dreaded going, envisioning myself just sitting on chairs with her and her sister while a few of Anita's old friends mumbled condolences about a loss I really couldn't feel. There was nothing to talk to Anita about. There were no good memories of my father that Anita and I had in common. But she was devoted to him, and I knew I probably should go. Dory said I absolutely had to go, and so I made her go with me.

At first, it was just as dreary as I'd feared. A few of Anita's relatives tried to get me into conversations about my father, but I had no idea what to say. Gradually, though, more and more people came, mostly from my father's office. They were drinking more than Anita's relatives. They started telling stories about my father, like the fact that he constantly failed to turn in his statistical reports on time, claiming that he couldn't keep the dates straight – but he had remembered everyone's birthday for the last twenty years.

"Your father was not a great legal researcher," one guy told me. "But he invented the legal doctrine that has guided this firm in all its litigation ever since."

"What?" I said this, though I had no interest in legal doctrine.

"The Unfairness Clause," he explained. "You know, when something just isn't right."

"That's a legal doctrine?"

"It became a legal doctrine, once your father got a hold of it. He had this basic idea that the law was supposed to be fair, and that we shouldn't get lost in all the legal claptrap. I think he really believed that. He was definitely a good influence on the whole firm."

I was pondering the Unfairness Clause when I saw Robert, my boss from my downtown law firm. "I just signed onto your father's old firm," he said, smiling at me warmly. "They said I had to come to the funeral. Tim, I would have come anyway."

Anita's sister was shorter, with frizzy grey hair, and without Anita's sharp bony edges or impeccable fingernails or coordinated jewelry. Anita was so straight-backed, her dark eyes so strained and red-rimmed, her face held together so stoically, her attention so focused on making sure that every detail of the wake was just right, that she really needed her sister to soften her edges with this crowd of well-meaning people. Before I left, I was going to say to her that no one could have taken better care of my father in his illness, but every other person in the room had already told her that exact same thing.

My mother did not try to compete with Anita's official wake, but after it was over, she invited all my friends to her house. "Come on in. Just relax," she said at the door. "We have beer and soft drinks, and Alan has volunteered to go out and get any kind of food you want."

"How are you doing, Tim?" she asked me privately in the kitchen.

"Fine."

"I know it hurts. He really loved you."

"Mom, I noticed something at the end. He stopped whining. He started fighting for his life. It didn't work, but at least he was fighting. I'm glad I was with him at the end."

"He was a good man. He just let himself get carried away."

"Mom, how can you say that? I watched him scream at you, throw things around. He was dangerous. How did you stand that as long as you did? "

"He was a passionate man. Sometimes he turned those passions against me. But he never hit me."

"When he jumped all over you like that, I knew I should stop him. But I was too weak back then."

She hugged me so hard she embarrassed herself, stepped back. "Tim, no one expected you to stop him. Or punish him. As I've watched you grow up, I've come to realize there's a lot of him in you. You are everything he could have been, if he could have kept control of himself."

The wake gradually turned into more of a party. The old folks sipped their Manhattans and Old Fashioneds. Jeremy showed them a lot of dramatic nature videos on the internet. Jeremy had his arm around Dory, but she still seemed miffed that he wouldn't move out into an apartment with her. Korean Kim told me the calculus exam "was not as hard as we had feared." American Kim rolled her eyes at his precise English sentence and gave me an I-told-you-so look.

"You and Kim have something in common," American Kim said.

"You both live in a basement." But there were some differences, she explained. I did not have to buy all my food out and eat it in the basement. I was allowed to use the front door, and the bathroom. I was allowed to talk to the other people in the house.

"My uncle is very strict," he tried to explain, "but he is a very good man." I didn't even need to look at American Kim to know she was rolling her eyes again.

The unspoken cultural compromise struck between the old and the young folks was that Dory and her friends could smoke their pot, but only out on the side porch. People kept filtering back into my mother's living room, though. My mother sailed in and calmly chatted up all the girls like they were her nieces or something. She pointed to the pile of pizza boxes and laughed and said Ben now owed her *two* home cooked meals. Jeremy shot me a look like – *this is your mother*? It was her, but with all the tightness taken out. This was the woman I remembered from when I was really small.

Alan came in. He tried to stay in the background at first, but soon he was sitting on my mother's leather ottoman, drinking beer and talking real estate with Ben and Tracey. Of course, because he was a social worker, his real estate talk was sprinkled with words like "affordability" and "low and moderate income," but Tracey and Ben were right with him. Ben looked fascinated, soaking up any tidbit of information about real estate, all with an air of calm confidence. Tracey let him ask most of the questions.

American Kim sat down next to me. "I know. I know. Miss State University. Far, far away. Working hard. You had your chance with me and you blew it. I want to talk about something else. When Jeremy and Dory move out of your house, why don't you rent out the room to Kim? What I told you about his uncle is only the tip of the iceberg. The man is really cruel to him, and he doesn't seem to know how to handle it."

"Sounds okay, but Jeremy doesn't want to move out with Dory."

"Oh, come on, Tim. If Dory wants them to move out, they'll be moving out."

I made the mistake of asking her what she did for Cameron's real estate company.

It had something to do with litigation over federal mortgage banking regulations. Because it mattered to her, I tried to understand, but the whole world of mortgage banking regulations sounded really dry and complicated. My father had done some regulatory litigation too, but he had always made it sound like he was on one side of a gang fight in an alley.

I met my mother again alone in the kitchen. "Tim, if Alan or I can help you in any way …."

"You've already done the best thing you possibly could have done – by hooking up with him."

"I'm so glad you like him! He's great, isn't he? Oh, and here's something. Your father left you a little insurance policy, $30,000. As part of the divorce, I made him keep paying the premiums."

I went to my father's gave early the next day with Dory. It was a little shocking because it was just a dirt rectangle with no headstone yet. I hoped, when they put on a headstone, that it wouldn't say beloved husband of Anita or some such crap as that. But it didn't matter. He was deep in there, cold as dirt, starting to rot. I didn't feel the way that people say you do, like there's an empty spot in your life now that he's gone. That spot had already been empty for way too long.

"Eileen seemed upset that I didn't call her until last night."

"I'd be pissed too." Dory had taken another half day off to come out to the graveyard with me. "She knew him too, right?"

"She met him once. He charmed her with his middle-aged gallantry stuff."

"That wasn't it. She wanted to be with you, or at least talk to you on the phone."

"Coming out here was a mistake. I thought I would get it over with – scream at him, curse at him, anything. I don't feel anything at all now. At least he was honest at the end. But the only thing I'm sure of now is I don't want to be like him."

"I don't understand. I just don't understand how people can make things so complicated."

"You're nothing like me, Dory. I bet you'll cry when your father dies."

We just stood there looking at the dirt rectangle. My father had wanted too many tears out of me when he was alive. It's not that I was glad that he was dead. If he had kept living, I would have loved to have brought Eileen down to match wits with him. They would have loved each other. I looked over and Dory was crying.

"I'm sorry. I shouldn't have brought you out here to show you the evil side of me."

"No, no," she snuffled. "What you said. I never actually imagined until just now that my own father will actually, really die someday."

I put my arm around her shoulders and we both faced the burial plot. The place was green and quiet, like graveyards are supposed to be. Dory lived in a soft universe where the sun always shined golden even on the tombstones and where the bad things like disappointment and disease and death are not anybody's fault. They are just acts of God, which is why she believed in God. I didn't believe in anything but friends. Dory had first dropped into my life as such a sexy young thing that I never thought we could actually be friends, but we were. Right then the two friends were looking down at that dirt rectangle, and the wrong one was crying. But at least somebody was crying.

"Stop for a minute." We were on the front porch at the house, just getting ready to go in the door. Even the pizza district was glorious in the fall. I turned her around and we watched as hordes of gold leaves shook themselves off the trees and swirled through the air and onto the street and the lawn and across the porch.

"Thanks for everything. You are really something, Dory. I mean that. I'll start working on Jeremy. He'll wake up to what he's got."

She tilted her head and smiled sadly. The wind ruffled her long golden braids, which wavered in the sunlight against her purple sweater. Those blue eyes were suddenly locked on mine. She put her hand on my chest.

"Don't hit me again, Dory. Twice is enough."

But hitting me wasn't what she had in mind.

What is the dramatic question?
By Pg. 115 I had wanted all to 'work' for Tim & Eileen.
Perhaps I should hope Tim escapes the boys mentality and seeks a professional life?!

Chapter 12

Eileen picked me up at my house about ten o'clock on the day before Thanksgiving. There would be another four hours of driving before we would reach her father's house in the suburbs of Washington or, as she called it, "D.C." I had never been embarrassed about the condition of our house before, but she looked instantly out of place there in her black skirt, silk blouse, silver bracelet, low heels. She said she wanted to see what she called "this famous house" anyway. I showed her all the rooms on the first floor. That took about twenty seconds. I told her I slept down in the basement.

"Yeah, I knew that. And that's where you do your weights too, right?"

She didn't say she wanted to see my bedroom, so after a long pause I asked her if she did. After another long pause, she said "No. You know what would happen."

I did.

"We're pushing it already as far as traffic goes. If we don't get there by three o'clock we'll be tied up in the giant D.C. Thanksgiving traffic jam until midnight." She said she had basically pulled two all-nighters, corrected papers until two a.m., just so she could get out of State by six that morning.

I drove while she nodded off, her head bobbing and jerking, until I convinced her to lie down in the back seat. We rode out of town, through county after county of low, green, tree-covered mountains separated by muddy rivers and fringed at the bottom with industrial plants, gas stations, convenience stores, and other useful or formerly useful structures. After a couple of hours the land flattened out, and we were sucked into the giant funnel of traffic draining the entire east coast through the narrow passage at Washington, D.C. We had to stop at one point. She got out of the back seat and went inside, and when she came out she said she felt a lot better and offered to drive. She still looked tired to me, and I insisted on driving the whole way. "But we can't stop any more. The traffic is getting worse by the minute."

But we did get there, even a little early. I saw a sign for Bethesda, the suburb where her father lived. "Take the exit north or south?"

"South." Soon, however, we were obviously going away from Bethesda. In fact, we were obviously going more and more into the city itself. It was a fancy part of the city, but it definitely was not any suburb. We went another mile or so in what I was sure had to be the wrong direction, but she seemed sure of herself.

"You want to take a right up here." We turned into a smaller street, but it didn't have any houses on it. "Okay, another right." An even smaller street. It had park-like greenery and some institutional-looking buildings, but still no houses. "Now, that driveway on the left, turn in."

"What? That's ..."

"... our hotel," she said. "We're not due at my father's until tomorrow."

"You're not mad?" she said an hour later.

"Wha..?" I was dumbstruck, out of breath, delirious with fatigue and joy, but definitely not mad.

"I did trick you."

"Believe me. That was okay."

"Okay?" She bounced over toward me on the bed. Leaning on

an elbow, her thick hair curtained behind her face, she touched my lips, then trailed her fingers slowly across my chest. "No one's ever made me feel this good," she said, her eyes wandering to my chest, which she began to kiss very slowly, making a noise in her throat almost like she was purring. "Maybe there's something I can do to make you feel more than okay."

"I have a feeling I'm going to find out."

There wasn't a lot of talk this time either. After it was over, she asked me to wake her in half an hour. "I have to get cleaned up and dressed. So do you."

"What? Why?"

"Surprise number two. We're going to see *Othello* at the Folger Shakespeare Theater tonight. I got us tickets."

We were back in the room by 11:00. Eileen had used up every cent she had on the hotel and tickets, and we couldn't even afford to drink afterwards in the hotel bar. We had bought some rum at a liquor store and brought it back to the room earlier. We were both quiet at first, maybe because we were so tired, maybe because we had just watched, from 30 feet away, Othello strangle Desdemona in a jealous rage. "There's one more surprise, number three" she said.

"You've got to be kidding me."

"I'm not really sure what you will think about it. I have the box your father sent you. His wife sent it back to me again just before he died. I can go get it out of my car trunk right now."

"I don't know if I want to see it or not."

"I thought you might say that. Was it awful, seeing him die?"

"Not worse than seeing him alive. I don't mean that. I mean he was more honest in the last couple of days than he had ever been, to me at least. If he would have lived, maybe we could've gotten to know each other. But I don't know."

"You haven't talked about him since he died."

"I don't know what to say. The whole thing, his whole life – I just don't get it."

"It bothers you, I can tell. But it shouldn't. You shouldn't be ashamed of how you feel."

We walked up the long stone walk toward her father's house, the house he had bought for his new wife. Sheaves of golden leaves were still hanging on the trees. The November air was unseasonably moist and warm. Eileen's father was a lobbyist, she told me. His client used to pay to put him up in a D.C. hotel during the entire congressional session, but he had gotten so used to the town when he was young he had decided to settle in there for life. I asked her what he was like.

"He's fine. He thinks I can do no wrong, so don't worry. It's not that he knows me that well. He was away at work, or wherever, most of the time when I was growing up."

He was standing on the stone front porch sneaking a cigarette. Tall and really thin, grey hair and wearing a suit. "Honey!" He threw the cigarette away and in the same motion opened his arms for her. I could tell he wasn't really sure she was going to walk into them, but she did. She introduced me as a friend. I liked that role right then, not having to impress anybody. It seemed like her father was the one who was trying to make a good impression, on her.

"Mike sends his love," she said.

"Are you two in touch now?"

"Oh yeah, all the time. Ever since Brittany dumped him."

"Why he ever got mixed up with her I'll never know."

In the living room I met Robin, his new wife. You always expect the trophy wife, but she was a chunk, short grey hair capped around a round face, no-nonsense eyes. Eileen's father would have to be described as smooth, but the word for Robin was solid. They gave me a beer and I set it on one of their fancy cork coasters. Then I met Robin's daughter, Kit, a tall girl who looked about sixteen or seventeen with a thin face, messy blonde hair cut just above her shoulders, and glasses. Eileen was playing the part of the sophisticated woman in front of Robin, rather than the role of chatty new sister with Kit, and so the kid got nervous. She answered Eileen's questions with hands folded on her knees.

There would be no awful scene at that Thanksgiving dinner table. To have such a scene, you have to have somebody willing to fight, but getting along seemed to be the highest priority in this house. But I couldn't help noticing an almost palpable note of resignation in the way her father and Robin talked to each other, as if they had long ago lowered their expectations of each other.

Eileen seemed to be reveling in her status as a fellow adult. She didn't tell her father or Robin much about my relationship with her, and I thought it best not to emphasize that I was a twenty-year-old community college student. Robin seemed pleasantly surprised when Eileen struck up a conversation right away, asking her casually about her job, her hours, the D.C. traffic, how she liked her house, why she picked various pieces of furniture. At the same time, Eileen challenged her father's every statement about economics or business or politics. Her father seemed happy that she was engaging with him at all; but it also seemed like he was a little uncomfortable with this new, sophisticated woman who was also his daughter. I could tell he wished his son were there. Kit, Robin's daughter, didn't really get into the conversation except when they talked about running.

"Tim runs too, and he bikes," Eileen told them both. "Actually, he supports himself working as a bike courier for a law firm."

"And you're in college too?" Robin almost insisted.

"Yes."

"I guess all that keeps you very busy."

"Yes."

"My father," Eileen said, "is a lobbyist for the American Tire Manufacturers' Association."

"Really?" I said, just happy that Eileen had drawn the attention away from me. "I don't really know what a lobbyist does."

"That's a good question," he said. Looking right at me and speaking in a really casual and confident voice, he went on. "My job is to make sure Congress has the facts before it acts on legislation.

Not newspaper stories, not ideological dogma, but hard facts. For example, right now we are making sure the committee is aware that the cheapest Chinese tires have a 65 percent greater rate of blowouts than any American-made tire."

"... so that Congress will raise tariffs on *all* Chinese tires," Eileen interrupted him, "even on the good Chinese tires, so his clients can raise the prices of all of their tires."

"Sure. They don't hire me out of the pure goodness of their hearts." He was completely unfazed by Eileen's comment. "But the one thing you need in a democracy is the actual facts. If the people elected to Congress passed laws based only on the knowledge that they actually have themselves, our country would be in a lot worse shape than it is already."

No one at the table seemed to want to keep this line of conversation going. I got the idea that everyone else had heard his spiel too many times already. He seemed perfectly willing to let it go. Things got quiet. Where was Ben when we needed him? He would have been asking these people how much houses in this neighborhood cost. I figured that this visit was Eileen's way of drawing up the outlines of a truce with Robin that might last the rest of their lives. She teased Robin about her husband still smoking. Although Eileen of course didn't want him to smoke, she couldn't hide the little bit of satisfaction she felt that even Robin could not cure him of this weakness. They seemed to be assuring themselves that this was the same guy they both had experienced, and that Eileen was now willing to share him with her. Robin's face relaxed and wrinkled with smiles. Eileen's father had pretended not to notice there might be something awkward in his daughter meeting Robin for the first time since that lunch meeting ten years before, when he was married to Eileen's mother. Eileen pretended as well. Maybe there really wasn't that much to be awkward about. I was just glad they weren't focusing on me and asking me how old I was.

Kit did not seem interested in joining any part of the conversation about Eileen's father. I turned to her. "I guess they put us together down here at the kiddie end of the table."

Kit took a quick breath. Her glasses were loose and kept sliding down her nose. "Um, I think my Mom's focusing on buttering up Eileen."

"That sucks. You're the real daughter."

She pushed her glasses up. "You don't have to advocate for me, Mr. Muscleman."

"You don't like the muscles?"

"I don't."

"I don't like your dorky glasses."

"I hear a lot of musclemen are gay."

"Everybody who wears dorky glasses is a dork."

Eileen's father took his bourbon on the rocks outside so he could smoke. Eileen and I cleared off the dishes. Robin called out to us to save the scraps for scraps. I looked at Eileen. "Scraps, the dog," she explained. "Scraps lives out in the garage. It's a long story."

Robin announced that she had made both pumpkin and cherry pie. She cut the pies and put the pieces on little plates and asked Kit to serve them.

"Hey, we have a lot of cherry down here at the kiddie end of the table." I looked right at Kit.

"Here, Kit," Robin rushed to solve the problem, "give him something other than cherry."

I looked right at Kit again. "That's all right. Cherry is all I want."

Kit stared at me while she dumped a piece of pumpkin pie just on the edge of her mother's plate. I silently dared her to make a smart-ass reply, but she thought better of it. Then nobody made eye contact for a while.

Eileen suppressed a smile. Robin didn't understand why Eileen had stopped talking, and for an instant that taut look came back to her face. Then Eileen focused on her main job, forging a truce. I forgot about Kit and just watched Eileen's face.

. . .

"Your father isn't coming back in?" Eileen and I sat alone on the glass-enclosed side porch while Robin and Kit cleaned up the kitchen. The weak afternoon sun shone through the high bushes outside and flooded the room with a reflected greenish light.

"He's in his office downstairs. You've seen about all there is to see of him, Tim, unless you want to talk about the American Tire Manufacturers' Association."

"Is he a big wheel?"

"Stop. He is what he is, and he was always okay to me when he was around. Mostly, he ignored me, but I've talked to enough girl roommates in dorms on enough long weekend nights to know that's what fathers do."

"So your mother is the one who raised you, right?"

"Yeah. But, my brother Mike, he was basically it for me. He still is, in a way."

Kit came in and plopped down with a glass in her hand.

"Tell the truth, guys." She waggled her index finger back and forth between each of us. "What's up?"

"They let you drink wine in the house?"

"On Thanksgiving. Your father smokes a lot."

"He always did. Back then, he did it in the house."

"My mother's always trying to get him to quit."

"My mother smokes too," Eileen said resignedly. "When I was growing up, the kitchen was always filled with a blue haze. That's probably why I never did smoke. How about you?"

"I tried it, but I don't like it. Anyway I don't have the time. I take three AP classes every semester, and I play tennis all spring and summer." Kit sipped her wine, swung her legs, took off her glasses and twirled them around as she talked. "It's so boring here."

"Tough to be such a loser that you don't even have a date on Thanksgiving," I suggested.

I knew she wouldn't flinch. "So, are you two going to sleep in the same bed tonight?"

"No."

"Afraid of my Mom?"

"Kit, you don't understand the relationship between Tim and me." I had no idea where Eileen was going with this. "There's this mentorship program in the psychology department at the university. They pick bright community college students, and we try to encourage them. I'm showing Tim around D.C. I took him to see *Othello* last night at the Folger Shakespeare Theater."

"So you're really not a couple?"

"He didn't have any place to go for Thanksgiving, and your Mom was okay with me bringing him here. Anyway, look at him. He's way too young for me."

Kit looked at me but talked to Eileen. "You're talking about him like he isn't even here."

I was trying to think of something to say besides "bwa bwa bwa."

"Kit, it's cool. She's showing me a lot." I looked right at Eileen. "She's letting me in some exciting places."

"I knew you weren't a real college student."

"I knew you weren't a snob. Oh no, I guess I was wrong about that."

Eileen put her hand up between us to get our attention. I thought she meant to tell Kit the truth before her little joke on me went too far, but just then Robin came in and said that Eileen's father wanted to talk to her. She went downstairs to talk to him alone in his basement office, leaving me alone with Kit. I didn't know how Kit would react if I told her that Eileen had been lying to her just to tease me, so I decided to stick with the mentor story until Eileen got back. But it got worse. She asked me how old I was and I answered that one truthfully. But then she started asking about the mentorship program. I suspected she knew the whole thing was phony and was just torturing me, but I couldn't be sure. If Eileen was there, and there was a table between us, I would have kicked her hard under that table.

I tried to turn the conversation toward Kit, asking her about her AP classes and her tennis – all the while implying, of course, that these were the activities of a dork who didn't have any friends. She was obviously a smart kid who was ambivalent about her conventional accomplishments and hadn't decided yet whether it was a good thing or not that she didn't quite fit in at school, or in this family. I wanted to tell her that she seemed perfectly fine to me and that things would probably turn out nicely for her, but I didn't want to get even that involved. The longer the conversation went on, and the more open and candid she was, the more guilty I felt for deceiving her. I waited and waited for Eileen to get back so we could come clean. Finally, I told Kit that I had to go for a run.

It was a relief to be out on the streets. There was just enough hazy light left to read the street signs. I memorized the names of the cul-de-sacs and courts and lanes and terraces and mews like breadcrumbs so I could find my way back through the development. The sidewalks ended at the main road, so I ran on the shoulder, against traffic, for a couple of miles, then back. As I approached the back door, a huge black poodle ran up and jumped on me, almost knocking me down. The dog just wanted to play, but it played rough. We started to have a good time running around the yard in the twilight.

"Oh, you've met Scraps." Eileen opened the door and came outside. She had changed into jeans and a sweatshirt. "Isn't that one beautiful dog?" She came out into the yard and wrestled with Scraps too, all three of us running, falling, rolling around while chasing and being chased across the yard.

"I didn't know you liked dogs," she said after we put Scraps to bed.

"At least somebody wants physical contact with me."

She punched me. "No whining, please. Couldn't you have waited for me so I could have run with you?"

"I had to get out right then. You left me in *bwa bwa* land with Kit. Did your father ever come back upstairs? What were you two talking about?"

"We had a drink together in his office. He asked me all about Mike, what his plans are now. He didn't say a word about you. He asked me why I'm not married."

We went in and sat alone on the enclosed porch again, the bushes outside the windows now black silhouettes against a faint rosy sky. Her legs were curled under her on the sofa, her running shoes set out neatly below her on the carpet. She asked me to help her close the windows against the cool air. I started to sit down next to her but changed my mind at the last minute. She noticed.

"I know this is hard," she said. "It was a bad idea, sleeping apart in the same house. It's just … I've never stayed in Robin's house before, and …."

"It's okay. But can you at least tell Kit the truth tomorrow?"

Kit helped me pump up a little inflatable bed in the basement. Eileen's father had closed his office down there for the night. It was one huge carpeted room that took up almost the entire basement, with Eileen's father's desk and office equipment and small bar arranged in a large alcove at the back. I had pushed myself hard during the run, but it was dealing with Kit and Robin and Eileen's father that had really worn me out. I lay on that bed on the floor trying not to think about what we did the night before in that bed in the hotel. From my spot on the floor I could see a few stars through the dark casement window.

I heard the door at the top of the stairs open and close quietly. My heart jumped, and I was instantly hard in anticipation of surprise number four.

But it was Kit. She tiptoed down the stairs without turning on the light. "Tim, shh, I hope I didn't wake you. Just sneaking down for another glass of wine."

"Oh." Fortunately, it was so dark there was no chance she would notice my condition. She passed by me in the utter darkness towards the alcove, where she turned on an under-counter light, poured herself a glass, and snapped the light off again. I could barely see her then, but I could hear that she stopped next to me.

"I poured you a glass too." I could see her now as she sat down on the floor next to my mattress. She sat with her legs under her, leaning slightly to one side, one hand on the floor for balance.

"Thanks. That's really nice." I leaned up from the plastic inflated pillow and took a sip. The house above was stone quiet.

"I didn't really mean," she said, "that you weren't a college student. I meant that you were not, like, in graduate school, or, in the same … age category, as Eileen."

"I knew what you meant. And no matter what I said, I don't think you're a snob. That was just part of me kidding you, like you were kidding me."

"Do you like this wine?" she asked.

"I don't know anything about wine, but I think I like it."

"I like it."

Her light blonde hair had looked a little scraggly at dinner – like she was sending a message to her mother and her new stepfather that she didn't need to impress them – but now it all hung straight and smooth and bright, whichever way she tilted her head.

"I can hardly see you." My voice came out higher than I'd like. "Let's turn on a light."

"Don't. I can see you fine. I'll get a little closer."

"Kit, you have to know something."

She stopped, took a quick breath. I could feel her bracing herself. "I'm. Not. That. Young. I'm almost seventeen. You're twenty. Eileen's 23. I'm as close to your age as she is."

"I didn't say you were too young. But I have to tell you some things about Eileen. Eileen likes you. She's excited about getting to know you. Can you tell that?"

"I think so."

"But, um, she'll do anything in the world to embarrass me, just for fun."

"What are you talking about?"

"That's just the way she is. She makes up stories about me just to embarrass me. Like tonight. You know, the mentorship program."

"What?"

"Think about it. If we saw *Othello* late last night at a theater downtown, where did we sleep last night?"

I could hear her swallow her wine.

"Together, obviously," she finally said in a whisper so low it could disguise any embarrassment in her voice. She took another sip. I could hear her swallow it. Took another sip.

"I'm not talking about last night," she said. "How's your wine?"

Eileen put her face in her hands the moment the car turned the corner. "That was tough."

"What? You were spectacular. You had them all eating out of your hand."

"I tried. You know what made it a little easier? I kept thinking all the time: if this detente with Robin and my father goes all to shit, I'll still have Tim."

I felt like a boy who had just been given a two-day lesson by a woman on how to act in the grown-up world. We drove out of the cul-de-sac and headed for the beltway that would lead us to the interstate north. She soon put her hands down from her face and relaxed, touched me on the shoulder, smiled. "You were great with everybody, even Kit. I want to be friends with her, but I think she likes you even better than she likes me."

I'm always trying to figure out to what extent not saying something to a woman is the same as lying. I said thank you to her several times, but the car droned along over the next several miles, and those two words didn't seem to be enough. "It seems to me," I said finally, "you could have your pick of almost any guy. I have no idea why you picked me. I *do* know how lucky I am."

We stopped at a rest stop and parked at the far end of the lot. While we were kissing, she ran her fingers over my chest again. "I'm kind of getting used to these muscles."

We were more than halfway back to the pizza district when she startled me out of my driving trance. "Did something happen between you and Kit last night?"

* My grown-up world was never so antagonistic.

When you're driving 75, it's amazing how far you can travel between question and answer.

"What do you mean?"

"It seemed like she wouldn't even make eye contact with you this morning."

"Um ... I told her last night we had been lying to her about the mentorship program."

"It wasn't lying. I was just teasing – teasing *you*."

"It fooled her, at first. I think she was a little hurt."

"I wish you would have waited and let me tell her myself."

~ Chapter 13 ~

"So, is this our honeymoon?"

Eileen was referring to the candles I had lit in my bedroom. She wouldn't let me keep them lit because the hot wax was dripping on the cardboard boxes I had set them up on. I didn't have any actual furniture except the bed, so I didn't have any other place to put them. I had brought a fire extinguisher into the bedroom in case something happened, but it still wasn't safe enough for her.

"Um. For our honeymoon, I guess we could go someplace better."

We were lying there, kissing lazily, fooling around. "I like this place," she said. "I like being here. I like being in your bed."

It was the night after Thanksgiving. She had mentioned on the way back from her father's house that she had a free day. "... but no money. Do you have any?"

"Seventeen dollars is all I have until next payday. But listen to this. In a couple of months I'm going to get $30,000 from my father's life insurance policy. It makes me feel weird, that I should get money out of this."

"What a sad way for that to happen."

I hadn't known if she would actually stay in our grubby house. Maybe I had been over-impressed by the neatness of her dorm room and by our stay in Robin's meticulous house. But she came right in, put her coat and pocketbook down on the stained sofa and walked into the kitchen after me so I could look for something to drink.

Right then, Dory came down the stairs on her way out of the house, and I introduced them. I had never seen Dory blush before. "Nice to meet you." Dory was obviously a little nervous.

"Nice to meet you. Tim talks about you and Jeremy and Ben so much I feel like I already know you all."

"Oh. Well, I was on my way out. Welcome to our humble abode." She went out.

Eileen looked at me.

I shrugged. "She usually talks a little more. A lot more."

But later, in bed, Eileen said she wanted to ask me something. "When your father died, nobody was answering the phone at your house, so I called the funeral home and talked to this guy who said he was a funeral counselor. When I said I was your girlfriend, he said, 'Oh, we already met. The way you've been at his side during this crisis has been admirable. You are really helping him pull through.' Was he talking about Dory?"

"Uh-huh."

"What did he mean, 'at his side all the time'?"

"She was great. She and my mother's boyfriend, Alan, stayed all night with me in the hospital the night he died. They slept on those plastic sofas in the waiting room. After that, she helped me do what I had to do, every step of the way. Not to dis my other friends. Everyone was really nice."

"But why did she blush when we met?"

Damn women notice everything.

"Tim, I'm happy she's your friend – if you can just tell me I don't have to worry about her being more than a friend."

If the honeymoon conversation had thrown my life halfway off the track I'd been following for the last ten years, Eileen's worrying about Dory threw me the rest of the way off. Ever since I noticed that girls were different from boys I had danced around committing to them. I had seen from my father's example that women could overpower your heart. They could make you turn your back on what you held sacred. They could run you over like a freight train. And so I'd always watched them from an ironic distance, toyed with them as from a parallel track. But Eileen was now plainly surrendering her heart to me. It seemed like the first real responsibility I had ever been given.

"You have nothing to worry about."

Neither did I. Everything I wanted was right there in front of me. There were no tracks, no freight trains, just journeys.

Ben had eaten Thanksgiving dinner at his parents' house. They gave him leftovers to feed the house on Friday. That was such a big hit he went out and bought another turkey and cooked it himself for the house on Saturday. Eileen and I were flat broke and very grateful for this. A couple of his friends from the auto parts store, Dory's real estate friends, and even both Kims came and stayed for dinner. I made sure to give Korean Kim a tour of the house.

Eileen was the newcomer here, and she didn't try to mess with anybody's head. She wore jeans and plain blouses, slightly less fancy clothes than Dory and her friends. There were a lot of opinions expressed about how to cook the turkey and the side dishes that Ben had planned. Eileen relegated herself to the role of sous chef, chopping or cutting up celery or apples or doing whatever else Ben asked her to. Ben seemed happy to work with at least one person who did not have an opinion about how everything should be done.

"I learned to keep my mouth shut," I overheard her explaining to him, "from years of trying to cook with my mother."

Ben's friends from the auto parts place had brought two folding plastic tables from the employees' lunch room at the shop. They were originally designed to be used outdoors, but we set them up and lined them up with our own tiny kitchen table. We had room for almost everybody, though a few had to sit on the sofa to eat – and a few had to eat standing up, hovering over the stove or leaning into the conversation at the table. Eileen and American Kim and Tracey sat at one end of the last table, consuming a bottle of red wine they had appropriated for themselves and chatting away. It seemed like they were on that girlie wave length where they all just suddenly believe they have all experienced basically the same life. The more they drank, the more they laughed.

I overheard Eileen talking to American Kim about *Othello*. "It was so intense. You wouldn't be able to get it from just reading the play. Not that I read the play."

"What's it about?"

"Jealousy, leading up to murder. Othello strangles his girlfriend right on stage." Kim looked skeptical. "No, really, it was great," Eileen insisted. "We both liked it." She paused. "I hope Tim didn't like it too much. Do you think I should worry that Tim chose *Othello* as the play he wanted to study this semester?"

American Kim grabbed me by the shirt sleeve as I was walking by. "Your girlfriend is okay. I promise I won't call her Miss State University any more."

In the middle of the dinner, I got a call from Robert, my old boss at the downtown law office I worked for. I knew from my father's wake that Robert was now working at my father's old firm. He offered me a job there. It was doing paralegal work, not bike courier work, and it paid more for the same number of hours.

"Sounds like a pity offer to me," Tracey shouted her opinion from the girlie end of the table. I was reminded of Tracey at the real estate party, modeling the new necklace Cameron had bought for his wife – then spending the rest of the night, like Dory, trying to keep out of his drunken embraces. She was over our house quite a lot now, and she never hesitated to give her opinions. "They're giving you a good job because they feel sorry for you."

"Yeah," Ben echoed her. "When things start out like that, with them giving you special treatment out of pity, eventually things will turn, and sooner or later all the other employees will start to resent you."

Dory disagreed. "They need you. They want your father back, and you're the closest thing they've got to him."

"What? I'm nothing like my father."

"They're guessing you are. And maybe you're not. But maybe when they get to know you, they'll like you even better than him. Give it a chance."

"You really think I should?" I was answering Dory, but my focus shifted to Eileen. "What do you think, Eileen?"

People looked over at her. I was sorry I had put her on the spot. "I don't really know much about it," she said at first. But everyone seemed to expect her to have an opinion. She thought for a moment, then tried again. "Just going on my instincts, I think Dory's right. I think they'll love you."

Jeremy burst in from outside and held both arms out to get everyone's attention. "Hey, everybody, I got a new job!"

"What is it? You didn't tell me," Dory said.

"Because I wanted to surprise you! You won't believe this. It's so easy. All I do is talk on the phone to people who want to buy cell phone service. They don't call unless they want it in the first place. All I have to do is get them to close the deal. If I sign up one a day I'll double what I'm making now. And I get paid an extra 50 bucks every time I get anyone to sign up for the Diamond Service Plan."

"Sounds great."

"I know what you're thinking, Tim. Selling out, sucking money out of people for some corporation's benefit."

"I didn't say that."

"Well, you're wrong. That's the beauty of it, Tim. The real beauty of it. Nobody needs the Diamond Service Plan. Nobody has to buy it. It's like selling toys. It's a toy they want to buy. Buy a bigger toy, put Jeremy through college."

Jeremy exited center stage and worked his way around to talk to me alone. "I can pretend all I want, but I'm just Joe College, average guy, doing whatever it takes to be smooth and get by. I'm nobody special. And if I want to keep Dory – and man, do I want to keep Dory – I'm going to have to, like, do whatever it takes to keep her interested."

"Does that mean you're going to move out with her?"

"Done. Decided, anyway. I was thinking, of all the guys in the world, how many would *not* want to move into a tiny little love nest with Dory? Nobody! Everybody wants what I can have, if I take just this one step. That's why I got the job. I'll have to trust you guys to tell me if it starts turning me into some type of corporate scumbag."

He leaned close to my ear. "If I have to talk a 100 people a month into the Diamond Service Plan so I can be the only noodle in her casserole, I'll do it."

"Shakespeare couldn't have said it better himself."

"No." Jeremy pushed himself off and pointed a wavering finger at me. "Shakespeare could have probably said it better. I admit that. If he knew Dory. But he didn't know Dory. So what the fuck did he know?"

Ben and Jeremy were watching television late Saturday night alone. The giant screen was filled end to end with Cat Woman crawling on her hands and knees in black leather. I sat down next to Ben on the sofa. "I have an idea for when Jeremy goes. I found the perfect roommate. Korean Kim. An *A* student. Quiet and clean. He really needs to get out of his house, and I think he has enough money to pay the rent."

Ben sat up right away, his eyes widening. He then looked down at his hands. I imagined he was counting on his fingers.

"The rent's too low. I'll need to raise the rent ten percent."

"He could probably manage that."

"I tell you what. If you show him the room and all, and he moves in here within a week of Jeremy moving out, and he pays the higher rent, I'll give you a $75 finder's fee."

"I don't know what a finder's fee is, but I'll take it."

Jeremy jumped up and clamped his hands on the sides of his head like it was exploding inside. "I can't believe this! This is disgusting. Tim, you'd be basically selling your friend."

"We're making a real estate deal," Ben said. "You believe in business, Jeremy, you just told us."

"And anyway, Jeremy," I said, "I think your real problem is you can't believe that you can be replaced for $75."

"I had a great time. I love your friends." Eileen was hugging me on the porch as she was leaving on Sunday morning. She had waited around an extra half hour for Jeremy and Ben and Dory to get up so she could say goodbye to them.

"Putty in your hands. That goes for everybody. Especially me."

"Just to be clear, to say it in the right words, you are mine, right?"

"You had me at 'honeymoon.'"

Chapter 14

I thought I was busy when I took eighteen credits and got all *A*s, ran twenty miles a week, pumped iron until my muscles were obvious and rode as a bike courier every afternoon. I had been doing all that with the idea that it was preparation – though I had never known exactly what I was preparing for. I still didn't know exactly what the goal of my life was, but my immediate days were busier than ever with all the decisions to be made.

"I'm transferring to State in January." I announced this at my mother's house at a little dinner she had for Alan and Jeremy and Dory and me. Having $30,000 insurance money coming does help you in being more decisive. I had already told Eileen about transferring, and she was ecstatic. She made me stay on the phone with her right then and look at the on-line catalogue of courses. There were hundreds of them, eight on Shakespeare alone. I was going up to see her again in the next couple of weeks, before the current semester was over.

Korean Kim moved in the day after Jeremy and Dory left. He of course could not match the entertainment value of Jeremy and Dory. Half of the fun of my old life had been making fun of Jeremy's Discovery Channel education and his pathetic attempts at weight lifting – and trying to be angry with him when he interrupted my studies by blowing cigarette smoke through the keyhole in my bedroom door. And Dory's night-time screams could never be duplicated. I would also miss the arguments with her about nutrition and her gentle insinuations that Eileen was putting me off – even though she was wrong, wrong, wrong about both subjects.

Ben and I started to clean up the house in preparation for Korean Kim's arrival, but then we decided that the only reason we were doing that was because he was Asian. Rather than engage in inappropriate ethnic stereotyping, we decided, we'd leave the slop as it was. After he moved in, Kim and I drove to school together sometimes, and he patiently helped me catch up in Calculus II. We were doing tests for convergence and divergence, and I had missed a week and a half of school and didn't even know what the words meant. But he and I rarely saw each other at the house. As expected, he did not bring any moaning women into his room. I kept the shitty basement room out of guilt for the $75 finder's fee I had taken.

I took the job at my father's old firm. It was humbling to see how much credit they gave me just because I was my father's son. The office bookkeeper pursued me, literally chased me down the hall the first day I was there, to talk about my father. This was quite a feat for him, as he was almost as wide as he was tall.

"I just wanted to say how sorry all of us are about your father. He was great. We loved him."

"Thanks." I tried in vain to think of something else to say.

"People are demoralized now. I'm afraid the office is going to shut down."

"But I thought you were going to be acquired by Liggett and Liggett?"

"We are still our own place for now. Nobody here buys into Liggett's billable hours philosophy. We like to think we're working *for* our clients, not just racking up the most billable hours against them. Your father was the leader of our passive resistance to the merger. It's been a happy place here, on account of him. Now that he's gone, I'm afraid things might fall apart."

Robert, my old boss at my old firm downtown, was learning the ropes at my father's firm, just as I was. "I was surprised," he said, "that there's no formal orientation program. And when I asked what they wanted you to do, a couple of lawyers said they needed help, but nobody took charge to make any decision."

"So, what should I do?"

He shrugged. "Why don't you just go up and talk to each of them, then tell me which one you want to work with."

"Wow, this is not like the place we used to work at all, is it?"

"Not at all. I mean, they're not young any more, but they still go out drinking together sometimes. They still play jokes on each other."

Kathryn was a real estate lawyer who was old enough to retire, but you could tell from the look on her leathery face she would never do it. She pulled me aside on my first day there.

"Your father said you were a straight-*A* student."

"That's true."

"From what he used to say about his school days, I doubt if he was a straight-*A* student himself."

I had never thought about that. "I have to tell you. I'm not anything like him."

"That might be good, in some ways. I've got permission from Robert to use you to help me negotiate some of these sale and leaseback transactions. Your father would never touch those."

I didn't ask her why.

"Do you want to know what it's about?"

"Yeah."

"These are complicated deals. The one I'm working on now is the Freedom Shopping Mall. We represent the bank financing the project – well, one of the banks, that's half the problem. There's a million little details – when the construction insurance kicks in, who pays for it, what happens if they don't pay, who is on the hook for any consequential damages, whether the construction bond is valid, whether the construction company owner really owns the property he has put up to guarantee the work, what happens if there's a detrimental zoning change, who pays if there's an unanticipated environmental impact affecting the construction plan, what is the definition of "unanticipated," how all this is affected if there's a change in the construction plans (as there almost always is) – a million other details."

"You, um, do all this yourself?"

"It's all been done before, a million times. My computer's full of sample contract clauses covering most of the issues that will come up. You just cut and paste. Ninety-nine percent of the time, the lawyers for the banks and the bonding companies and the construction companies and the architects and the landowner and developer just agree on one of these standard clauses. That's where you would come in."

"Me?"

"Every one of these clauses has to be agreed to by the lawyers for every one of these entities, and sometimes the county government has to approve some of them too. I don't have time to do that."

"How would I do that?"

"It's not that hard. I have a list of the contact people for each of the players. You run the clauses by the contact people and get their electronic signatures agreeing to them. You just have to be detailed, and careful, and persistent. Sometimes the simplest thing has to be run up the whole chain of command at one of these entities, and then there's a delay. But if anybody actually objects to a contract clause, you don't have to worry about it. It's my problem then."

"Sounds doable."

"It's not rocket science. Sometimes the other law firms want to change things because they have their own favorite language that they want to use. Just ask me when that happens. Usually it's okay. After a while you get the hang of what's a meaningful change and what's not."

"Sounds exciting," I said, straight-faced. She looked at me.

"It's not," she said. "It's a job. Somebody has to do it. But when you get into the more significant negotiations, you feel like you're an important part of a big project."

"At my old firm, all they did was fight with other lawyers all the time."

"Litigation. I never do that. Your father used to do it once in a while – just for laughs, he always said."

She started me on it that afternoon. It was tedious, but mostly cooperative with the other side, and not nearly as hard as calculus. And it paid much better than being a bike courier.

My mother put on another dinner, this time with Alan's help, and I was allowed to bring along Ben and Jeremy and Dory. While we were joking around before the dinner even started, Jeremy pulled something out of his pocket. "Here, Tim, since you're leaving to go to State, I'm giving you a going away present." It was a cellphone, a small one. "This one's so old we can't even recycle it."

"How much does it cost a month?"

"That's the beauty of it. Zippo. The Diamond Service Plan, which as a company representative I get for free, has free talk and text for family members, 'family' being defined extremely loosely. Welcome to the family. I mean, I was worried for a while you were going to lose that awesome girl over a simple failure to communicate." He couldn't just let it go at that. "I'm still afraid you're not smart enough to keep her without my constant instruction." He pointed to the phone. "Use. This. Call Eileen. Many times. Pick up when rings."

My mother liked Dory a lot and always referred to her as "that dear child" when we were alone in the kitchen. Alan had helped me arrange for a student loan for my first semester, as the insurance check I was supposed to get hadn't come through yet.

"Tim, I think you'll be happy at a place like State," he said over after-dinner coffee. "I'm convinced you can learn almost any subject. You'll probably have a chance at State to see a whole lot of options and, you know, decide what you really like."

"Maybe that's what I have to do. Decide."

Jeremy and Ben went into the living room to sample some

after-dinner port that Alan had brought along. My mother excused herself to go back in the kitchen, leaving Dory and me alone together. Dory and I had not talked alone since the day we visited my father's grave. I couldn't explain to myself what happened between us that day. I hoped it wasn't as bad as I feared.

On the porch that day, she had touched me and stepped forward into me, and we had put our arms around each other. Then she had melted her willowy body into mine and I had pulled her closer, so grateful for her touch and for helping me in those days after my father died. In a minute I was sobbing, then crying, about my father, thinking about how much we might have been to each other. She held me quietly and let me cry. We held each other for a long time, her head on my shoulder, her own tears christening my neck with the new experience of sharing pain with another person. No one had ever drawn that kind of honest weakness out of me before.

It seemed like the most natural thing when we both got aroused. I held her to me, moved my arms down toward her waist, sadness blending with sweetness. Then mostly sweetness. But then she moaned her famous "OOOOHH!" and we could no longer pretend it was just sisterly love. We untangled ourselves long enough to get through the door and fall onto the sofa. We didn't care if it was dirty. We weren't thinking. We weren't worrying about anyone walking in. The sorrow was swept away for a minute by the pleasure we were giving each other. Afterwards, the sorrow came back, and she let me lie next to her and softly cry until I was all cried out.

Only when my crying was over did Dory come into focus for me as the girlfriend of my best friend. And she read my eyes.

"I don't think Jeremy loves me," she said. "He says he does, but he won't move out with me. This house, you guys, that's what he really loves."

"He loves you."

"What about Eileen?"

"I wish she could have been here the last couple of days, for the funeral and all."

"Oh."

Now, Dory just looked at me across my mother's dining room table. She was trying very hard to give me her usual sunny smile.

"I was right," I said. "He loves you. He's moving out with you. He's changing jobs so he can afford you."

"We can never tell him," was all she said.

Dory found a little apartment right away, and Ben and I helped her and Jeremy move out. Half of everything Jeremy owned didn't make it past the trash pile. At times that morning, he looked really sad to be giving up his sweats with the holes in the knees and his broken old games and toys. But mostly he talked about living with Dory in a real apartment in a place that was just theirs and where he could pay his share of real market rate rent and demand standard conveniences such as air conditioning and faucets that shut all the way off. They threw a house-warming party the second night they were there. The place was new and immaculate, and Dory had made fruit salad and a cheese plate and some kind of spinach pie with a vegan crust. American Kim brought some pigs-in-blankets. Ben and I brought a bucket of KFC. People drank beer and made hard drinks, and there was a faint smell of pot in the air.

As I was looking at the table, I noticed that people seemed to be avoiding a lot of the food. American Kim crept up behind me and whispered in my ear. "Dare you to take a bite of that vegan pie."

"What? What'd she say?" Jeremy was standing right on the other side of the table.

"Nothing. Nothing," I said. Jeremy looked from one of us to the other, then down at the table. He caught my eye again, picked up a knife, cut a huge piece of Dory's untouched pie and put it on his plate.

"You don't know enough to take the really good stuff that's offered to you."

Dory was dressed kind of fancy and acted at first like she was some kind of real estate agent giving us a formal tour of the amenities, but a few seconds into the two-minute tour she was giggling. It was basically a small beige box with white trim, with strangers living on the other side of every wall. They had a cute little kitchenette, a cute little dining/living room and a cute little bedroom. Jeremy's rumply old bed seemed too big and out of place in the clean, bare bedroom. They did have the best view in the development. If you looked across the parking lot and between two other buildings, you could see the lights of the tall buildings downtown.

Jeremy seemed intent on listing its pros and cons. "No pool, no party room, no workout center. But no condo fees! We can't hear the neighbors through the walls, an' we sure as hell hope they can't hear us. See, hardwood floors in the living room."

"I love hard wood," Dory said innocently, but Jeremy caught my eye and bent over in loud exaggerated laughter. I hadn't realized he was drunk. Dory whacked at him. Ben was not drinking or taking anything. As usual, he didn't have a date. The place was crowded with people and without much furniture to sit on. Ben was wondering out loud how someone got to be the owner of a building like this. A couple of girls decided to try to explain it to him. There was nothing at all about Ben's appearance that would make the female heart race, but his aura of calm competence had almost the opposite effect. He was like a walking anxiety cure for some types of women.

Jeremy walked over and leaned against me. "You think I did the right thing, moving in with her?"

"You definitely did the right thing. Why did you drink so much tonight?"

"Try'na make a good impression. She's got a lotta friends. Hey, think about this. Can you believe it? Dory and me are fucking like bunnies. You got Eileen buying you hotel rooms and tickets and sleeping in your bed, and Ben is putting his warm comfort spell on all those twitchy young pussies on his side of the room. One, two, three. Life is good."

Jeremy was not feeling as well the next night when we met for a pizza and beer down the street. He had a hangover, but it wasn't just that. I figured it was the spinach pie, but he swore that the pie had been "absolutely okay." Instead of philosophizing constantly, as he usually did, he was just drinking his beer with a mopey look on his face.

"You're not talking." Ben finally said. "Something's wrong."

"It's weird. I found out I'm really good at selling the Diamond Service Plan. They already gave me a raise. My boss says I could sell anything."

"That's a problem?" Ben said.

"No, but is this what I'm going to do for the rest of my life? Ten years from now, will I be some bloated cell phone executive getting in his limousine and buying off politicians? That's not who I want to be."

"What does Dory think?"

Jeremy thought about that. "She asks me if the people I work with are nice. That's what she cares about mostly. She has no concept of thinking about what the company you're working for is doing for the world."

"She cares about things," I defended her. "She must care about animals, or else she wouldn't eat that crappy vegan food. She cares about the earth. She cares about her friends. She's nice to everyone." They were both looking at me. I realized I had gone on too long in praise of Jeremy's girlfriend. "And maybe one day you can combine your phone company experience and your Dory experience and invent the Orgasma-phone."

"You don't understand what I'm saying."

"I understand this. Dory's the best thing you will ever have in your life. Don't screw it up with your crazy-ass philosophy."

Jeremy talked to me alone on the way home when we left the bar. "You know, I feel kind of sorry for Ben. We both are moving on, but he's still stuck here doing the same thing."

"I wouldn't worry about Ben. He told me he's going to start fixing up the house as soon as I move out – so he can sell it and buy a better one."

Chapter 15

"Can you come up here right away?" There was something different in Eileen's voice on the phone.

"Yeah. Like we said, this Friday. I'll be there by eight o'clock."

"No, I mean now." Then I heard the urgency in her voice. "Can you come right now. Please."

I left within half an hour. She had arranged for her friend Jen to meet me at the door to the dorm and come up with me to the room. Jen's face looked softer than it had the other time I had met her here.

"What is it?" I asked as I followed her up the four flights of stairs.

"I'm not trying to be mysterious," Jen said. "You just really need to talk to her."

Jen knocked, opened the door, let me in, then disappeared. Eileen was sitting straight up in her wooden desk chair, but with her head down. When she looked up at me I could see that she had been crying. She was looking at a framed picture she held in her hand. I saw who it was and immediately knew what had happened.

"When?" I said, my own voice quavering.

"Yesterday morning. His last patrol before he was supposed to come home."

"Oh, I'm sorry."

She cried again but sat there still, shrunken but self-contained. I wanted to grab her in my arms, squeeze the pain out, breathe for her. I wasn't sure that was my place. I found a chair and pulled it next to her and put my hand over one of hers.

"I know your brother was everything to you."

She held my hand tight, still looking at the picture of Mike in her other hand. She pushed the picture away. "I have *nothing* now."

I just looked steadily at her. "You two were really close, I know."

"I wanted you to meet him. I really wanted you to meet him. With you and Mike knowing each other, I just felt, I don't know, it would just kind of complete the circle somehow. Now it never will happen. I'm sorry I'm crying so much."

"He had to know. He had to know how much you loved him."

She kept sobbing. I couldn't think of anything else to say about Mike. All I knew is that she idolized him and kept in constant e-mail contact with him ever since his life was thrown off track by his divorce. She was closer to him than to her father and maybe even her mother.

I walked to the window and looked out over the campus. I asked her if she wanted me to get her something to eat. She stood up and walked stiffly over, then swayed into my arms.

"Thank you for coming," she said.

"Let me know what you need. Anything."

"Just keep holding me for now." Over time her tears stopped, her sobs stopped. It almost seemed like she was asleep.

"Would you take me outside somewhere? I have to get out of this room."

She said she was going to her mother's house in a few days, after they flew his body back from where it was now in Germany. She stumbled over the word "body." I asked her if I could go with her to the funeral. She was surprised that I thought I had to ask. Dusk was settling in outside. She said she was ready to go downtown.

"I think I should carry this picture with me downtown." Her voice was weak.

"Why?"

"I don't know. I don't want to leave it here."

"Why?"

Her eyes looked lost. "It would be like I'm forgetting him already."

"Um, it's really just a picture. Leave it here."

I deliberately steered us to a place we'd never been to before. She hadn't eaten anything all day, but she refused to order anything except a diet soda. But even that revived her a little.

"I can't possibly know what you're feeling," I said. "I never had a brother."

"I need to tell you something about Mike. I want to get it off my mind before I have to go down there for the funeral. I was thinking about this all day before you got here. You know how I would always say we were so close, that he practically raised me? That wasn't exactly true."

"Eileen, *exactly* doesn't matter now."

"Yes it does. When I was seventeen years old, he and Brittany came over for Christmas, and I realized I hadn't seen him since the last Christmas. That's how it was, exactly."

"You knew him in college. You said you were imitating him the first two years."

"Sort of. I heard stories. You know, family legends about wild college days. When I was a teenager he never came back for me, like I secretly hoped he would. The truth is he hardly ever talked to me after he left."

"But you had gotten close since he went in the army, right?"

"We tried, I guess. I still felt like a stranger. I never told him about you."

"You always said you wanted me to meet him."

"I did. I really did. But maybe that was just to show him I could get a real guy's attention after all."

x x x

"It's not unusual to idealize a relationship with absent older siblings. It's normal, Tim. She shouldn't worry about it." This was at my mother's house a few nights later. It was just my mother and me and Alan. Alan didn't think there was anything unusual in what Eileen had said. I didn't feel disloyal to Eileen to be discussing her with my mother or even with Alan. The two of them were utterly kind and discreet. And hundreds of miles away.

I didn't know how to help her. I remembered how nice it had been for me to have Dory help me through the whole thing when my father died, showing me step by step what to do. I made some calls to Eileen's mother and her father. They were bickering about the funeral arrangements. Eileen's father talked for a while about a military burial, but I guess his heart wasn't in that, and then he wanted him buried near Bethesda, near where he lived. Eileen's mother had moved to Northern Virginia and had joined a Christian church late in life. The church was another 50 miles further south of D.C., and she wanted Mike to be buried there. I had to tell Eileen that her parents wanted her to choose. I told her exactly what Alan told Anita when my father died, that it didn't make a damn bit of difference what the arrangements were. She talked to her mother and decided to go with her mother's plan.

When I got back to the house it was late afternoon, and Ben and Korean Kim were at the kitchen table. Ben jumped up when I opened the door and rushed up to me.

"We all heard. Sorry about Eileen's brother, Tim."

"Thanks. What's the deal here?"

"Kim's been pestering me all day about what's the right thing to do. I didn't know. So he finally talked to the other Kim. She told him to buy a card. I think she meant for Eileen, not for you. But he's very proud of his card and he won't let me touch it."

"I'm very sorry to hear about Eileen's brother," Kim said when I sat down at the table. "I offer you my condolences, and I have this card for you."

Just then Jeremy and Dory came in. Jeremy began to pace up and down. "Stupid war! Stupid fucking war! Everybody who could read knew there were no weapons of mass destruction before it even started."

"Don't be such a smartass about it." I tried to calm him down. "It doesn't help Eileen now. And what were we doing at the time the decision was made to go to war? Lifting weights? Watching the Discovery Channel?"

Dory noticed that Korean Kim was still holding up his card. She took it from him very gently and read it. She sat down next to him and explained that I didn't need to be sent a card, but that Eileen did. She said that it was a very beautiful card, though. Kim still looked perplexed.

"What we have to do," Ben announced calmly. "What we have to do is, all of us should sign the card, and then we should send it to Eileen. The appropriate thing also would be for each of us to share in the cost of the card. That's how it should be done." This was not how Ben normally talked. He was adjusting for Kim. He also knew that each of us shelling out a buck and a quarter for the card would be meaningless – unless you were from outside of the country and it was important that you feel like you were following the proper American custom. One after another, we all said "great idea," and started searching in our pockets for money. Kim seemed transformed, very pleased to be doing the right thing. He turned the card over, wrote down the price, and divided it by five. I noticed he got it wrong.

"I think my whole family is looking for people to blame," Eileen said to me in the car on the way down to the funeral. "It seems like the ex, Brittany, is coming up first choice. I talked with my mother on the phone for hours last night. She's just crushed. I can't imagine. Her firstborn. But you know, she said she rarely saw him either after he was married. Brittany's fault too. According to my mother."

I asked her if she thought Brittany would come to the funeral.

"I don't care. She might not even know about it."

"She knows. Your mother asked me to call her. She's remarried."

"Did she say anything?"

"'Thank you for letting me know.'"

Recently there had been a Christian group who protested at servicemen's funerals, chanting that they deserved to die because of some medieval religious doctrine that God had recently authorized them to enforce. Eileen's mother's church friends weren't these red-eyed, raw-meat Christian crazies that I'd feared, or anything like that at all. It was a very nice group of people, and they didn't treat Eileen's mother like the relative newcomer she really was. Her mother was a big woman, square-shouldered, her aging blur of a face softened by thick grey hair and modest gold earrings. They had scheduled the funeral in the afternoon for her convenience. Several of the church members went out of their way to seek out her father. He stood there, tall, thin, distracted, suffering, and still handled all comers as easily as the professional handler of people he was. I watched Eileen's eyes as she watched out for her mother, guiding her throughout the ceremony, and afterwards during the long car drive to the graveyard. She stood between her mother and father and held onto both of their arms at the grave. The December light was fading by the time the ceremony at the grave was over. Then people got in cars to go back to her mother's house, five miles away. Eileen and I drove back toward her mother's house in her car.

"Can we stop the car?" she asked.

"There's nothing here."

"That's what I want."

There was a frostbitten old apple orchard on one side of the road, decaying magnificently in the orange autumn sun. She got out and asked me to walk with her under the trees.

"Can we sit down?" she said. "I just want to get away from people for a minute."

The dry leaves crunched as we sat down on the ground next to each other. The orchard sloped down and then up again onto the next hill. The sun was going down over the edge of that hill, filtering the lavender sky through the skeletal branches.

She looked serene, a breathing bronze statue in a black mourning dress, raven hair tinged with copper. She sat with her legs straight out in front of her, her arms close to her sides. The moment I put my hand around her waist she burst into tears.

"This is tough, I know. But you're doing great."

"I can't thank you enough for coming. I know you don't have much time."

"Time's going to wait for us today."

The sun sank very slowly behind the hill, and very gradually the air started to get cold. I pulled her up and led her to the car, hand in hand. This side of this country road was exactly the place on earth I was supposed to be at this moment. She seemed defeated, but wasn't that the way you were supposed to be at a funeral?

Back at her mother's house, Eileen pulled herself together to handle the horde of relatives and family friends – and two new friends of Mike from the army. Eileen told them Mike had written about them in his e-mails. They seemed pleased about that. They were holding themselves off from flirting with her. Eileen had even persuaded her mother to invite her father back to the house. That meant Robin would be coming too. Her mother had never spoken to Robin since her husband had left the marriage to live with her seven years ago, and the string was not broken that evening, as the unspoken agreement was that Robin would stay in the front room, which her mother avoided.

Her father was collapsed into a big armchair, with Robin standing more or less comfortably at his side. Eileen waited on him gently and graciously, almost as if she needed to remind him that he still had a competent daughter who cared for him. It wasn't necessary for her to entertain him though, as he was never at a loss for words and talked easily with whoever was passing by. But then, Eileen was the same way.

At one point, just as she was turning away to talk to a cousin, he stopped her.

"When I saw you at Thanksgiving, I was impressed at what an elegant young woman you've become. It was like you had grown up ten years right in front of my eyes." It sounded to me like a boozy compliment an uncle might give to a niece he hardly knew.

"It couldn't have been right in front of your eyes, could it, Dad – since you've hardly seen me in ten years?" He was not fazed, and she apparently hadn't expected him to be. Then she settled where he started, on "elegant." She lowered herself gracefully onto the arm of his chair and touched his arm. "But thanks."

"Thanks for getting me and Robin invited here," he said. "I know I wasn't the greatest father. You know that. At least Mike got out of the house before the worst of it."

Eileen, who did not get out of the house before the worst of it, kept her hand on his arm, her touch momentarily holding back both his reflexive glad-handing and the inconsolable grief showing in his eyes. He was for the moment under her spell, and she used her spell like truth serum.

"Mike never really found what he was looking for, did he?" she said.

"He got mixed up with that banshee, Brittany. Is she here, by the way?"

"No. She chose not to come. Was he always unhappy with her, from the beginning?"

"He didn't say that, but I know all the symptoms now. Things were always going to get better when he got a better job, when they got a bigger house, when they got a dog, when they took up running together, tennis. Maybe having a kid would have done it. I don't know."

"They all seem like good things."

"Yeah, I thought so too. He did whatever she wanted. He really tried. I couldn't see how any woman wouldn't fall in love with him. But to tell you the truth, honey, I don't think Brittany ever loved Mike."

"I didn't know any of this back then."

"What? You told me you two were always such pals."

The truth serum worked both ways. "We weren't quite as close as I made out."

Eileen stood up and left her father so she could mix with the other mourners. She caught me admiring her from across the room and gave me a sad smile as she moved into the kitchen to help her mother. Back in the front room, her father introduced me to everyone who came up to sympathize with him. His manners were smooth but his eyes were in pain. He was drinking whiskey steadily, but his conversation was clear. One of my jobs was to keep his glass filled. I was admiring the way he kept on even keel and pushed through his grief to be nice, and even entertaining, to two of his nephews and their wives who had gathered around him. Then he turned to me and handed me his empty glass, accidentally calling me Mike.

Eileen's stepsister Kit was sitting alone on a chair in a corner of the dining room. She looked away when I walked up to her.

"Hi, Kit." She still didn't look up.

"I guess you have to be nice to me anyway because it's a funeral." Her voice was strained.

"What are you talking about?"

"Oh God, you don't even remember! I'm such a total dork."

"I remember everything. It's all good. Won't you talk to me? You're practically the only person I know here."

"They made me come. I feel like half the people here hate me and my Mom."

"Did you know Mike?"

"I met him once."

"I never met him."

"He was nice to me." All of a sudden she was fighting back tears.

"See, you have more reason to be here than I do."

"I don't usually cry. Not that I've ever been to a funeral before."

"This is my second one ever. My father died a few weeks ago."

"Oh. Was he old?"

"No."

"Was it like an accident?"

"Cancer."

"Oh, that's scary."

Ten minutes later I saw Eileen in the kitchen and persuaded her to come out onto the landing outside the back door.

"At least your mother and father aren't slugging it out with each other," I offered.

"Kit tried to talk to my mother, and my mother, my nice, civilized mother – I don't know what she was thinking – looks right at Kit and says right to her face, '*What are you doing here?*' Kit was really upset."

"Oh."

"It's not an easy time for anybody," she conceded. We went back in the kitchen where she stopped and took a big slug of the drink she had been making for her father, swallowed it down slowly. "Hey, after everybody leaves, do you think you and I can be alone together?"

"Go for a run?"

"Oh, that would be great."

She went out to serve the crowd, and I stayed behind outside after making a drink of my own. The house was part of a typical development of vinyl houses. From the landing, you could see the glowing yellow windows in the backs of the houses on the next court. The whole development seemed artificial, perched like a temporary encampment on the edge of the surrounding fields, not really dug in to the earth. Almost everyone at the wake was making accommodations, talking to people they didn't like, avoiding certain sensitive subjects. Perched on the edge of their chairs, they strengthened fragile alliances, extended truces, established their own form of temporary community gravity. I used to be self-conscious around any group other than my old friends, thinking I would screw things up somehow, spill a drink, insult someone by accident, throw up on a rug. But after going through two funerals I realized that all of the above is bound to happen anyway, that what matters is how we handle it when it happens, that to spend your energy monitoring yourself for errors is to miss the point of why we are together. I knew

Eileen really needed me today, and that was gravity enough for now.

"Where should we run?" It was a good question. Eileen's mother's house was in a suburb so far out in the county that the only real choices for long runs were dark country roads or superhighways.

"Let's go for the country roads," I said.

"It won't be so bad. The moon's coming up. Let's head back toward that apple orchard for starters. I remember how to get there."

I went ahead of her. Because of this, she had to yell out the turns to me, but there were only a few turns. No street lights, hardly any traffic, the beginnings of a moon. The narrow road wound through long, sloping, gentle hills of open fields – but it was sometimes lined with overhanging trees on both sides and so dark it seemed like we were running in tunnels. We were totally warm and running smoothly within a mile.

She wanted to stop and rest at the fence surrounding the apple orchard. The spidery tree branches crisscrossed in front of the moon. We stood facing each other, out of breath. She looked happy for the first time that day. "This is great. I don't want to go back to my mother's house yet," she said.

"There's plenty of miles left on these roads."

"Do you think we could go to the graveyard?"

We ran toward the graveyard. It had been only a few hours since we were there, but even though the moon was up and giving off a little light, we could hardly find the site. Another rectangle, this one newly filled with black dirt and covered with heaps of flowers glowing even in the weak moonlight.

"I just want to be with him one last time." She looked at me like I might object.

"Sure. Do you want me to go so you can be alone?"

"No. Would you stand here with me." She was holding onto my arm and looking down at the grave, her eyes two black patches of darkness. I could hear her breathing slowly, deeper and deeper. She did that for a long time, as if she were trying to breathe his soul into hers. I thought about Mike as much as I could, based on the pictures of him I'd seen and what she had told me about him. His death had made no sense at all. His life had just run away with him and plunged him off a cliff. At least that's what his family thought. All the funny stories and joyful reminiscences about him were about the times when he was just a kid. They all talked as if he had been lost as an adult. I hoped Eileen's fate would be different. I hoped she'd learn her own heart. I hoped she'd follow it, no matter what.

~ Chapter 16 ~

Ben was rushing around picking up pizza boxes and other trash and jamming it into the garbage can which he had installed in the middle of our front room. "Help me guys. Quick, if you can. The lady next door, the cop, is coming over."

This was something new. It was a Saturday morning, and I had been studying quietly for my Shakespeare exam. Then Jeremy and Dory had dropped in on the way to their weekend jobs. But we hadn't spoken two words before Ben had burst in with the garbage can in his arms.

"What? Why would she come over?"

"I invited her. I'll explain in a minute. But she's coming, and she might look around a little bit. If I can just get rid of the big crap. Can you help me get just the big stuff into this can before she comes?"

We threw all the boxes and papers and bottles in the can, then went around and picked up all the glasses and dishes and put them in the sink. We picked up all the clothes lying around and threw them down the basement stairs. Jeremy and I shook out the little area rug, which was covered in something that looked like peanut shells. We found the lamp shade for the lamp next to the sofa. Ben looked over in that direction. "Okay, but let's not highlight the sofa. Turn the light off."

Ben straightened out the curtain on the window that looked out over the front porch. "Here she comes. Oh God, she's bringing her kid!" We knew she had a little boy, maybe three years old. "This place is like a nightmare for a kid." We all looked at Dory.

We knew our neighbor was the one who called the health department on us last spring, when the grass got so high. Since then, I had said hi to her once in a while, but I didn't even know her name. She was probably in her late twenties, brown hair often pulled back into a tight bun, not as tall as Dory but a lot more substantial. The few times we'd seen the kid hanging around with her outside, she had pushed him behind her like we would be a bad influence or something.

"Okay, guys, thanks." Ben turned to us. "Here's the story. The one-minute version. We got another health department citation. I called the county and found out it was her again. I can't let this keep happening. We have to get her to stop filing complaints. We have to … um …"

"… make friends with her." Jeremy finished Ben's sentence just as we heard a knock on the door.

There was not much we could do about the condition of the house. Before he opened the door, Ben looked around, took a deep breath. Then he opened the door with a calm smile on his face. His eyebrows were slightly raised, like he was surprised that she had even felt the need to knock. "Come on in. I have my roommate here, and these are two of my friends."

"Oh, I didn't expect such a crowd," she said. "And I guess you didn't expect little Timmy. Saturday's usually our alone time together."

"That's great. Hi!" Ben knelt down on the floor to make eye contact with little Timmy. The little kid just stood there, holding on to his mother's hand. Ben stood up and invited her in and introduced us all.

"Tim and I have lived here for a year and a half," Ben said. "It's embarrassing that we're only introducing ourselves now."

"Oh, modern life," Cindy the policewoman said. Her eyes searched the floor for things that little Timmy should not get into.

For the moment, he seemed to be getting into Dory, who was sitting on a pillow on the floor, holding her arms out to him.

"Can I hold him?" she asked Cindy.

"Sure, if he'll let you. He'll want to play with his little truck at the same time. Careful he doesn't clock you on the head with it."

Then there was an awkward silence that Ben took advantage of to get immediately to the point. "I want to apologize for that porch rail. I have no idea how that porch rail got torn off like that." Ben knew exactly how that porch rail had gotten torn off like that. "I just wanted to assure you that it will be fixed within the next couple of days. I'm not going to wait the 30 days like they gave me on the citation. Why don't you sit down?" Jeremy and I practically knocked each other over scrambling to get one of the kitchen chairs for her. Nobody wanted her to sit on that sofa. "Would you like a soda or coffee or something?"

Policewoman Cindy knew she was being played, but she didn't seem to mind. Dory was keeping her little boy amused for the moment, Ben couldn't have been more diplomatic, and Cindy wasn't so old that the memory of early ratty living arrangements had entirely faded from her memory. Ben told her that he worked in an auto parts store but that he had put in several applications for jobs at real estate companies. He said he had learned a lot just by being the owner of this tiny little place. "And Dory has a job at a real estate company."

Dory seemed preoccupied with little Timmy, who was driving his little plastic truck on her face. "Does this mean he likes me?" she laughed.

"Timmy, stop that," Cindy snapped.

"Oh, it's alright. I don't get the chance to play with little kids much."

"I've been meaning to ask," Cindy said, "if he bothers you when I let him go outside on my porch. I see him babbling at you sometimes."

"No. Of course, no." Ben acted like the concept was ridiculous. "He just likes to talk to us when we walk by. I'm more afraid of us being a bother to you."

"Cindy, that's an awesome cell phone you have there," Jeremy interjected. "Can I take a look at it?"

"Sure. Police issue."

"I've never seen one like this. And I'm in the business."

"The cell phone business?"

"Yeah. I sell this thing called the Diamond Service Plan. It's mostly for streaming movies, sharing movies, simultaneous text, talk and movies, things like that. But I don't think we can add it to a law enforcement phone like this."

"I have a personal cell phone too."

"Oh. You really are a connected person."

"Have to be. Life's complicated."

"I promise you," Ben said, "as your neighbors, we won't be another complication for you. Just let us know any time we're bothering you."

"Thank you."

"And really, anything we can do to help …."

Cindy laughed. "I do have problems. Nothing you kids can solve. But thanks."

"It must be hard." Jeremy met her eyes. "Being a cop must be a tough job. And you have a three-year-old to take care of too."

Cindy nodded. "Yeah, I'm sure you noticed I'm raising him by myself too."

"Very tough, I imagine," Jeremy said.

Cindy took a sip of the glass of water that Ben offered her. "I got an ex-husband who questions every move I make with little Timmy. I swear I'm going to get one of those GPS bracelets for Timmy so every time my ex calls questioning me about where his son is I'll just text him the exact coordinates. I wonder if that could be done automatically. Can the Diamond Service Plan do that?"

"Honestly, I don't really know. But I'll find out this afternoon and get back to you by tomorrow." Jeremy paused. He looked disappointed in his own answer. "And if the Diamond Service Plan won't do it, I might be able to find some old GPS equipment around the office. People trade it in and we have no use for it. Sometimes they just dump it on us to get rid of it."

The plan of mollifying Cindy seemed to be going well. Ben introduced me as a paralegal. "And last year, he had the highest GPA of any a full-time student at Badger."

"Please, Ben," I said, "it was actually a tie. I was tied with 41 other students last year."

"Still, a 4.0, I guess," Cindy said. I shrugged modestly.

"I went to one year of community college," Cindy said, "but I really wanted to get out on the street. My boyfriend was a cop. Everybody says I'll have to go back to school if I really want to get anywhere."

"I don't see why people think everybody has to go to college," Dory chimed in from her seat on the pillow on the floor.

"That's kind of what I think. Where is it, exactly, that everybody's trying to get?" Right then her little kid left Dory and ran over to Cindy and hugged her knees. Cindy smiled, almost as if this were a demonstration that there were better things to do with her time than getting somewhere.

"Thank you guys," Ben said after she had left. "I think she likes us. Jeremy, are you really going to sell her the Diamond Service Plan?"

"I don't think it will do what she wants." Jeremy was rushing out the door to get to work. "But I'll try to help her. She seemed nice."

Dory hung back to ask me how Eileen was doing.

"Oh. Not too good, I guess. I drove her back to State the day after the funeral. She cried the whole way. I couldn't really help her."

"I know you helped her."

I had a strange conversation with Kathryn at work. I told her I was going to State in late January, but I'd like to work as much as possible over the semester break and maybe come back next summer.

"You're good at this," she said. "The job involves a lot more tedium than your father would have tolerated. But I see you like to get the details right. And now I hope to find out if you're good at persuading everyone to get on board, like your father could."

She stopped for a second, looked down at her desk, then raised her eyes to me and went on. "I apologize if I'm mentioning your father too often. He was a big presence around here. But you are your own person. I understand that, really. By the way, I've already asked them if you can work here full time over the summer, if that's what you want."

"I do." There was no set date when my insurance money was to be paid, and I'd been dreaming of making enough money to take Eileen some place fancy to see some Shakespeare plays this summer. Comedies this time.

"Okay. I've already put you in for a slot at a higher level. You'd have to do more varied work, including some for other attorneys, but it would be a 75 percent raise. There's one catch. You couldn't wear those, um, *courier* clothes you've been wearing – at least not all the time. There would be a few days when you'd have to carry things for lawyers going to court. You'd have to wear a suit."

A few days before, American Kim and I had watched from inside the floor-to-ceiling library windows as the snow began falling on the Badger campus. It was supposed to be just a dusting, but the ground was so frozen that every flake stuck. I had just finished my Calculus II exam, my second last exam ever at community college. We were waiting for the other Kim. The two Kims were the only two friends I'd made at Badger. American Kim and I had worked on the exam until the last second. Korean Kim had finished early, but he had promised to come back and meet us here.

"Oh my God." I collapsed on a sofa facing the snow scene. "Comparison tests. Partial fractions. I never want to see any of that crap again."

"Trigonometric substitutions. We wouldn't have had a prayer without him. I bet you didn't get your precious *A*."

"No, I think I did." This had been a close one, though. Calculus

It could have ruined my perfect record. I ignored Kim's sarcasm. The night of the real estate party, when she told me Eileen wasn't really my girlfriend, she had been wrong. So she wasn't always right.

"Let's celebrate. Let's take him out and see if we can get him drunk."

I studied her face, that smooth skin behind those thick, black-framed glasses. Her eyes had already wandered away toward the scenery. If Kim was flirting with you, you would know it, I decided.

It had been her idea in the first place for Korean Kim to move into the house with me and Ben – after she began to suspect his uncle was abusing him. Ben and I just did what she said. That was because we trusted her. She was not the kind of person who would foist off a stupid idea on her friends.

"Yeah, let's take him out," I said now. "But it would be impossible to get him drunk."

"Tim, with all due respect to your straight-*A*, weight-training, fitness-fanatic lifestyle, I don't think you know anything about drinking. I guarantee you I can get him drunk."

"I bet you can't."

We made an actual bet. A very bold bet on her part. She was quite sure of herself.

She told him it was the American custom to go out drinking at the end of the semester. At the bar, she made him clink glasses with us and told him he had to drink in unison with us, swallow for swallow. Korean Kim complied with all of our directions, but when it was time to drink he took only the tiniest sips. You could tell he didn't like the taste. We tried changing to jello shooters, but he almost gagged on them. Nevertheless, he religiously followed the clink-drink-rest routine with us like he was supposed to. American Kim and I had each finished two beers and were ordering and consuming a string of shooters before he had drained two inches out of his glass.

"Kim and I want to say something," I began, "while we're still coherent."

Korean Kim interrupted. "I want both of you to know how much you have helped me."

He slid both of his full beer bottles over to me. The plan of getting him drunk didn't seem like it was going to work. I suspected the other Kim had given up when she ordered another round of shooters and automatically took his.

"Oh, come on," I said. "*We* need to thank *you*. We both know you don't need us at all. We've been sucking your brains out all semester."

"*Sucking my brains*." I could see him right then registering this new American idiom in his mind. I knew he would remember it forever and always use it in the exact right context. "See? *Sucking my brains*? Where would I ever learn that in an English class?"

"Anybody could talk to you in our dumb-ass American slang."

"But you don't understand. Maybe everybody could, but nobody did, except you two."

When he left to go to the men's room, the other Kim and I assessed our chances. "He hasn't drunk more than two ounces of beer, and he's the one going to the bathroom," she giggled.

"This isn't going to work."

She was on her fourth shooter by then. She had drunk to the point where she was not quite as funny as she thought she was.

"You seem very happy," I said. "But of course you remember our bet. I think that will be a unique, intimate present from you that he will remember and appreciate for the rest of his life."

She sat up straight for a second, pushing her short hair back behind her ears. "No way, Jose. That was a joke. If you think I'm really gonna do that with him ...." She threw her head back and laughed so hard I was afraid she'd fall off the little wooden chair. He came back to the table then, looking back and forth between the two of us, recognizing that he didn't comprehend the situation.

"Kim here," I said to him, "has a present that she wants to give you. We have to go back to the house. She can only give it to you in the house."

"Oh, a present is not necessary."

"Okay," she quickly jumped in, "no present. Good. End of story."

She gave me a look that convinced me I had better let it go. I ordered a soda for poor, confused, sober Korean Kim, and we ordered food. American Kim kept working on the shooters.

"Ahh, you're the same as him," she said to me, putting down her half-finished burger. "You never get drunk. Bunch of tightasses." Elbows on the table, she propped her face up in her hands. Her hair fell forward, all but concealing her eyes, her glasses almost slipping off until she batted them back up. Then she shook her hair out of her eyes and waggled her head at me. "Stupid bet! It was your lecherous idea. I think you just liked fantasizing about it yourself."

"Why would I fantasize about a baloney sandwich when I can have steak any time I want?"

She threw her shooter on my shirt. There was instant contrition on her face. "Oh, Tim, I'm sorry. I might have had too much to drink." But then she laughed and could not stop herself. Korean Kim was busy at the bar, asking the bartender for a towel.

"Kim, American Kim here has disrespected me. Do you know what that term means?"

"I think I do," he replied.

"No you don't. No you don't," I said quickly, sharing a smirk with the other Kim.

"I believe I do," he said. "And furthermore …."

"*Furthermore*? *Furthermore* what?" American Kim was giggling like a teenager and trying to look superior to him at the same time.

"Furthermore, does not this lack of respect call for the appropriate social controls to be applied?"

American Kim thought this was hilarious. "Right. I'm going to be put under control by one nerdy-headed body builder and one calculus genius who can't even finish a beer. Bring it on."

"We need to teach her a lesson, Kim."

"Oh, you two are so full of shit. You are so not up to it."

She was starting to cause a disturbance in the bar. Korean Kim and I stood up to leave, but she refused to go. I quietly wrestled her out the door. Outside, I pinned her arms behind her. Korean Kim walked a few steps to the side, watching us closely. As I was pushing her forward, she would kick back at my shins with her heels.

"You asshole, you jerk, where are you taking me?"

"To the house. I'm not leaving you out here on the street."

She was struggling wildly, except she would pretend everything was normal whenever anyone passed us on the street. "I'm not going to that house. You had your chance with me, Tim, and you blew it."

"Then we'll tie you to this light pole."

Korean Kim did not look like he thought this was a good idea.

"You guys are going to be so sorry."

I dragged her to the house, but she stuck her arms and legs out so wide we couldn't get her through the door. I looked around.

"The porch sofa!"

"Don't put me on that filthy old thing!"

I lay down across the porch sofa and started to pull her down.

"Sit on top of me. You won't even have to touch it."

"Touch what?"

She yanked me halfway off the sofa. I tried to stand up and reach for her and everything suddenly swirled around and I think she yanked me again and I know I crashed into the railing and it collapsed and I fell off the porch into the bushes. The next thing I remember she was kneeling over me, laughing.

"Are you okay?"

"Yeah. I'm fine. What happened?"

"Oh, you are going to hurt tomorrow!"

She and Korean Kim helped me up, and we all went inside. She was drunk enough that she didn't mind sitting on the almost equally filthy inside sofa. She picked up a pillow and whacked the little dusting of snow off my clothes with a severity that felt like punishment. She begged Korean Kim to go get some more beer. It occurred to me that, for all we knew about him, he could be 40 years old. While he was gone I noticed I was bleeding from a long scratch on my face. She tried to get some music website to come up on the TV but couldn't figure out all of the remotes. It all seemed hilarious.

He came back with the beer really soon. She thanked him profusely and kept talking about giving him the money for it, but she kept forgetting about it before she found her purse. She chugged half the first beer down in one gulp. I was already dizzy but tried to keep up. He sat across from us on a footstool that was actually in much better shape than the sofa. He was attentive to everything we did. His attention to our every slurred word and deed made us both want to show off.

"Here's to calculus!" I had finished my second beer of the new supply with a dizzy sense of accomplishment.

He nodded and smiled.

"Here's to techniques of integration!" American Kim thought that was worth another chug.

"Here's to partial functions!"

"I think you mean partial fractions." He couldn't help himself.

"Right. Partial fuck-tions. Here's to partial fuck-tions!" The two Americans drank to celebrate how funny we were.

I had a vague memory of Jeremy and Dory arriving and trying to carry her out to the car, but they must not have made it because I met her in the middle of the night crawling down the hallway towards the bathroom. Around noon the three of us found each other on the indoor sofa downstairs.

American Kim spoke first. "I so deserve this headache. But maybe it will clear all the calculus out of my head. I've never been so done with anything as I am done with calculus."

"Last night," Korean Kim said, "I thought you two were going to hurt each other. But you are still friends, I can see."

"I don't think you understand alcohol."

"That would require a lot of experience, I think."

"Oh yeah."

He was a real student, of both schoolwork and life, but I could tell by the look on his face that he was wondering if alcohol was something he really wanted to learn.

My whole body felt awful. I was still in the same clothes. The

dried blood still felt sticky on the side of my face. “Thanks for sticking with us, Kim,” I said to him. “I’m sorry we got so wasted. I don’t remember everything I did. I just remember I thought we were being really funny.”

Kim lifted her face out of her hands. “We were boring and crude. We tried to get you drunk. We really don’t deserve a friend like you.”

“Did the non-alcoholic beer I bought taste as good as the genuine product?”

American Kim and I could not bring ourselves to look at each other. Or to speak. “For the both of us,” I finally mumbled, “thanks for being our friend.”

“This is my home,” he said, pointing upstairs. “You are my friends. You have helped me. You have sucked out my brains, but I am sucking America out of you.”

~ Chapter 17 ~

The transition to State was a little more complicated than I had expected. Before her brother died, Eileen and Jen and another woman had signed a contract to rent a house off campus, with the lease starting at the beginning of the year. I couldn't even help her move. Because my insurance money hadn't come through, I had to arrange to take a student loan for my first semester's tuition and work as many hours as I could at the law firm over semester break to earn a little spending money. At the law firm, Kathryn agreed to put in a request for extra hours, and Robert made sure that the request was granted quickly. Kathryn really did need me, as there was a whole pile of backed-up unsigned contract clauses and unresolved issues, and it was really difficult to get anyone on the phone or to answer their e-mail over the holidays. I got a little of it done, and Kathryn seemed happy, but I was disappointed about not seeing Eileen over the holidays. She had to spend most of that time at her mother's house. She said she was trying to keep her mother busy. She told me her mother had no memory of insulting Kit at the wake and was mortified to hear that she had done that. Eileen's friend Miriam flew in from California to stay with her at State for the days just before classes were scheduled to start again.

The pizza district never felt so much like home as when I was leaving it. It would be weird to be around all full-time college students now. It would be weird not to know anybody there but Eileen. The house I lived in in the pizza district would never be the same, as I was sure Ben would be well into his renovations by the time my semester at State was over – and that he would sell it as soon after that as he could. I attended every one of the little parties and drinking sprees that went on over the holidays. I didn't have any regret about leaving my mother because she seemed so happy now with Alan. I did wish I had more time to get to know him.

Jeremy actually did get a GPS device for our next-door neighbor, Cindy. He made a lot of money selling the Diamond Service Plan over the holidays, and he didn't seem to feel as guilty about being a good salesman as he had previously. He told me the GPS device actually would track little Timmy and send the coordinates in real time to her cell phone.

"What a coincidence," Ben said. "You found the exact device that Cindy needed in the trash at work." Ben looked at me.

"Oh. You bought it for her. Right, Jeremy?" I said.

Jeremy shrugged. "It was worth it to get her off Ben's back."

I drove up to State a day before the dorms even opened. Eileen was back from her mother's house by then, her old college friend Miriam had gone back to California, and Eileen said I could stay with her in her new house just off campus. I could take only as much stuff as would fit in my little Nissan. My mother and Alan and my friends were going to bring up the rest in a week or so. Eileen's new friend Jen met me at the door.

"Tim, right? Come in. I know we ran by each other a couple times."

"Right. I guess we finally are meeting for real."

"Eileen wanted me to get to know you. She's out at the grocery store right now." She stood in the doorway wringing her hands without saying anything more. I got the idea that the plan had been for Eileen to be here when I showed up. Jen did not look like the kind of person who liked being the center of attention. I closed the door behind me and asked for a glass of water. I followed her into the kitchen.

"You're a psychology student too?" This gave us something to talk about for a minute. She was a psychology graduate student like Eileen, but she was into the bio-statistical brain research side of the profession. At first I thought I understood what she said about it, then I just pretended to understand it, then I admitted that I had only gone as far as Calculus II and passed that only with the help of a Korean math genius.

"I get a lot of blank stares like that when I try to explain what I do," she admitted. "Eileen at least knows the terminology," she smiled. Then she looked like she was searching for something else to say. This was a new kind of awkwardness for me. Jen was Eileen's friend, and I knew I should make some kind of effort. I couldn't think of a thing to say. I wondered what Ben would say in a situation like this and suddenly – aha! – I thought I'd ask her about the house.

But she beat me to the punch. "If you're half as great as Eileen says you are, you're a great guy." She said this in the same flat, blasé tone that American Kim might use to describe a teacher she wasn't particularly fond of. I got the idea that Jen herself was not in the market for a boyfriend.

Still, I recognized her remark as a compliment, and I was stumped. Fortunately, just then there was a bump and the door swung open and Eileen came in with a pile of plastic bags full of groceries. Jen immediately ran over and took all of them and disappeared with them into the kitchen and didn't return.

We embraced. "So glad to see you," she whispered in my ear. I held her tight. There was a slight catch, like a sob, in her chest. I had forgotten how exquisitely dark and sleek her hair was, again with a trace of a lilac scent.

"I wish you could have been with me at my mother's." She sighed. "My mother and I are not at all alike. I felt like I was suffocating. Getting your calls every night was like coming up for air."

It didn't take a minute to get to her bedroom. I had almost forgotten the soft strength of her kiss, her strong runner's legs. I was awestruck to be touching her again. Her eyes seemed even larger, darker, and they stayed open, focused on mine as we moved together. Then we lay side by side.

"What's the matter?"

"Nothing," she said, too quickly. This is the kind of lie women say that isn't really meant to be a lie. It was a test to see if I cared enough to ask her again. I asked her again. "I've been thinking since my brother died," she went on, "there's so much that's false in the world. Mike's marriage to Brittany was a sham, and he didn't even know it. My father lied to my mother for years. Mike went off to a war started for a fake reason. And I've been just as bad. Maybe if I hadn't pretended all those years that Mike and I had a close relationship, we could have actually been close. Maybe everything would have been different then."

"You didn't cause any of this."

"Thanks, Tim. I guess I know that in my heart, but it counts more when you say it." She pulled closer, pulled the sheet up over us. "Sleep with me. I mean actually sleep." But she still had more to say. "I'm so glad you moved up here. There's so much to show you. I think you'll love it." She propped herself up on her elbow. "Stop me if I talk too much. I'm excited. Maybe it's just a rebound effect from being so sad. Nothing to do with you, of course."

Her house was on the town side of the bridge over the ravine, so it wasn't that far a walk to the eating places there. Jen could tell that we wanted to be alone, and she declined our invitation to join us. It was my idea to go downtown. I thought that her house, her living arrangements, her courses – everything – was new, all new just at the time that her family had been devastated, and so maybe it would do her good to talk in a familiar setting. We went to a place we had been a couple of times before. Actually, it was the first place we had ever gone together.

She smiled at me tentatively. "My mother, um, doesn't seem too happy about my dating you. Wait. It's just grief, Tim. I think she wants to mourn Mike, and it rubs her the wrong way to think I'm hanging around so happy with a guy so soon."

"She's barely even met me."

"She's afraid I'm making you an instant replacement for Mike. I tried to invite you down there over the break, but every time I brought it up she would suddenly get upset over something."

"At least I know where I stand with her. Listen, I know about blacking people out. I blacked out my father and Anita for ten years."

"Wasn't it you who got hurt the most from that?"

The bartender brought over our plates. Hot Mexican on a cold January day. I had a much better fake ID now, and they brought us a pitcher of beer.

"Are you going to teach again this semester?"

Her eyes lit up. "Oh yeah. I'm doing two classes – or study sessions, they're actually called. I'm teaching an extra session because another graduate student just dropped out last week."

"You had to take over that class?"

"No. I volunteered. I think I might like teaching."

"I wish I knew something I liked – I mean something that people want you to do, that pays money."

"You have plenty of time. You'll find something you like."

She ordered a second helping, and a huge dessert. She looked at me. "Rebound eating," she explained. "I hope." She dove her fork into the key lime pie, but then she pulled it out and put it down. "I do feel like things have shifted a little since Mike died."

"Like how?"

"Some of them are little things. Kit, for example. I don't know how there could be this great kid practically right in my family and I didn't get to know her earlier. Now I feel like I need to get to know her right away."

"You would be a great step-sister to her."

"I want to talk her into coming up here sometime this semester. You'd like to see her too, wouldn't you?"

"She's a good kid."

"And a bigger thing. I've relied on Miriam so much. She was my only close friend for my last two years of college. It was so nice of her to come and stay with me last week."

"But …?"

"Things are a just a little different with her now. Not in a bad way. What it is, I think, is I'm not relying on her so much any more. Because everything has shifted."

"How?"

"Because now I'm relying on you."

I kept sipping slowly on my beer. It seemed like the best one I'd ever had. The people at the next table left and another set of people came. The waiter came over to take their orders. They quietly told him what they wanted. He wrote their orders down; then he went away. The earth spun slowly on its axis. Soon he would come back with their food. They would probably like it. Then they would leave, happier. There was a way things were supposed to work. Sometimes they did.

"So when you become a psychologist, are you going to work on me?" I said.

"What's your problem, Tim?"

"Maybe fear. Fear all the time of making the wrong decisions."

"Oh, you're serious."

"I am. My default seems to be withdrawal."

"You're thinking about withdrawing from me? Is this your way of telling me that?"

"No. Not at all."

"Even after what happened at the grave?"

"Your brother's grave?"

"Yes. You don't have to pretend you forgot."

Eileen had stood at the edge of her brother's grave, head down, eyes blacked out in the weak moonlight. She breathed so deeply and for so long it seemed like she too was dying. Then she knelt down on the grass right at the edge of the plot. I knelt down next to her and put my arm around her waist to support her, but she pushed my arm off and threw herself down forward, lying on the grave, face flat into the dirt, like she wanted to bury herself too. Time passed, the moon rose higher in the sky. I put my hand on her back to see if she was asleep. She pushed it off. The moon rose higher. Every sound I made, every touch, would cause her to start sobbing again. Finally I forced my arm around her waist and pulled her gently up and off the grave. She was limp, shivering. I had to stand her up and wipe the mud off her face. She clung to me for a long time, then let me take her hand and lead her out of the graveyard and back down that country road.

"What keeps me halfway sane about that," she said now, "is what you told me earlier that day. There is no right way or wrong way to mourn."

I spent the night in her room. She was still going through this cycle of feeling ready to go on with her life without her brother, then feeling guilty for feeling that way. Long after she fell asleep I kept thinking about that cycle and came to the conclusion that I couldn't help her with that. Her pain would still come, probably for a long time. I hadn't gone through that cycle when my father died. There was just that one long crying incident with Dory. But there was no right way or wrong way to mourn, I told myself.

Chapter 18

The State campus at was a lot less enchanting in January than it had been in the fall. The soft skies and dramatic foliage were gone. The trees were now black skeletons against a freezing sky, and the fallen leaves were banked on the edges of the roads, alternatively frozen solid or sodden with slush. My dorm room was in a different part of the campus than Eileen's old dorm room, and it didn't look out over anything but a weedy field with a line of pine trees on the other side. But without my paralegal job, I had so much free time it seemed like I was on vacation. I found a carrel high up in the library with a window that had a great view of the frozen campus, and I spent a lot of time studying there.

We met every day that first week for lunch. She talked me out of signing up for 21 credits and trying to catch up to her academically.

"Really, Tim, there's not that much time in a week. We want to run, right? We want to see each other. And not be wound up all the time tight as springs. I want you to have a good time up here. With me."

On one of the warmer days we ran on the road along the lake. We worked out in the fitness center on the others. We made love mostly in her rented house on the bed that came with the rental, surrounded by the Jacobean-flowered wallpaper that some art student once upon a time thought was an appropriate statement for a bedroom. Then we would have at least one drink later at the kitchen table with Jen before I ran back to my dorm. We made love in my dorm once. She pretended not to notice that I hadn't even gotten my sheets yet. When my friends from home had to postpone their trip to bring my stuff up, she made me a little gift package with extra running shorts, an extra pair of underwear, and deodorant. Apparently I hadn't brought enough of these items to suit her. We studied in my favorite carrel in the library. Her cheeks were always flushed when she came there right after teaching class.

I didn't make any friends in the dorm right away. My roommate was eighteen, and he was out partying every night past midnight. He wanted to be called Slide, and he claimed he once played Australian football in a league in Illinois and it was so cool there it would be too much of a letdown to play any of the lame sports here. I found myself wondering if he was the kind of guy Eileen would have gone out with in her early years of college.

She took me to her mother's house during the first three-day holiday. Since I already knew her mother didn't like me, I negotiated it down to a one-night stay. We arrived at her suburban Virginia house late Saturday afternoon. Her mother was out at the store when we arrived, so we took another run, not nearly as far as the graveyard this time. On the way back, we ran into a whole bunch of kids playing on a court near her mother's house. I got the idea they didn't see a whole lot of adults come by on foot.

"Did you guys run a marathon?"

"Are you a weightlifter?"

"Are you married?"

Eileen got them to let us take a few shots at their portable basketball hoop. They talked us into choosing sides and playing against each other. They thought it was hilarious that Eileen was a better shot than I was.

One thing that her mother hadn't liked about me was that I was so young, but she did seem a little mollified now that I was a regular college student at State. We took her out to dinner at a faux rustic dinner theater where we watched a really silly play about some bungling nineteenth-century English highwaymen. Eileen had planned it, and it was a great choice. Her mother had a few drinks and was laughing until tears came to her eyes.

The next morning they made a huge production about preparing a fancy brunch for the three of us. "I really want to help," I told Eileen, "but I don't want to stick my nose in. If your mother is afraid of me replacing Mike ...."

"Helping us fix a meal? That certainly wouldn't bring up any memories of Mike. I never remember him even so much as making his own sandwich."

"So I should help?"

"Um. Well, maybe your first instinct was right. Maybe you should hold back, at least this time."

They rushed around the kitchen making a complete brunch with eggs and bacon, waffles and pancakes, toast, jam, oranges, cake, coffee, and mimosas. After watching them for a few minutes, I understood a little more why Mike had never been involved. Eileen and her mother didn't agree on how anything should be done, but they nevertheless resolutely plowed on, working parallel to each other, obviously trying hard not to object to everything the other one did. At one point I saw Eileen stop completely for a full minute, take a deep breath, and just stare out the window. I could see why she had never made it to the status of most-favored child. Eventually, though, the two opposing teams did produce a huge and delicious brunch.

"You can clean up," Eileen announced.

Because Eileen's father didn't actually leave the house for a long time after the marriage was really over, he had paid all the bills for years. But her mother had been smart enough to read the handwriting on the wall, and she had kept up her job at a non-profit agency, and kept up her contacts. She had accounting training, and apparently that was something really in demand in the non-profit world. By the time Eileen was a junior in high school, her mother started working more hours, switching jobs as she became known as a valuable asset in that community. Eileen said she had hardly noticed her mother back then. "I was too cool. I was going to be like Mike. I couldn't wait to go to college and just get away."

"So, are you more like your mother or your father?"

"I don't know. I never thought about that. Even at my age now it's hard to admit that I have anything in common with either one of them. Do you have an opinion on this?"

"I do."

"And you're going to tell me, I bet."

"Yes, I am. You have your father's easy way with people. I've seen you make people feel comfortable even in horrible situations. And you have your mother's common sense. It's a great combination. People really like you. I think they can sense you'll be good for them."

She pursed her lips. "Maybe I should believe you. You are the only guy I've dated who met all the suspects. I don't think anybody's ever investigated me so thoroughly before."

"You came up clean, ma'am."

Eileen wouldn't let me take Psych 101. She said I'd distract her. I signed up for Western Civ, more Shakespeare, Russian History, Biology, Statistics. I took statistics because it was a prerequisite to a lot of graduate courses, including psychology and political science. I figured it couldn't be as hard as Calculus II, and this time I would have two tutors, Eileen and Jen, if I got into trouble. We went out with Jen a couple of times. Eileen told me I was wrong when I guessed she was not interested in guys. That was hard to tell from the way she was dressed – and especially from her hair, which you could tell had the potential to be a thick, beautiful honey-blonde mane, but which most of the time looked half-greasy and was shoved behind her ears.

"Why don't you like, give her a makeover?" I suggested to Eileen one night.

"You want to try saying that directly to her?" That shut me up. "Really, I'm a graduate student, and I guess I'm doing okay, but Jen is a real scientist. She's the real deal. There's no way I'm going to make suggestions about her looks." So we went out with her and let Jen be Jen. It was a lot of fun. She had that frowzy but sarcastic big-sister demeanor that a lot of guys obviously felt comfortable with – though, apparently, comfortable didn't translate into enough excitement for them to ask her out.

"You notice how nobody hits on Eileen when the three of us are out?" she laughed one night. "Nobody can imagine that you're out with me."

"You just need the right guy, one who is infatuated with bio-statistics," I told her.

"Yeah. There must be thousands of them."

I needed Eileen to know how much I loved her. In most of the measurable criteria of love – time spent, experiences shared, dreams revealed, complaints heard, laughter echoed, orgasms reached – we were already in the 99th percentile. It was nice – perfect maybe – but it seemed maybe too plain and obvious to me. I wanted to do something she wouldn't expect from me, something that would show her how much she had changed me. And so I did something that was strange to me but that would maybe be really plain and obvious to almost anyone else. I bought her a gold necklace at a jewelry store, with a pendant gold heart. The edges of the heart were bordered in tiny emeralds. I spent way too much money on it. I felt like a rube, buying this silly, flashy thing; but I wanted to show her I was willing to feel like a rube – for her.

A heavy snow was blowing in my face all the way to Eileen's. She was going to fix me a Valentine's Day dinner in her house. Jen and their other roommate, Diane, had walked to town together, planning on making fun of all the couples on their solemn Valentine's Day dates. As the snow piled up and the wind blew harder they called to say they had met some funny guys and were going to sit it out where they were until the bar closed.

"You should know, I'm a pretty poor cook," Eileen said as she spread out on the table a printout of a recipe for some kind of casserole.

"Yum. Internet food. Can't go wrong." I noticed she didn't have a single candle or any other type of romantic thing around, and I wondered if I'd overdone it with the pendant.

She put the dish together and put it in the oven. "My mother is a really good cook. I don't understand why I could never learn from her." I didn't say anything.

We just sat there and drank beer at the kitchen table. There was not much that had to be said. We both knew we would be living together if the school didn't require transfer students to live in the dorms for their first semester. She'd already told me that what we were feeling had electro-chemical analogues in the brain that you could see on an MRI. Those hot spots always faded with time, she said. I told her let them fade. I told her I had measured her by every yardstick, run her through my battery of friends, investigated her, and she had passed.

"I have something for you," she said. She left the room and came back with a box with UPS stickers all over it showing every place it had been since it had first been delivered to me last summer.

"Why don't you open it now?" she said.

"I still don't want to."

"I've been carrying it around in my car trunk for a month. It's the only Valentine's Day present I have for you. Please open it."

I took it from her and put it on the table next to my plate.

"It comes with a letter now," she said. "Your father's wife sent it the last time she sent the box to me."

She got a kitchen knife and I cut off the many layers of tape that had accumulated on the box. Inside, there was a lot of brown packing paper and another box. The other box had once been bright white. It had a cartoonish drawing in primary colors of Sherlock Holmes with an oversize magnifying glass in his hand. In large, red, block letters were the words: SECRET CODE BREAKING KIT. In smaller letters: (Ages 10-12).

"What?" Eileen was puzzled. "Open it up. Maybe there's something different inside."

"No, there isn't. I remember this. When I was little I was into mysteries and codes and secrets. I used to have this game. I mean, it's the same one. Look, that's all it is."

"Oh. Did you have, like, a special attachment to it or something?"

"No. I only played with it a few times."

She went out of the kitchen and came back with the letter. It was from my father, obviously written in the hospital at different times with different pens, in a wandering scrawl, but with his perfect grammar.

> Dear Tim,
>
> This box keeps coming back to me.
>
> I took this by accident when I left the house ten years ago. I always meant to give it back, but I just kept forgetting. When I sent it to you last summer, I did it only because I thought it would be a good conversation-starter.
>
> Cancer seems to have served that purpose instead. I can't tell you how much our little talks in the hospital have meant to me. If my cancer was the only way for us to get close again, it has been worth it.
>
> I think we have finally cracked the code that kept us from communicating for so long. Please keep the box this time. It seems to have brought me luck. Maybe it can do the same for you. And please come see me again soon.
>
> Love,
>
> Dad

Eileen put her hand on top of mine. "Oh, that's so sad. You can tell he thought he was going to live when he sent that."

"Yeah."

"I wish I had come down when your father was in the hospital. I wish I had gotten to know him. And I really apologize for not coming down to the funeral."

"He remembered you."

"Oh."

"You had no way of knowing he was that bad off. But you know, I did tell him about you. I told him you and I were going strong."

She smiled sadly. "That makes me even more sorry I didn't make the funeral." The wind started shrieking even louder outside the windows. "There's not going to be any school tomorrow, and we're out of beer. Wait! I think there's some rum here that Jen bought." She jumped up and found it right away.

"Before we get too far," I had a half-empty glass in my hand, "before the night gets too old, I brought you a Valentine's Day present too." I pulled out the little box and slid it across the table towards her. She looked puzzled.

"Jewelry? This is not like you, Tim."

"I'm trying to keep you guessing."

I hadn't gone to all this expense without checking out the opinions of my friends in the pizza district. American Kim told me exactly what would happen when I gave the pendant to Eileen. In a situation like this, she told me, the woman will say she loves it whether she likes it or not.

"In other words, the woman will lie," I said.

"No, Tim. Listen. If you want to know whether she likes it or not, you have to wait a couple of years and see how often she wears it. That's the only way."

"That's crazy *and* dishonest."

"No. It's not dishonest. It's a required ritual. All women understand it intuitively. You just don't get it."

That didn't make any sense to me, so I just gave the pendant to Eileen and waited to see what would happen. She held the pendant up to the kitchen light and tilted it around so that the emeralds sparkled from different angles. Then she dangled it from its chain under the light. She didn't say anything about whether she liked it or not. She put it down before saying anything at all. Then she grabbed my hand and started to say something, but tears came to her eyes, and she got a little embarrassed about that and let go of my hand to wipe them away. She said she loved me. ! *

She told me the next day that she liked the pendant. I understood then that she would go through the rest of the steps of the ritual that Kim had described. I would find out in two years if she liked the pendant or not. But I finally understood it didn't matter at all whether the pendant was aesthetically pleasing to her or whether its color matched her complexion in certain kinds of light. The only thing that mattered was that she loved me. The ritual was just a woman's way of putting the most important things first. I hadn't been mature enough to understand this. Maybe the box was working, helping me to crack another code. It certainly was bringing me luck.

* This is a big scene and should be shown and not told. And we need Tim's responsive feelings, better in dialog somehow? Very good is his insight toward maturity!

Chapter 19

There were two feet of snow on the ground by the time we woke up early the next morning. Jen, and Eileen's other housemate, Diane, had come in long after we had gone to bed and woke us up with a lot of loud laughter and boot thumping, but the house was quiet in the morning. It would be hours before they woke up. The school was closed. The wind was gone, but the temperature had dropped. The sunlight reflected off the snow and exploded with brightness through the window in her bedroom. The house was warm, though. We had never before woken up together like this, with such a still but dramatic scene outside, with all ordinary events cancelled, with the house all to ourselves for the moment.

"Good morning! What should we do?" she greeted me. We were still in bed, lying side by side. I spread my fingers and sifted through her hair, then pushed it back so I could see her whole face. I traced her exposed cheekbones. She was staring at me, looking just as overwhelmed. Our feelings were probably just those hot spots in the brain that, she had assured me, would cool with time. Right then, however, it seemed like time didn't exist. She raised her eyebrows as if to ask her question again.

It turned out she had an idea of what we should do, and it turned out it was more specific than I had guessed. "I want to be on top," she whispered, her eyes suddenly shy.

I had never done that before. She crouched over me on all fours. I couldn't see very much because first her hair, and then her breasts, were in my face. I could feel her grab me and then I felt her working her way onto me, every inch announced with a quiet gasp. Then she sat up and slid all the way onto me and I almost lost it right then, but I managed to hold myself back, the tension seeming to heighten my sensation, even my vision. Her breasts glowed white in the preternatural sunlight from the window, her nipples bright pink, surrounded by their softer pink halos. She started to move and I could see her mouth open and hear her quietly breathe: *oh-oh-oh-oh*. I didn't look in her eyes at first because I was afraid it would end too soon. But she kept moving and breathing and I needed to watch her. She stared at me, and then she began working on me, watching me gasp in response to her every twitch and wiggle. Then she stopped and leaned her shoulders back. I thought she was showing off her breasts, how they actually pointed up when she was in that position, but then I felt her fingers on my legs, stroking the skin on the inside, going further and further up. And then as she stroked me, rode me, showed off her body to me, she looked in my eyes and sweetly smiled. That did it. I must have made some kind of noise that foretold that I was losing it. She cried out herself just as I came with a groan that might have awakened the dead but apparently didn't stir Jen or Diane from their drunken comas.

"I didn't know anybody could do that." I was still catching my breath. "I mean control my body like that. It's like you're wired into my nervous system."

"I've been reading magazines."

"What?"

"You know, women's magazines. My mother had a lot of them around the house."

We ate some cereal in the kitchen downstairs. Still not a peep from Jen or Diane. The snow hushed every noise outside. We could hear the refrigerator click on and off, the faint roar of the furnace in the basement. "Promise me," I said, "we'll move in together at the end of the semester."

"Maybe you can move in right now. You can still officially live in the dorm as far as the university is concerned. Let me talk to Jen and Diane."

"Why don't I demonstrate to them how helpful I can be? Do you have a snow shovel? I'll dig out the walk, and their cars."

"I remember the landlord showing us a shovel somewhere."

I found the snow shovel in the basement. I did the walk and dug out her car. The snow was over two feet deep, but it was dry and light. The air was colder than anything I had experienced in the pizza district. The cars were covered in almost identical igloo-shaped mounds of snow. After I finished Eileen's car I started on Jen's. About this time the plows came through and walled in both cars with a bank of heavier, scraped-up snow. It took another hour, but it was good exercise – and a good excuse to hang around until lunch time.

She met me at the door, looked past me at all I had done, and then got this weird little smile on her face. "Would you mind very much if I asked you to do Jen's car too?"

"I already did it."

She looked at me, glanced out at the street, looked back at me. "No you didn't. I don't know whose car that is you just dug out, but it's not Jen's."

"Oh shit. Shit!"

"Hers is the one parked behind mine. Diane's is the one behind hers. Just saying. I have to walk downtown anyway to buy something for lunch. It'll take me a while."

It was really fun playing house with her. I never thought I could enjoy such a simple thing. Jen got up in time for lunch, dressed like Eileen in a sweatshirt and jeans.

"Where did you go last night?" I asked.

"Hard to remember. The anti-Valentine's Day fun got old pretty quick. But we wanted to leave you two alone. At one point we were at a place with a band. It's possible we got up and sang along. I recall thinking we were really good."

"I can't wait to see the reviews."

"Our set might have been cut a little short. Oh God, I feel awful. I can't eat this. I'm sorry. Thanks for making it anyway. I'm going to go lie down."

"This wasn't the time to ask her," Eileen said after she went back upstairs.

"Oh, I agree. I don't think I should even be here when you ask."

"If you live here, it's not going to be just our house, like it was last night and early this morning. Could you live with Jen and Diane too?"

"I like Jen. Don't really know Diane. It'll be fine. They can't be any crazier than the people I lived with in the pizza district."

"I'd rather we could live alone together."

"Me too. Eileen, I never had a better Valentine's Day. And that was even before you showed me your new tricks in bed."

She just put her head down and, smiling to herself, took a bite of the tuna salad sandwich she had bought at the carryout.

I searched her face. "Are you reminding yourself that the hot spots will fade?"

"Yeah, I am." Still smiling, she didn't look up. "But maybe that's not the important thing."

She kept on eating. "Honestly, this is the best sandwich I've ever had in my life."

In the silence that followed I heard a buzzing sound from the next room. It was my cell phone, which I had left inside when I went out to shovel snow.

"That thing has been buzzing all morning," she said. "I thought about answering for you; but you know, even if we were married, I don't think I would do that."

I didn't get to the phone in time, but I brought it back to the kitchen. I scrolled through the numbers. "Look at all these people who called me. Almost everybody I know from home. I bet they're thinking about cancelling coming up here this weekend because of the snow. There must be a cell-phone frenzy going on in the pizza district." She looked on as I scrolled through the callers: "Jeremy, my mother, Dory, Ben, Jeremy again, Dory again, my mother, American Kim, Dory, Ben again, unidentified (that must be Korean Kim), Jeremy, Ben."

"If you had a more modern phone, you could text message them all back at once."

"I probably should listen to these messages first to see what they're saying."

"I should call Dory and thank her," she said suddenly.

"Why?"

"For taking care of you at your father's funeral. When I didn't come. The least I can do is thank her."

"I don't think you need to call her." But I could not keep the fear out of my voice. Eileen picked up on it immediately, searching my eyes. "She would do that for anybody," I continued in desperation, not meeting her gaze. This was even less convincing, I could tell. I snapped the phone closed, too quickly. My hands were shaking. I couldn't look her in the eye. She had already guessed. Her face went white, and she seemed to shrink down in the chair.

Chapter 20

"*Sociology 317: Definitions of Normality.* What the hell is that?" My friends had finally arrived. American Kim was sitting at the table in the restaurant we went to together, looking over the State catalogue. My mother had come up with Alan, and they had brought Jeremy and Dory and Kim and Kim. Because they only rented three rooms, and because neither Kim would sleep in the same room with the other, Jeremy had to share a room with Korean Kim while American Kim bunked with Dory. At the restaurant that evening, no one responded right away to American Kim's question about the *Definitions of Normality*, because another subject came up.

"Where's Eileen? Does she have a class this late?" my mother asked.

"Um, we're not dating any more."

There was a deafening silence at the table. I looked up, ready to face their questions, but there were none. Dory would not meet my gaze. Alan looked at me, nodded to acknowledge that he had heard me, then looked down at his silverware.

"Hey," I said, "give me credit. This was an all-time record for me. Five months."

"I hadn't realized it was even that long," my mother said.

"I'm very sorry for your loss," Korean Kim said, looking around.

"Nobody died, Kim. But thanks."

"Sorry, Tim. She was cool," Jeremy offered.

"Thanks. I'll be okay."

"And according to this catalogue, there are 8,746 other female students on this campus. If I …."

"Shut up, Jeremy," Dory interrupted.

"Hey, I'm just saying. You know what I heard the other day? Even if your girlfriend's one in a million, that means there's 8,000 others exactly like her in the world."

"You're not funny." Dory's comment silenced the table again. I took a sip of my beer. There was some clacking of silverware against plates.

Alan seemed to have the knack for knowing when a subject should be changed. "Maybe the idea of *Definitions of Normality* is to get you in the habit of constantly questioning all of your assumptions about what is normal."

"Why would you want to do that?" Kim screwed up her face. "If you question everything all the time, you couldn't put one foot in front of the other."

"But how could we ever change things if we automatically accept everything that currently exists as normal?" Alan persisted.

I laughed. "Alan, you're talking to a future businesswoman here. She doesn't want to hear about no stinking habits of questioning everything."

After dinner my mother and Alan excused themselves, and I hung out with the rest of them, talking about college and real estate and Jeremy's job and the pizza district. I was trying to talk American Kim into finishing college here.

"They're supposed to have a good business school here at State," I told her. I could tell she would succeed in any business field she entered. She attacked life like it was a field hockey game against a slow and clumsy opponent.

"Yeah-yeah, I'll think about that some other time. This weekend I just want to play."

"Do you know anybody else up here?" Dory changed the subject.

"I mean, Eileen wasn't your only friend up here, was she?"

"Of course not. I have a roommate, other friends in the dorm. In fact, I've been nominated to be president of the Transfer Students' Association."

Korean Kim perked up. American Kim put her hand on his arm to restrain his enthusiasm. "He's just kidding us. I'm sure there's no such thing as the Transfer Students' Association."

"Now that you're single again" – Jeremy already had enough to drink and was not above embarrassing people – "maybe you should hook up with Kim."

"I think I'm going to limit my search to women who have not thrown me off buildings."

Kim laughed. "Actually," I said into the silence that followed, "Eileen and I are still going to be friends." That comment changed the focus of the humor. Now the little snorts of laughter from Jeremy and American Kim were aimed at me. Korean Kim didn't get the joke. Dory didn't seem to think it was funny.

The whole subject embarrassed me and put a damper on the conversation. Korean Kim took advantage of the silence to talk American Kim into taking a walk to look at the Engineering Building. I had a very vivid memory of that building from the time Eileen and I ran in there to shelter from the storm, and I would have liked to see it again, but neither Kim seemed to want me along now. Dory seemed content to stay back and manage Jeremy. Jeremy was drinking sodas now. He finally understood that my breakup with Eileen was not funny to me. So he told us funny stories about customers and other people he had met on his job. The wireless company he worked for was thinking about sending him to a convention in Las Vegas. He said Ben was becoming friends with Cindy the policewoman next door, and Dory had even babysat little Timmy once.

"You like little kids, don't you?" I said to her.

"Sure. I want to have at least five one day." At this comment, Jeremy made an exaggerated gulp and set his glass down on the table hard. He looked at her, his eyes wide. "I mean some day. In the future. If I ever get married."

"Sometimes," he said, "I can't see a minute into the future. It's so hard deciding what to do. Choosing one thing rules out so many others. Dory doesn't think that way. She gives me faith that anything I do will be okay. That's why I love her so much." He picked up his glass. She was smiling at him sweetly. "Oh, and also because of the way she screams out when we're making love."

She hit him on the shoulder.

When Jeremy left for the men's room, Dory searched my eyes.

"Why'd you break up? Did Eileen find out?"

"Yes."

"You told her?"

"Not in so many words. But she knows."

"I'm sorry, Tim. If you want me to talk to her ..."

"No!"

"I feel so awful. I did something so wrong it can't be fixed."

"I guess that happens sometimes."

"Not to me, not ever before. At the time, I thought you .... Never mind."

"You're a good soul, Dory. I did it too. I'll have to live with the consequences. She's really hurt. But maybe I can fix it up."

"She'll come to her senses. I know it. She won't pass you up."

"I guess that's what I was hoping everybody else would say, too."

I had a conversation alone with Alan the next afternoon in a breakfast place. "You know what I think, Tim?" he gently suggested. "I think you are a natural born scholar. You seem to really enjoy learning everything. I can see you with a PhD someday. If I were you I'd just go for it, study anything I wanted, let it all hang out."

"At one point I tried to learn everything there was to know about this Shakespearian play, *Coriolanus*. I don't know where that got me."

"Your mother talks a lot about you, how smart you are, how driven."

"She's worried that I'll drive myself off a cliff."

He shrugged. "She's a mother. They worry. To me, there's nothing to worry about. You have a wonderful set of friends. You have a lot of interests. You're persistent. You'll find your way."

"What I can't understand about you, Alan, is why you're not the President of the United Nations."

"It took every diplomatic skill I ever had to get your mother to pay the slightest bit of attention to me."

"She was hurt."

"She seemed to be hurt very badly. But imagine! She still took a chance. *On me!*"

Most of the weekend, my mother and Alan paid for everybody's meals. They even went into a bar with us once and paid for all of our drinks. They treated us like we were all their own cherished, grown-up children. I caught my mother and Dory once having a long conversation about vegetarian food through a cloud of pot smoke in the hallway outside of Dory's room.

"There must be a place where we can dance," Dory suggested one evening. "Here. Here's one," she added, looking at an advertisement on the placemat.

"I've never been there, but it's supposed to be lame," I said.

"Come on. We'll liven it up."

Dory and Jeremy and the two Kims got up, and Alan got up to go with them. I tapped American Kim on the shoulder and teased her about being paired with the other Kim. "Actually," she said, "he told me he's been taking dancing lessons."

I looked over at my mother, and I could see her eyes were tired.

"I'll stay here and babysit this old lady."

"You don't want to dance with Kim?" This was just after they were out the door. "She seems nice."

"Kim's a good person, but maybe not my type."

"I thought your father was my type. Alan is so different, but I really like him. He's not at all what I thought I was missing all those years. Maybe I should have found somebody like Alan a long time ago."

"That's impossible, Mom. There's nobody else like Alan."

"Oh, thank you." She blinked back tears. "I'm so happy. I don't deserve it, I know. I guess I was waiting all those years – I don't know, for your father to come to his senses maybe? He seemed so unhappy ever since he got mixed up with Anita."

She ordered another martini. I raised my eyebrow.

"See? Your mother's getting a little wild in her old age." She took a sip, put the glass down. "So, you're still trying with Eileen."

"Yeah. The breakup was not my idea."

"My experience is, wanting something really badly is not enough to make it come true. I guess I'm saying don't wait forever."

"It's not exactly forever yet. We're talking last Thursday."

The next day we went for a hike, went bowling, went to a movie in town. Jeremy paid for all of our movie tickets.

"Diamond Service Plan?" I looked at him. He gave me the thumbs-up.

I even got them to stay an extra day so Jeremy could go to my European History class. It was about the Reformation.

"What did you think about the class?"

"It made me feel stupid. I didn't even know there was a Martin Luther Senior. I don't know. At least it gives me an idea of how much I don't know."

We all met again at the motel the last day in Alan and my mother's room. I brought up some snacks. I was hoping to talk to them some more, but they were all packed and ready to go.

"I thought you had chemistry class at 11:30?" Dory said.

"I could skip it."

"Don't, Tim. We gotta get going."

I skipped chemistry class anyway and ran up into the hills. Then it would be statistics class, then back to the dorm. Then studying in the library for the night, in the same carrel where Eileen and I used to meet. Then the dorm, sleep, and starting all over again in the morning. This was my new life.

~ Chapter 21 ~

Eileen leaned forward over the kitchen table with her face in her hands. My cell phone lay flat down on the table between us. She looked up, her face pale, breathing shallowly, her gaze not quite up to the level of my eyes. All I could think was I had failed the biggest test of my life. I could have stammered out a list of excuses, tried to make her feel guilty for not showing up at my father's funeral, blamed Dory, asked for pity for the poor boy whose father had just died. There were plenty of excuses, but how could we live a life together founded on excuses?

"Do you love her?" Her voice was weak.

"I like her a lot. She's my friend."

This was just making things worse. But I wasn't going to lie.

"Did you tell her you loved her?"

"No. She was kind to me that day. That's mostly what I remember."

"What's wrong?" Even Slide, my self-absorbed roommate, noticed that I was in my bed with the lights out whenever I was there. "Don't you even eat?"

"Yeah. Yeah. I guess I forgot today."

"You definitely forgot. It's one o'clock in the morning. We're going to the B Cafeteria. Come on."

He was the only person whose name I knew on campus besides Eileen and Jen and Diane. His friend came into our dorm room then, and Slide and Greg and I crunched a shortcut through the knee-high snow to the walkways leading to the all-night cafeteria. I had suggested calling out for pizza, but there was a lot of verbal fumbling around, and it went on and on until I realized the real problem was they had no money, while the cafeteria was already included in the meal plan.

"Do you have, like, junior standing?" Slide asked me tentatively as we sat down at the table in the half-filled, all-night cafeteria. He seemed a little intimidated by me because I was a little older and had muscles and had once brought a woman to the room.

"No. I have 63 credits, but not all of them transferred. I'm a few short of junior standing. What are you guys majoring in?"

"You can't really major in anything your first semester here. There's a lot of required courses that count for any major. You have to take them first."

"Except for physical therapy," Greg added. "If you're wanting to be a physical therapist, you have to decide before you show up here the first day."

"Is that you?"

"So far," Greg grinned. Greg was short, stocky, with muscular arms. He looked like my idea of a physical therapist.

"Find anybody to play Australian football here?" I asked Slide.

"Ah, we met some other guys on the floor. We're thinking of starting an intramural basketball team. There's a dorm league, you know. We're actually a little short" – he looked at Greg, who made a face at him – "on members, that is. If you want, you can join the team. There are no standards."

There was a lot of kidding between them about their dismal love lives. It reminded me a lot of Ben and Jeremy and me, shooting the breeze and taunting each other in the bars at home, in a time that now seemed ages ago. I didn't want to join in, and they didn't ask me to. I was eating a giant yogurt with fruit in it. Something told me this would be a good start, since I hadn't eaten in more than 24 hours. Suddenly I realized that Slide was talking to me.

"So, will you be bringing Eileen again to the dorm? She is one beautiful lady. You should see her, Greg. She's a knockout."

Greg snapped to attention on hearing this. And so, for the second time that week, I had to tell a rapt audience that Eileen wouldn't be coming around any more.

"They're bitches. All bitches, I'm telling you," Greg suddenly snarled. I guessed that Greg didn't know anything at all about girls except that he had never been able to get one.

"No, this is all on me. It was all my fault."

"So, you boinked another broad, did you?" I thought I heard a trace of a lilt in Greg's question. And the contrast between that faint musical lilt and the crude wording of his guess made me smile, then laugh. Then all of us were laughing. I decided to let it go at that. All so funny. They didn't need to know the whole story, and they didn't really want to.

That last morning in her kitchen, Eileen would start crying, then apologize for crying. Every time she apologized, it worsened my shame. Then, for a while, she just sat, staring ahead at nothing. I figured she was planning her life without me.

"I never had a single thought, even for a second, about any other guy," she said. "Ever since we met." Although her voice was quiet, the distinction she was making between her and me was very clear.

"I can't say that," I confessed. I always knew there was something wrong with the way I related to women, and that it would come out sooner or later. I always suspected I wouldn't be able to love a real woman like her.

"Is that all you have to say?"

"I shouldn't have dragged you into my life." My mind stumbled, searching for something more to say. The problem was, I wasn't even in the same category she was in, the category of normal, decent people. A decent guy would talk to her even now, would think of something to say that wouldn't hurt her worse. But right then I didn't feel even close to decent.

"Maybe you should go," she said then.

I walked out fast without my coat or gloves. Without the box. What did it matter? I found the snow shovel out near the street where I had left it in my rush to come in and eat lunch with her. I picked it up and laid it quietly on the porch. I didn't want to knock on the door and make her see me again. I kicked my way through the snow all the way back to my dorm. She was the only real girlfriend I'd ever had. I was 0 for 1, in a game I was probably never meant to play.

It was that very next weekend that my friends had come up to visit. They were nice enough not to interrogate me about losing her. Only Dory knew the reason. After they went home they kept trying to contact me. Ben called me and talked about his renovations to the house. Jeremy told me about his job and about some furniture Dory was buying. My mother called and said she was changing the house around, going for a more modern look.

They were all good people. I tried to sound upbeat on the phone. But the things they told me about, the things they were doing, seemed so unimportant that I had to fake my enthusiasm. They sensed that it was fake, but I couldn't do anything to make it real. After a while, it became very painful to talk to them at all. I didn't think I was doing them any favors by putting on my sham show of concern. After a week or so I stopped picking up when I saw their numbers.

I started running a lot more, mostly on the treadmill but a few times in the cold, lung-searing air on the roads above the town. I tried to think about the true meaning of my relationship with Eileen. I must not have felt the bond between us as strongly as she did or I wouldn't have messed with somebody else. Probably I was incapable of that kind of love, as my past history seemed to prove. She could probably see all that, and that's probably why she simply said, in the end, "You should go."

You could take a final statement like that and at least have solid ground upon which to build a new kind of life. That's what I started out to do. I knew I was a good student, and my body was in shape, and I was curious, and I had a lot of drive. I appreciated Alan reminding me of all that. So my first plan was just to forget all women, stop wasting my energy pursuing the fantasy of having a partner.

That didn't work out too well. My life without Eileen started off okay, moving along on its own inertia. I kept the same study habits, including using the same carrel in the library where we used to study together. It was okay the first day, but on the second day I found a tiny gold-colored medallion with the school seal that had fallen off her key ring. I picked it up and starting wondering if she had noticed it was missing. Then I started wondering about when she had bought it, where she had bought it, why she had picked that particular little trinket. I couldn't get these thoughts about it out of my mind. So I picked it up and walked over to a trash can in the hall and threw it away – but then I thought she might want it back some day, and I went out and got it back out of the trash. But I didn't send it to her. I didn't take it with me either. I left it in the exact same spot I found it. The first thing I did when I came in every day was to look to see if it was still there. It became important to me that it still be there. It seemed like it was the psychological cornerstone of the room, keeping my study session from flying apart.

The little medallion was only the beginning of the compulsive thoughts. I had to find different roads to run because the snow melted enough to uncover the tree trunk we leaned against that first time we ran up in the hills. In the fitness center, I had to shake my head and hum a tune to keep from remembering the specific treadmill she used. Fortunately, in the dorm, Slide was still intimidated enough by me that he never asked me what was going on with her, but I could tell the question was always on the tip of his tongue. I started seeing parallels to my betrayal of Eileen even in Shakespeare's history plays.

These reminders of her were like pop-up ads everywhere in my brain. You can ignore them, and I guess after a while you hardly notice them. I was waiting for that to happen. But it took such an effort to ignore them that everything else seemed dull, black-and-white, routine. Classes began to seem like a grind. I had to read things over several times before the contents would sink in. I had to ask Slide to repeat even the simplest things he said. I was becoming stupid.

In two or three weeks I realized it wasn't working and I was a mess. I needed to see Eileen. I walked to her house after dinner on a night I knew she would be there. Most of the snow was gone by then, the ground covered by just an inch or two of dirty, crusty white.

Jen answered the door. She seemed surprised to see me, but not unhappy. She had me wait in the kitchen. Eileen came in wearing jeans and a sweatshirt, her hair pushed back behind her ears. I could have brought the medallion to serve as a conversation-starter, but I hadn't been able to. I could not risk removing it from its place.

"You look beautiful."

She shrugged and gave me a tight smile. Her face had regained its full color. She kept standing in the doorway to the kitchen, as if she didn't want to re-enact our last meeting sitting at that table.

One thing I'd learned from my years of experience with my father's whining was that neediness was not attractive, no matter how abject you feel inside. And so I didn't beg.

"You were my best friend up here," I started. "I miss that a lot. I wish we could at least stay friends, talk sometimes."

"Are you friends with Dory?"

"I am. And with Jeremy. And Ben, and American Kim. I haven't talked to any of them in weeks."

"What kind of friend is that?"

I wasn't good friendship material either. How did she have the power to see through me like that? "I just have this feeling," I persisted, "if I could be your friend, I could build back my other friendships – be like a whole person, even if I'm not suited to be anybody's lover."

Her voice was suddenly strained. "Nobody has ever gone to the trouble of knowing me before. It's hard to explain how good that felt." Then she put her stuff down on the steps in the hallway. I hoped that meant she was coming in the kitchen, but it didn't. She kept talking from the hall. "And I already really miss watching you take on State."

Then she did come toward the kitchen so she wouldn't have to talk so loud. "It would hurt too much to be just your friend," she said. "I think we need a clean break."

"We should forget each other ever existed?" The thought completely blew my mind. But I could see the logic.

"Everyone knows that's an impossibility." Jeremy had called every day until I finally did pick up. "It's written in the stars or the constitution of the universe or something: you can't be friends with an ex-girlfriend."

"Well, sign me up as Exhibit A on that one."

I was trying again to talk to my friends on the phone. At least I had something to report on that was interesting to me. But I realized as soon as I started talking to Jeremy that I didn't really want to talk about my final break with Eileen. Jeremy simply suggested I start going after one of the other 8,746 females on campus.

I actually took his advice. There was a nice-looking girl in my Shakespeare class who was really smart, and she wasn't so beautiful that she already had to have a boyfriend. I sat next to her that day, and afterwards tried to talk to her about the play. She said hi, but as soon as I said the next thing she stiffened up like she was grossed out by my talking to her. It didn't get any better when I asked her a question about her interpretation of *Othello*. She clearly didn't want to talk to me. I got out of there right away.

I wore a different shirt the next day to my statistics class so nobody would notice my muscles. I had started being embarrassed by them. I started to talk to the girl next to me about why we had both decided to take statistics. I thought this would be a good conversation starter, because most people taking statistics are not interested in becoming statisticians but are taking the course because it is a prerequisite for something else. She was a very serious-looking strawberry blonde whose slightly frowsy hairstyle reminded me a little of Jen's. She said she was going into political science. It occurred to me right then that I didn't have a good answer as to why I was taking statistics myself. And when she asked, I froze up. I mean I could hear myself saying words, but it was just some kind of rote thing about statistics being a requirement for so many majors that I was keeping my options open. It didn't seem like it was me talking at all. She said something like "that's nice" and turned back to her notes. I didn't blame her. It must have seemed like she was talking to a robot.

I didn't give up trying to meet girls, but I got the same kind of response all week, until I realized it was me, not them. The more women who rejected me, the weirder I felt. The weirder I felt, the worse my approach was. I also had the same kind of experience with guys. Slide was the only person who was different, and even we were playing artificial roles. I was the slightly older, slightly more experienced person who knew enough about calculus to help him when he got stuck. I knew a lot more about women, it was assumed, and I let him assume that, but I provided only tongue-in-cheek answers to all his questions about the subject. I felt a bit phony for being so flippant about the subject, but I was sure he didn't want to hear me whining about how much it hurt to lose Eileen.

I never called Jeremy back about my progress with the 8,746 women, and I didn't pick up his calls after that. All 8,746 women on campus could intuitively sense there was something wrong with me. I could tell Jeremy that – which would just make him think I was going crazy – or I could not talk to him at all.

I tried to get interested in events of the world. People were being laid off by the millions. The pointless war dragged on. Both political parties seemed to hate each other more than they cared about what was happening to the country. College students were being shot by the dozens by deranged fringe students, and it was clear that nothing was going to be done to prevent it from happening again. The only groups that got anybody's attention were interest groups or hate groups. They say you can help change things, but it seemed to me that was just a joke. I stopped reading the newspaper, stopped clicking on the supposedly interesting stories, left the room whenever the news came on.

I kept ignoring my friends' calls. I cut down on my running and spent more time studying. At least, I spent more time in the carrel in the library. I was more worried every day that the medallion would be gone when I got there. I wasn't allowed to hide it, so I just had to hope and pray that it was still there each day when I arrived. I was allowed to pick it up when I was in there, so I spent some time – I don't know how much time – fingering it, flipping it over, examining both sides of it in various angles of sunlight. I didn't have the capacity for study that I used to have. I used to read everything a least twice, answer all the obvious questions in my head, then go back and re-imagine the material while changing one important aspect in my head, then figure out how the result would be different. This was easy to do in math, but it worked for Shakespeare and history too. It was the kind of thinking an *A* student did. I couldn't do that any more. The words on the page and on the screen were not alive with ideas any more. Now they were just flat things to look at and memorize.

One night I took a call from Dory. "Not good," I said honestly, in answer to her question. "I think the Eileen problem is spreading into the rest of my life."

There was a long silence on the phone. "Maybe she would have dumped you anyway. Maybe she's just using what we did as an excuse."

"She thinks there's something wrong with me."

"What's wrong with you?"

"She implied if I was a real man, really in love with her, I wouldn't think of anybody else, even for an instant. And so she suspects I'm in love with you."

There was another long silence on the line, and her voice was different when she came back on. "That's such crap. We had a sweet moment. I don't really see anything wrong with it. What's the sense of being young if you don't let yourself get carried away once in a while?"

"Once in a while?"

"I'm trying to do better these days."

"Not Cameron?"

"No, no! God, Tim, no!"

"I don't believe you. I don't believe you ever cheated on anybody before." There was an even longer silence on the line.

"Anyway, I'm trying to follow the rules now," she said, then hung up quickly.

I began staying away from Slide too. I spent more time in the weight room. The one thing I could still do well was grow even bigger, freakier muscles. Why not? I really was a freak. I came back from the weight room one afternoon and sat staring out the window, even though I knew I was supposed to be helping Slide by showing up for his intramural basketball game. I knew he might have to forfeit the game if I didn't show up. I knew not showing up was a really scummy thing to do. I wasn't going to go. I was not only a freak but a scumbag too. Might as well show my true colors.

Slide came back to the room to get me, though.

"I forgot," I blatantly lied. Seeing him there right in front of me, I couldn't admit to him that I had intended to leave him in the lurch.

"Tim," he said, still panting from his rush to get me on time, "I think you might have problems." I realized this was hard for him to say because he was still a little bit intimidated by me. "I mean serious problems. Maybe you need to get some kind of counseling or something."

"Is that going to help win the basketball game?"

"No. So please, let's do the basketball game first."

Soon after that the physical pain started. I stopped the extra weight workouts, but that didn't help. It was just a dull pain, throughout most of my body. It was there most of the time, but it was worse whenever I had one of those pop-ups about Eileen, or when I started thinking over my life. I still went to the carrel, but I don't think I was studying any more. I spent a lot of time staring at that medallion. I would still listen to my friends' messages, even though I would never return them. Dory was going with Jeremy to Vegas. Ben had finished the electricity and drywall on the entire second floor. Kim was now dating Kim. They all seemed to have real lives, as compared to mine. My entire past life seemed like a façade, a façade that was now crumbling.

I even came up with a diagnosis. I started thinking back over my entire life, back to when I was a little kid. I had never been honest with anybody. I betrayed Jeremy, screwed up Dory's head. But long before that, I had cowered behind my mother when she was being berated by my father. And then I helped my father lie to her. I thought about Alan and how he had so much faith in me, and now I couldn't face the fact that I would definitely disappoint him. I couldn't study any more. All that achievement in community college had been just a cover-up for my fear of facing the world. My mother would find out soon enough what an empty role I had been playing.

I kept wishing I could start over, be five years old again, grow into a different person brave enough to stand up to his father and honest enough to be trusted as a friend. That wasn't going to happen. I didn't have the capacity to help anyone. I was just a downer, a charity case to my friends, my mother, Alan. And I was 0 for 1, zero percent worthwhile to the only woman I could ever love.

They would all be better off if I were dead. I realized this while standing on the bridge over the ravine. The bridge had iron fence rails five feet high to keep people from jumping. It hadn't stopped the last person, a freshman girl from China. She took her leap in the middle of last semester's final exams.

They can never stop us. We defectives will always find a way to eliminate ourselves. Nature must take its course.

I pulled myself up and sat on the rail of the fence. Just then I heard a sound I hadn't noticed in this town since the night when Eileen and I first made love, the sound of a freight train in the distance. Mine had come. I stared down into the icy ravine. I started to push off. I could feel my corrupt soul tear itself away from my body. Good riddance.

Chapter 22

The police stopped because of the scuffle. It was me versus three huge guys. They had me down on my back on the bridge. They were even stronger than they looked, and I was helpless to get back up. A police siren went off next to my ear. They rolled away from me and we all got up and faced the cop getting out of his car, radio in hand. One of them kept his arm cinched around mine so I couldn't make a dash for the rail.

"What's the problem here? Are you alright, sir?"

"I'm fine," I said.

"Were these guys assaulting you?"

"No. They're not trying to hurt me, officer."

"We come by," one of the guys explained. "He's sitting on top of the rail, leaning out. Looked like he was getting ready to jump." He was the biggest guy I had ever seen in person, a huge black dude with a jagged beard but a very gentle face – had to be a football player, had to be a defensive lineman. "We pulled him back. Now he's fighting with us."

"Is that true?" the cop asked me.

"They're not trying to hurt me."

"That's not what I asked. Why were you on the rail?"

I realized this instant was going to be a defining moment in my life. If I told the truth I'd be taken in for observation, maybe kept in a mental ward. I would still be defective, but I'd be a walking defective, a chicken defective. People would spend big parts of their professional lives listening to me whine about Eileen.

"I was ... *writing a poem*." I spread my arms, hands up, rolled my eyes, like this should have been the most obvious thing in the world to them.

"What were you writing it on?" The cop wasn't buying it.

"A piece of paper."

"Where's the paper?"

"Probably about 100 feet down now, at the bottom of the ravine somewhere."

"I suppose the pencil's down there too. What was the poem about?"

"About ... a freight train. The power of a freight train."

He let the other three guys get up, but he put cuffs on me and made me sit in the back of his car with the door open while he completed his investigation. I caught the eye of the giant guy who saved me. Save me again, was my message. I think he was 99 percent sure I had been jumping, but he looked really unhappy when the cop cuffed me.

"Did any of you gentlemen actually see him try to jump?"

Giant guy mumbled no. The guy next to him, almost as big, white, dark hair, shook his head no. The third guy started to nod yes, but when he saw what the other two were doing he just shrugged his shoulders.

"Anybody hurt?"

No all around.

I tried to look as unconcerned as possible when the cop looked me in the eye again. The other three looked nervous. I couldn't tell if they were afraid the cop would run them in on some excuse or whether they were afraid they were making a horrible mistake in backing up my story.

"All right, I'm going to write an incident report. No arrests. I want all your names and IDs. Then I want you, all three of you, to escort Mr. Poet back to his dorm. He's got to be upset, losing that poem and all. And when you're done that, if you remember any more details, call me at this number."

He uncuffed me and let me out of the car. Trying not to be obvious about it, they stood between me and the rail. I made a point of walking very slowly off the bridge with the three of them close behind.

They followed his orders precisely, escorting me not only the entire mile-long walk to my dorm but also into the dorm and up to the door to my room. No one said a word. I turned around at my door.

"Thanks. I mean that."

"We covered up for you. Don't make fools of us, man," the third guy said.

"There's another way. Look for it," giant man said.

I figured I would try to go on. I tried to keep up a little curiosity about what would happen next. There was nothing to lose. Every second of life now was gravy. I could still do enough rote learning to get a *B*-minus in most classes. I'd hear other students ask the kind of searching questions I used to ask, but I no longer cared what the answers were.

I asked Slide to do me a favor. "There's a carrel I sometimes use in in the library."

"What's a carrel?"

"It's like a little room. Nobody owns it, but if it's empty you can go in there and study."

"What's *study*? Just kidding."

"Anyway, in carrel 542, there's a desk. There's this little thing in the room on the floor near the back leg of the desk." I told him exactly what the medallion looked like and where to find it. "Will you go get it?"

"Is it valuable or something?"

"Not at all. I'm asking you to do something with it. And this is going to do me a lot more good than any counseling. Take the medallion and throw it away. Throw it someplace far away. And never tell me where."

"Radioactive?"

I looked at him. "Yeah, basically. But only to me. I promise I'll make every basketball practice if you do it."

Slide did exactly as I asked. I still couldn't study in carrel 542, but I could use any of the others on the floor without obsessing over anything. I was somewhat afraid that getting rid of the medallion would just cause some other obsession to crop up, but that didn't happen. So I continued slouching through the rest of the semester with my *B*- minus plans. The Eileen pop-ups, however, continued, bringing with them the conviction that life had passed me by.

It wasn't hard to figure out her schedule. I stood at the far end of the parking lot one afternoon and watched her walk to her car. It had snowed that morning, and she had a lot of things in her arms. She looked great, but she was having a hard time getting her car door open against the snow with only half a hand free. For a moment I indulged in the fantasy that I could walk over and help her, but I knew my place. It was great to see her for real. I also figured out where she ate lunch on Wednesdays, and I realized I could sit down at the opposite end of the giant cafeteria without her even knowing I was there. She was eating with Jen, and I had a moment's fantasy then that I could meet with Jen some other time and talk to her about Eileen without creeping both of them out.

One day I walked into the fitness center and she was right there on a front row treadmill, her body and hair reflected in the 30 or so mirrors they had on all the walls of the giant room. Nobody could hide from anybody, and so I just walked up to her and said hi. She stumbled and almost fell off. I jumped toward her, but she regained her balance. She then slowed the machine down almost to a stop.

"Can we go over there and talk?" Her voice was just loud enough to be heard over the idling machine. She jumped off and turned to go before I could answer. I had forgotten how cut her legs were.

There were some benches lining one wall. We were sitting next to each other, both facing the same way. There was an awkward silence. Finally, she turned to me.

"I'm worried about you," she said.

"Why? I'm okay."

"Have you made any friends?"

"One. My roommate. He calls himself Slide."

"What's his real name?"

"I don't know. He's a freshman. You know, a lot of drinking, video gaming, card playing, leering at girls."

"You're so beyond that, Tim."

"I know. I do a lot of running by myself, weights, studying in the carrels – not that same carrel." Then I sighed dramatically. "When I first got here on campus I hung out with this older woman, but she doesn't want anything to do with me any more."

"That's not funny. You know I'm having a hard time."

"I'm not exactly frolicking around the campus myself. But I'm hanging in there. I have like a *B*-minus average so far."

She sucked in a quick breath. "You're so much smarter than that."

"Sometimes I still try to be the person that you falsely imagined me to be."

"It wasn't my imagination." Her eyes teared up.

"I didn't come here to make you cry. Look, maybe we can do something that will make us both feel better. Maybe go for a run some time. Really, we could maybe do just that one thing together. Just that."

"I don't think I could face that same road up in the hills, the one with that tree trunk."

"Maybe someday, some place. That's all I meant."

"Maybe some time when the weather's better?"

I was really proud of how cool I was pretending to be about that. This was not the time to push it, so I stood up, said I'd call her some time, and began to walk away.

"What about your workout?" she called after me when I had almost reached the entrance.

"Oh. Yeah. Um … I …. I'm just going to leave now."

"Would you come back here just for a second? I forgot to tell you something." I was at her side in an instant. "I've been talking with Kit. She's going to come up here in two or three weeks. You remember her, right?"

I laughed. "Oh yes."

"Well, she remembers you too. She wants to see you when she comes up here. I told her … I told her we're still friends. Are we friends enough that you would come and see her, talk to us when she comes to visit? She likes you."

"I like her too. I'd love to."

"Maybe we'll get a break in the weather and we can all run or something. They say it never gets warm here until early May, but I guess there's always a first time."

When I got back to the room unexpectedly early, Slide was waiting for me.

"You've been working out an awful lot lately. Decide to take it easier today?"

"Yeah. Why? Are you calling another unscheduled basketball practice?"

"No. It's you. Look, I don't mean to try to get into your head. I don't know a tenth of the stuff you do. But you've looked so sad the last couple of weeks. Did you ever get any counseling?"

"I did. You actually met my counselors."

"Those guys didn't exactly look like the Three Wise Men."

"I'm not kidding. Those guys really helped me. And what you did with the medallion – that helped a little, believe it or not. Honestly, things are looking up."

"If you say so."

I sat next to that frowsy-haired blonde in my statistics class and chatted her up just because I knew I could do it now. Her name was Susan, and she seemed to regard the social life of the campus as nothing more than an obstacle slowing her down in her path to becoming the chief of staff for some muckety-muck politician who I bet would be a woman. She was very cagey about what her politics really were. I tried to figure out if she would go out with me if I asked, but it really didn't matter because I wasn't going to ask. I had no plans of dating as long as I would see Eileen in a few weeks when Kit came to town.

I called her, left my number, maybe too many times. She finally took my call.

"Eileen, do you think I can get that box back? The one my father gave me for my birthday?"

"Of course. Is that really the only reason you called?"

"Also, I'd love to talk to you."

"I can't. I'm not trying to be mean. I can't describe to you … my mind goes spinning … remembering things. It lasted for days after I saw you in the fitness center. It's not helping anybody."

"Maybe if we talked about something real, in the present …."

"I just … can't."

"You won't even try? We always talked …."

"Tim. I …. I can't even do this. Every time I hear your voice, even over the phone, I … I get wet."

I did some drinking with Slide and Greg. They were both very funny in their self-deprecating ways. They seemed like freshman versions of the two guys Eileen and I met in the bar on our first day of running up here. I did a little drinking in the bars alone. A few days after my phone conversation with Eileen, I got a message from the campus mailroom that a box had arrived for me. I signed for it and took it back to my room. Slide was more than a little curious about it. I told him it was just a sentimental present from my father. But as I looked at the outside of the package, I had a sudden fear that she had also enclosed the Valentine's Day pendant, returning it to me. That fear grew beyond all reason. I was happy when I saw the package was still the original size, but I still couldn't be sure she hadn't stuffed the pendant inside until I opened it up. And I had to do this in front of Slide. When I opened it up and checked all around and assured myself that she hadn't enclosed the pendant, my relief was so great I laughed out loud. I had to hide from Slide that I was laughing out of relief. Explaining this kind of stuff might make me seem even crazier than I was.

One day Dory called me every hour on the hour until I finally picked up.

"Tim, your mother is worried about you. She's talking about driving up there again. You don't answer people's phone calls. Why won't you speak to your friends when they call?"

"I'm having a little bit of a hard time up here."

"Is it Eileen?"

"That's maybe going a little better. I think we actually could be friends."

"Friends? That's good, I guess."

"How are you doing? It's been a long time since I got the daily report from you at the breakfast table."

"Yeah. Good. Jeremy is so sweet. On the way back from State, he was driving, looking at the road, and all of the sudden, out of the blue, he says, 'I think maybe I could do five kids, but absolutely no more.'"

"Are we talking about the same Jeremy I used to know?"

"I know. I started to cry, and he thought he said something wrong."

On a Friday, coming back from my last class, I came into my room to find Jeremy and Ben shooting the breeze with Slide. "What are you guys doing here?"

"Came to repossess your phone," Jeremy said.

"You obviously don't know how to use it," Ben added, "like, to return calls."

"I'm sorry, guys. I was going through a bad time for a while."

"He was," Slide interjected. We all looked at him. I hoped he would shut up.

Fortunately for me, by the time we got to a bar downtown, Jeremy had reverted to his old habit of regaling us with his own problems. Dory was not happy about the trip to Las Vegas he had won as the top local salesman for the Diamond Service Plan.

"She wouldn't even go with me."

"Did she have to work?"

"No, it's something else." Ben and I had learned from long experience that the rest of the story was coming, and that we wouldn't even have to ask. "Okay, I'll tell you. At the convention, they assign to each top seller an assistant, like a super concierge. These people take care of everything for you. At the meeting, personal stuff, everything."

"What's Dory's beef with that?"

"She didn't like that they're called the Diamond Service Girls. And that they were optional but I signed up for one anyway."

"So, Dory's solution was to let you go to Vegas alone to be taken care of by your Diamond Service Girl?"

"Yeah, and it worked. She got really mad, and then I got so upset my stomach was churning the whole weekend. I was afraid to even make eye contact with my Diamond Service Girl."

"Why'd you sign up for a Diamond Service Girl in the first place?" Ben asked.

"I don't know. Can't a man dream?"

Ben told us about his renovation of our old house. He'd done the drywall on some of the rooms, but he said it took twenty times as long as he'd planned. He was getting ready to hire professional drywall people and electricians and roofers to get it done quickly. To do this he had to take out a loan, and he had to get his father to co-sign the papers.

"I bet Dory's real estate girlfriends are all excited about this," I guessed.

"Not really. Tracey helped me get an idea what the house would sell for if I fixed it up. But none of them are interested in how it actually gets fixed up. They just want to see it done, and then see how it sells."

"That's shitty," I said. "They want to see it sell but don't really want to hear about how you're fixing it up."

"Are you kidding? It's great. I need to get it done. I don't need anybody's remodeling ideas. This is not the Taj Mahal."

As the evening wore on, and we talked about everything we used to talk about, except Eileen, and there was nothing radically new to talk about, I started to wonder why they had come. Nothing really exciting or different had happened to Jeremy or Ben since their visit up here three weeks before. Despite their occasional enthusiasm for our conversation, I started to suspect they were here doing a job.

"Dory sent you two, didn't she?"

Jeremy put both hands on the table, palms up. "Dory knows best."

Chapter 23

Some wishes do come true. Just as Eileen had hoped, there was a highly unusual burst of warm weather in early March, the weekend that Kit came to visit State. Kit looked older than I remembered her, probably because of her clothes. She looked sophisticated in low black heels and a black skirt and a plain white blouse, but she wore her hair in a girlish ponytail. And she also had on goofy multicolored earrings. Eileen wore a bright green jumper over a buttoned-up white silk blouse that emphasized her dark hair and eyes.

Eileen spoke first when I met them in front of the library. "How do you like our elegant walking-around-the-campus clothes?" She was talking for the two of them, keeping her emotional distance from me, but it seemed like she was trying to do it in a nice way. Eileen seemed proud to be playing the role of the big sister showing Kit around. Kit was nervous. She met my eyes and said my name and held her arms close to her side. I hugged her quickly, let her go, and we were on our way.

"Where should we go now? Kit and I are done with the walking tour, and the yummy cafeteria brunch."

"See a class?" I suggested.

"Been there. Done that." Kit was dismissive.

"Watch a chemistry lab?"

"Oh, yuck. I thought you were a Shakespeare person."

"He thinks he's an everything person. That's his problem, Kit."

They changed their clothes and we went for a run. We ran through town, the next stop to be determined by whatever struck Kit's fancy as we flashed through. Kit had just started running last fall – she said just to help her tennis game – but she could already keep up with us. Eileen and Kit ran side by side and I ran behind, watching them, pretending to myself they were my women. We jogged down to the docks on the lake.

They were so far ahead of me they were already chatting up a yachtsman by the time I got there. Jack, with his trimmed beard, looked like the professorial type, but he was way too young for that role. He said he was on the school sailing team. He was showing them the school's 26-foot racing sailboat, talking a mile a minute. Kit was acting wide-eyed with amazement, angling for a ride. Jack was waxing ecstatic about the wonders of the "sea," as he called the lake. If Kit was actually listening to what he was saying, she might not have tried so hard to flirt her way onto the boat.

He didn't seem to be getting the hint, so Kit finally asked flat out. "Oh, come on, will you take me for a ride?"

"You can get a whole new perspective on your environment, gliding over the silent sea powered only by the wind. You know what the wind is, right? Nature's breath."

Kit took that as a yes.

"Can I go?" she looked at Eileen.

"There's some real wind out there," I noticed.

Jack just kept talking. He had progressed from the silent sea to the tides, but he now seemed to be focusing more on Kit's legs.

Eileen didn't answer but instead asked me a question. "I don't know the first thing about sailboats. Tim, do you?"

"Not a thing."

"You can go," she said finally, "but only if I go too. And I'm only going if Tim's going too. Tim, will you go?" I said okay.

Jack had trouble untying the last knot as we pulled away, and he took a knife from his belt and just cut the rope. We promised to do some of the work if he gave us directions.

It didn't start well.

"For God's sake, a sheet's a rope!"

"None of us have ever been on a sailboat before, Jack! If this isn't working, maybe we should go back."

"Noooo!" Kit had her feet spread and was flexing her knees, riding the bouncing bow of the ship like it was a skateboard. The boat started to lean and dip into the water as it went faster. A big ferry passed and Jack crossed through each side of its wake. Both times the boat lurched and dipped, and the wind sprayed the cold water over Kit up front.

"Kit, get back here!" I'd never seen Eileen so worried. Kit either didn't hear over the wind and the rush of the spray, or she didn't want to hear. There was an aluminum thing like a fence rail at the V at the front of the boat. Kit climbed over it and stood outside the rail, poised like a figurehead, gripping the rail with her hands behind her. We were already far from shore. The more Eileen and I complained, the more Jack made the boat lean over and dig deeper sideways into the waves.

"She'll fall off!" I shouted at Jack.

Jack started talking about the moon and the tides. I looked closely in his eyes, and they were so vacant I realized that something had messed with his mind. Eileen started to crawl toward the front to get Kit. Kit had climbed back from her perch on the bow and was now sitting on the deck, dangling her feet over the edge in the rushing water. I would have pushed Jack away and steered the boat myself if I had any idea how. He seemed to control the thing by constantly pulling the ropes attached to the sails and at the same time moving the rudder. I was afraid the boat would flip if he let go. We had life jackets on, but I didn't think we would last long in the cold water. Jack was tilting the deck closer and closer to vertical. I couldn't get him to talk about anything but the moon.

"Coming about," Jack said very quietly, as if speaking to himself. I had no idea what that meant. The boat lurched to the left and this huge metal pole attached to the sails swung low and fast over the deck. I saw it coming and yelled just in time for Eileen to duck. It missed her head by about six inches. Up front, Kit was in no danger of being hit by the pole, but she fell backward onto the deck as it sharply leaned the opposite way. She scrambled around crab-style to get her balance and slid across to the edge which was now almost underwater.

"What the hell?" I screamed in Jack's ear.

"Coming about, coming about. Boom! Do you see the water, man? Do you really see it. Can you feel the *depth* of it?"

"Did you know that was going to happen?" I screamed. "That pole could have killed Eileen!"

"Boom. Appreciate this *depth*. If you could only see what I see. Feel. Go in so deep. Oh man!"

Jack's brain was obviously somewhere else. The boat was tilted so steeply that Kit's dangling legs were knee-deep in rushing water. She held both hands onto a wire cable that ran like a railing around the edge of the boat. Jack pulled the rope even tighter, and the deck tilted so sharp! Eileen had to lie flat and grab the high edge just to keep from falling off. I started to fall and grabbed at some ropes with one hand. Jack looked like he was about to go too, so I grabbed him with my other arm. I was holding Jack in place so at least he wouldn't let go of the whole thing. The boat was now almost on its side. I couldn't see Kit.

"Cut it back!" I yelled in his ear.

"Want me to tell the wind to stop?"

"Turn back, then."

"Tell the wind to stop. Ha ha ha ha ha ha."

I knew Jack was going to keep tilting the boat until it flipped upside down. We were pretty far away from the town and the sun was starting to go down. I had to get the boat level, and under control, but I had no idea how. Jack's brain seemed entirely disconnected from what we were doing. He seemed to be sailing from pure muscle memory. If I pushed him too hard I might break the spell of his

muscle memory. Eileen was flattened against the deck, her legs and arms spread-eagled, just trying to hold on. Kit was soaked and was bouncing against the wires. Jack was babbling, smiling.

"What the fuck are you on?" I yelled at him.

"Ha ha ha ha ha ha. Magic Mushroom! Want some?"

"Here's the story." My left arm was already around his chest. I used all my strength and squeezed until he couldn't breathe. I held him like that for 30 seconds. Then I let him take one quick breath. Then I did it again. And again. I was counting on my idea that the magic mushrooms hadn't completely destroyed his instinct for self-preservation. I squeezed him even longer.

"Straighten the boat up and turn it back, gently," I said in his ear. "Gently. Otherwise, this is your last breath." I let him breathe once. Then I squeezed again, a little harder. I didn't let up. My arm was over his chest at an angle and I had to squeeze extra hard to stop his breathing, and I was really afraid I might break his ribs. But somehow his muscles knew how to react even while his mind was gone. He made little adjustments and the boat slowly righted itself. I gave him another breath. The boat started to turn back. Another breath. I gave him another breath every 30 seconds until the docks came into sight. Then I let him breathe freely.

There were people milling around at the docks. Just before the boat got there, however, Jack steered it away towards the wooded shore close by, then jumped into the water and swam to the shore. The boat bottomed out with a jolt that knocked all the rest of us down. The people on the docks were too busy helping us pull the boat in to go after him. Kit was quiet, shivering. Eileen took her aside and held a blanket around her while I explained to the people on shore what had happened. Some of the people on the docks said he'd been hanging around the past few days. I told them he said he was a student.

"Not any more. He just hangs around town now and bothers people all day."

. . .

While Kit was taking a hot shower at Eileen's place, Eileen went upstairs to get out of her wet clothes. She came downstairs in a thick white robe with her hair wrapped in a yellow towel like a turban. She was dressed just like she was on that first night we made love. I thought it might be a signal. I was instantly turned on so much I couldn't think clearly. She stopped and looked up at me. I had forgotten how long and black those lashes were, how they amplified every entreaty and hesitation in her eyes.

"We haven't really talked," she began. "Maybe that's my fault …."

"I miss you," I croaked. I put a hand out and touched the waist of her thick robe. I meant it as a sweet gesture of how much I missed her. But her eyes flickered downward to where she could see my erection that was plainly obvious under my soaked running shorts. She jumped back and pushed my hand off her robe. There was probably desperation in my voice as I whispered her name and searched her eyes.

"Get off!"

There was passion in her voice, but there was also something in her expression I had never seen on any woman before, an unmistakable tinge of fear. She was afraid *of me*. That realization froze me, but it had no effect on my erection. I felt like a dirty animal in rut. Fortunately, Kit called down from upstairs just then to say that the bathroom was free and she'd be ready to go downtown in a few minutes.

"I guess I should go."

Her voice was normal now. "Why don't you go and get changed. We'll meet you downtown in half an hour." I turned to go. "Maybe take a cold shower," she added.

We all had on casual, dry clothes by the time we met again in a bar and restaurant downtown.

"You know, Kit, Tim saved our lives today."

"What?"

"You didn't see him squeezing the life out of Sailor Jack? Sailor Jack, who was trying to dump us all in that ice water?"

"Really? He was doing that on purpose? God, I'm such a dork. Jack was trying to flip his own boat?"

"It wasn't his boat." Eileen was trying to be kind and hold back on the sarcasm. "We should have figured that out when he had to cut that rope before we even got started. The boat belongs to the school. He isn't even a student. Look, I never should have let you go with him. It's my fault."

"No, it's not. I started it. God, I must seem really dumb to you two."

"Take it from your new step-sister. There's kind of a general rule of life for women. If you meet some amazingly charming guy on the street who wants to take you off alone somewhere right away, your chances of ever coming back are about 50-50."

Kit sat quietly then. She was wearing one of Eileen's sweatshirts, her elbows close to her sides, her two hands palms down on the table, her eyes darting back and forth between Eileen and me.

"I wasn't scared. I thought it was fun. It's just so embarrassing that I didn't even know what was going on."

We ordered burgers and sodas. Eileen spiced mine up with rum that she had brought in a bottle in her pocketbook.

"Yo ho ho."

"Here's to Sailor Jack."

"So, are you two guys still pretending to be not dating?"

"We're not dating. Really this time," Eileen said quickly.

"That's right," I said. "Seriously."

"But you two are still hanging around with each other. What's that all about?" Kit was enjoying teasing us. "Tim, I can understand why no one would date *you*. I guess, with your twisted ego and distorted muscles and all, nobody but a high-schooler would think about screwing …."

"High-schooler?" Eileen's eyes widened as she stared at Kim. "Why did you say 'high-schooler'?"

"I mean ...." Kit blushed and couldn't finish the sentence. The table went dead quiet. The longer the silence lasted, the redder Kit's face got. Eileen looked back and forth between Kit and me.

"It didn't happen, Eileen," I said. "Nothing happened." My voice was strong and calm, like it is when I have nothing to be embarrassed about.

Eileen's face relaxed. Kit, her face still red, was sitting up, breathing deeply and nervously like she was getting ready to say something. I was afraid she was going to make things worse. Eileen knew that *something* had happened, but she wasn't asking any questions. I thought I'd do a preemptive strike before Kit would suffer a complete guilt trip and go into the minute-by-minute details of her attempt to seduce me. "Although," I added, "this horny little teenager, confused by misinformation given to her by her new step-sister, might have made a pathetic suggestion or two."

Eileen took a slow drink of her rum and coke. Yo ho ho. She looked at each of us. She took another drink. Then she looked at us again, started to say something, stopped.

"I'm sorry," Kit said, in a thin little voice. Her hands were clenched on the table like she was determined to hang onto her spot there.

Eileen looked like she was trying to recalculate her relationship with Kit. I knew a lot about Eileen's family relationships. Her relationship with Kit was one of the best she'd ever had. Kit obviously idolized her. Eileen really wanted to get to know her and to try to be a role model for her. Eileen had never gotten to know her brother in any deep way, and I was sure she would never throw away this chance of knowing a sister. I could see that forgiveness is sometimes necessary in families. Maybe it had been harder for me, an only child, to understand that. I could tell right then from the way that Eileen looked at Kit that she wasn't going to recalculate anything. She swished her drink around, poured a little bit more rum into my glass. Then she poured some in Kit's glass, smiling when Kit looked up in surprise.

"So you refused her advances, Tim," Eileen suddenly turned to me, in all apparent seriousness. "Was that because you had already banged Scraps the dog?"

"Why would that stop me?"

The fact was, Kit was a bright teenager but was not magically wise beyond her years. Eileen forgave her for coming on to me. I wished my own thing with Dory had been just a clumsy, failed, forgivable attempt like Kit's. Still, Eileen seemed intent on at least making Kit squirm a bit.

"So, Kit, sailing off with Captain Jack today wasn't your first impulsive moment with a new man?"

Kit would not be flustered. "I guess they don't all work out." Then, with the bravest little smile, she added, "Lucky for you."

We began sharing our rum with Kit every round. We dragged the dinner out for over an hour. I was enjoying watching Eileen trying to connect with Kit. I saw so much of Eileen's quiet self-confidence in Kit that I had to keep reminding myself that they were not blood relatives. We talked about lots of things, world news, family news, high school, college, books. Kit seemed to want to be a real sister as much as Eileen did. Taking advantage of the ambience of affection and amnesty in the room, Kit apologized also for going off into the side room alone at Mike's wake.

"I'm sorry I acted so immature that day."

"I should be the one apologizing," Eileen said, "for the way my mother treated you."

"She didn't think I belonged there."

"You did belong there," Eileen stressed. "She was just upset. I read her the riot act about how she talked to you."

"I didn't even know anybody even saw that," Kit said. "I had been watching you all that day. You kept your mother and father from fighting. You kept your mother from falling apart. I don't know how you did it."

"I agree," I said. "You were wonderful that day."

Eileen hesitated, looking at me. "It's really nice of you guys to say that. But, as long as we're confessing .... This is supposed to be a secret between me and Tim. I had a moment, a real bad time, later that night, after the wake. I couldn't have gotten through that without Tim."

Kit's fingers were still pressed onto the table, but her anxious look was gone. "It had to be the toughest day in your life," she said quietly. "I can't imagine …."

The waiter brought more sodas. We added more rum. Kit didn't ask Eileen to explain about her bad moment.

"Let's stop talking about sad things. Let's talk about today," Eileen said. "Have any of us ever spent a crazier day? How did all three of us get sucked into taking a boat trip with a guy who was so obviously drugged-out?"

"Maybe we were all a little over-excited," I suggested.

"Where in the world did that Sailor Jack guy come from?" Eileen wondered.

"And where did he go? Where is he, like, right now?" Kit looked toward the door like Sailor Jack might walk in any second.

"And Scraps. What about Scraps?" I threw in. "She never writes. She never calls."

"*He*, you mean."

"*He?* Oh shit."

"So you're not normal either, are you, Tim?" Kit was growing more and more self-confident as the night wore on, and as she consumed more rum.

"Depends on your definition of normality."

But all definitions of normality seemed suspended for the night. We went to another bar and drank sodas and watched an awful country and western singer who walked off the stage in the middle of one of his songs and didn't come back. Some college guys at the next table started flirting with Kit. She was rolling her eyes like they were subhuman creatures, but then she became totally tongue-tied when one of them pulled up a chair and actually tried to talk to her. After the guy gave up on hitting on her, she got chatty and wanted our opinions on every movie she'd seen and every book she'd ever read. One minute her eyes were flashing with excitement, the next she was asleep with her head down on the table. The bar ran out of soda. Going back up the hill towards Eileen's house, we walked with Kit between us, arms around her waist.

Chapter 24

The next day I received my first e-mail ever from Eileen on my student account:

> Tim,
> Kit and I will be forever grateful that you saved us from that drugged-out sailor yesterday. I hate to think how that could have turned out without you. Thank you. I have always felt safe when you're around, and yesterday you demonstrated one reason why.
>
> I had a wonderful time with you and Kit last night. I don't understand all of the dynamics, but I feel closer to her than ever, and you were part of that. She's going to come up again this spring. Would you be willing to do it again – except for the sailing?
>
> Now comes the hard part. I seem to see you a lot accidentally on campus lately, on the parking lot, in the cafeteria, at the fitness center, etc. This is way too big a campus for that to happen so often by chance. Your hiding and sneaking really bothers me, mostly because I think you are so much better than that.

"What's it say?" I had told Slide that I had gotten an e-mail from her.

"Long story short, she wants to be friends."

"I can't see doing that. I can't see how any guy could be friends with such a beautiful woman. I mean, you know, after you were lovers once."

"I know, but I need to see her, one way or another."

"That medallion had something to do with her, didn't it?"

"Yeah. Pretty much every crazy thing I do has something to do with her. Does every guy have problems like this, Slide? Did you ever fall for a girl so hard you couldn't think of anything else?"

He shook his head. "Nah, not really. Girls don't like me that much." I wondered why. He was built okay, had okay features, even a sculpted, movie-star chin. Maybe he looked a little weak around the eyes. He had made some friends from the basketball league, mainly on the team that he started, and he had the knack of enjoying the low-key, fun, time-wasting activities that flourished in the dorm. I had thought he was a total jerk when we first moved in together, but I was wrong.

"Anyway," he said, "there's an emergency basketball practice tonight right after dinner. You'll be there, right? We have a game Thursday that was just put on the schedule." I knew the game hadn't been put on the schedule by some unseen force. Slide had just decided right then to have another game just because he liked being the coach. The guy made me smile.

After basketball practice, when Slide was out playing poker or video games somewhere in the dorm, I decided to take a closer look at the box. I thought about taking it to the library so I could do it alone, but I didn't want to create another medallion-type situation. When I opened it, though, I could see that never would have happened. The box had a transposition cypher, invented by the Spartans, with instructions on how to use it. It had a cipher disk and something called a St. Cyr slide for decoding. These were basic codes that any ten-year-old boy could use. I didn't want to be that simple boy again, but it was good to remember where I started. The box was pre-Eileen, pre-pizza district, pre-parents' divorce. I spent over an hour carefully working out the example codes. It was silly and a little tedious, but it made me feel better. It had the opposite effect as the medallion.

"Sir. In the back row, last seat on the right. I don't see you on my seating chart."

I had told my mother that there was absolutely no need for a suit at college, but she brought it up anyway, hidden at the bottom of a bag of regular clothes. When I found it, it was rumpled beyond belief, and it didn't get any better, since there weren't any hangers in our room. I also wore sunglasses, a tie, and a straw fedora that Slide had rustled up for me when I decided to sit in on Eileen's class.

"Yes, you. Wearing the suit. What is your name?"

"Suit … um … Rumpled Suit … Rumpled Suitskin. That's my name."

She didn't miss a beat. "Mr. Rumpled Suitskin, what are the barriers to a common cognitive perception of an event?"

"They are legion."

"Could you be more specific? Which barrier is exemplified by the Greek philosopher Heraclitus's saying: 'you can't step into the same river twice'?"

"I don't know that saying."

"It has to do with the singularity of experience. The river is not the same in the next instant, nor are you the same person stepping into it," she explained. "In other words, the observed object and the observer are both constantly changing, and an accurate, communicable perception is thus impossible."

"I don't know about any of that stuff. Round my way, river's so full of crap, you can't even step in it once."

Slide didn't know whether to be amused or alarmed every time I left the dorm room in my Suitskin outfit to catch Eileen's class. I think it was my air of confidence that caused him to start believing it was cool. That and because he couldn't get over the fact that I'd slept with her. He kept calling her beautiful, perfect, *etc.*, until I couldn't resist messing with his head.

"'Perfect skin?' You've got to be kidding, Slide. You haven't seen that hideous tattoo."

"Tattoo? Of what? Exactly where is it?"

"She's embarrassed about where it is. That tattoo …. I guess it's sort of an intimate thing. I shouldn't really talk about it." But I had just made sure he would think about it, a lot.

"Mr. Suitskin, do you have a response?"

"How can people believe something and know the opposite is true at the same time?"

"You mean, like cognitive dissonance …."

"No. I mean how can an idea get stuck in somebody's head so hard they still believe it no matter what the evidence is?"

"This is beyond the scope of 101. Perceptual distortions are a very interesting subject, in which I'm not an expert."

"You're not? You personally have not known something to be true and denied it at the same time?"

"These kinds of problems are covered pretty well in Psych 302, which you might have an interest in. Abnormal Psychology. Perhaps I can discuss the more advanced courses with you during my office hours."

"Exactly what are you doing?" she started off.

"I can tell you what I'm not doing. I'm not hiding. I'm not sneaking around. I'm not getting you publicly associated with me in any way. I'm not disrupting the class. I never even say a word in that room except when you call on me."

Eileen was teaching both her original class and another one left over from a graduate student who had dropped out. Fridays were joint study sessions between the two groups. I picked Fridays because everyone in Section A would think I was somebody from Section B, and everyone from Section B would think I was somebody from Section A. I explained to Eileen that everyone would assume I belonged there, and nobody would be upset.

"But what are you doing? You're taking a full load of classes already. Why are you wasting so much of your time going to my class, which you haven't even signed up for?"

"I should have signed up for it. It's very interesting. And the teacher's really good." I was afraid this comment would annoy her, but I could see she was pleased. "Actually" – I could hear my voice go a little shaky, and I worried that this in itself would scare her – "I think we're friends now, at least when Kit's in town. But it's not quite enough for me. I need to see you just a little bit more. I can do it this way. And I'm actually learning something. I don't see the downside."

Her sigh filled the tiny graduate assistant office. She looked like she might have thought of a downside, but she didn't say what it was.

I skipped a chemistry class and ran up into the hills. The valley below was almost as pretty at the end of the winter as it had been in the fall. Black spikes of trees slit through the white snow and into the sky. A patch of evergreens curled around the outlines of distant hills under high cobwebby clouds. Smoke rose from the stacks of little businesses in the town. Eileen was not going to report me for the Rumpled Suitskin bit. I had found an acceptable form of madness. Find a way, the giant guy had told me.

I had never just walked back from a run before. My feet grew cold in my running shoes. Soon the road descended out of the farm country. There were still a few old scattered white clapboard buildings perched not far from the top of the hill. I focused on a two-story white house with a collapsing porch and an overgrown lawn. Its bleached white siding glowed a brilliant, splintering white in the bright afternoon sun. I was struck by the splendor of its decay. The house was just as beautiful in destruction as it had been in design. Nature lets us come and play for a little while, then takes everything back. We are all splintering, bleaching in the sun, rotting in the cellar. Squirrels are scampering around in our heads. We lose everything eventually. Sometimes we lose our sons and brothers before their time. The big mystery is not why so many have given up, but why so many more plow on.

Spring break was embarrassing. Everybody was working long hours, including Ben, who was remodeling the house. I couldn't sleep there, so I ended up sleeping at my mother's. Alan lived in his own house but ate dinner with my mother every night. They both seemed very happy I was staying with Mom. I didn't tell them about my new *B*-minus standard of scholarship or any of my other problems up at State. I noticed that all of those problems did seem a little bit smaller from 300 miles away.

What did seem more immediate was the absence of my old life. I indulged myself in a run around the old neighborhood. I started thinking about my old bike messenger job, the legal job with Kathryn, the stark little basement room where I used to do my weights, kidding around with Jeremy and Ben, my original, innocent messing around with Dory and her real estate friends, and the two Kims. Jeremy blowing smoke through the keyhole. But there was no point in being nostalgic. You can't go back to nineteen any more than you can go back to ten. What I seemed to need now was a code-breaking kit for twenty-year-olds.

Dory came over alone one night. Alan smiled whenever she was in the room, and my mother positively gushed over her. It made me jealous. I told myself if they got to know Eileen they would like her better than Dory. When we were alone, I told Dory the truth of what was going on at State, even including Rumpled Suitskin.

She squirmed a little when I told her all this. "If it will help, I swear I'll drive up there right now and tell her it was all my fault."

"It wouldn't help. It wasn't your fault anyway. I'm on a kind of psychological quest up there now. I'm going to keep going with the crazy."

"What did she say when you apologized?"

"Apologize? It's not like I accidentally stepped on her toe or something. I mean, I turned into an insect in her eyes. And the only thing you can do with an insect is squish it."

She put her face in her hands. "I hate hearing you talk like this. You might not be a hero, but you're not an insect." We heard my mother's and Alan's voices from the other room, and she lifted her face and put herself together quickly. "I hate seeing you like this."

"I love seeing you like this." She looked angelic, sitting on my mother's sofa with her perfect posture, every part of her body long and tall and thin, her long plaits arranged in a circle around her head like a blonde halo. A girl could make one mistake and still be an angel. But angelic was not my type. "How is Jeremy?"

"Good. I guess you heard about the Diamond Service Girls. I got over that. He says he owes me one." We looked at each other and let that hang in the air for a minute. "He's going to real college next year. Two more years. That's a long time. We might be fighting over that a little."

"He worships you."

"I love him too. That's not always enough, my mother says. It will be years. He'll be 50 miles away, with new people all around. What are my chances?"

"Dory, I know Jeremy. I know you. Your chances are exactly 100 percent."

Alan asked if he could talk to me alone before I went back to school. I thought he was going to give me some advice about Eileen, but that wasn't it at all. "Tim, I have strong feelings for your mother. I love her." He paused as I stared at him. "I want you to be completely honest with me. I know I'm not anybody's dream man. So please take as long as you need to think about this. Do I have your permission to ask your mother to marry me?"

Chapter 25

I skipped Rumpled Suitskin for a week, and when I came back to her class I changed his voice. Now there were new images of Eileen popping into my mind. She was struggling her way to the front of the boat to save Kit. She was frightened by my crude attempt at sex. She was talking with Kit like they were lifelong girlfriends. She was forgiving Kit for trying to seduce me. She was on the other end of the phone line, secreting with desire.

Slide was calling more and more basketball practices. I learned to play a little bit. At first they told me to just outrun the other team down the court on defense, stand in the middle with my arms up, and lean my body into any guy who came near me. Eventually I figured out what a zone defense was and became a little more helpful. We had so many practices I eventually learned how to shoot a real simple, five-foot shot, and how to push my way in to get that shot. I went out with the team a few times after practices. I found myself thinking they were nice kids.

Even going to her class only once a week, I could tell that Eileen was really excited about psychology. It was supposed to be just a study session, but she couldn't help but teach. She taught about the history of psychology from its origins in seventeenth-century philosophy, and you could tell she thought the study of human consciousness was way more important than the study of the oceans, or the galaxies, or the atom. She peppered her discussions about cognition or perception with examples from real life, half of them starting with phrases like: "Like, you know, when you're a kid and you've screwed up and your mother says ...." She asked them to interpret the psychological implications of sayings, famous and obscure, and kept asking until she got a conversation started. She was fascinated by animal studies and the potential in those studies for trying to draw the line between animal and human consciousness.

I'll never
Be such a gosling to obey instinct, but stand
As if a man were the author of himself.

"That's from Shakespeare's not-so-famous play, *Coriolanus*," she said one day, without even a glance at Mr. Rumpled Suitskin in the back. "Coriolanus is saying that overcoming your animal instincts is an important part of being human. Sounds okay, but then he goes on to use that theory to make a horrible mess of things. Authors like Shakespeare, philosophers, and thinkers throughout history have been trying to figure out what makes human beings tick. That's the subject matter of psychology. And isn't that really the basic question of the universe?"

I wanted to talk to Jen in person. I tracked her schedule and found her in the cafeteria, alone. I went right up to her and sat down. "Hey."

"Hi, Tim. I was out of town at a conference, but I heard you went out with Eileen a couple of weeks ago when her step-sister was in town."

"Yeah. Kit. We both like her. We had quite an interesting time."

Jen had her hair all pulled back in barrettes now. It was better than her frowsy mop look, but she still tended to clap her hands on the sides of her head as if there were ghost hairs she had to brush back. "Eileen says Kit might come up here again before the end of the semester. Are you planning on going out with them again?"

"Hope so."

Again, the hands. "Damn. I keep doing this. I know in my mind I have my hair pulled back tight, but my hands keep forgetting."

"Maybe you should consult a psychologist."

"Heh heh." She took a breath. "But, Tim, do you think it's really fair to keep stringing her along, after you dumped her?"

"What?"

"She told me about this Rumplestiltskin business. I'm going to be honest with you. I told her to file a complaint. She should be creeped out by that, honestly."

"I hoped she wouldn't be creeped out."

"She's not, at least on the surface. When I told her to file a complaint, she said it wasn't so bad. In fact, she said, 'At least, he reads the material.'" Jen did chuckle at that.

"It's not so bad. It's only once a week."

"She's really hurt. Don't play with her, Tim."

My mother was on the phone, stopping and starting, hemming and hawing.

"Mom, this has something to do with you and Alan, right?"

"Yes. And it involves you too. Alan is a very good man. He makes me feel so comfortable. It's different from being with your father. There's not nearly so much drama."

"Dad was big on drama."

"Yes, and he was a very passionate man too – with a very tormented nature, I've begun to think. Living with him was like being on a roller coaster ride. I don't miss that drama now. Maybe that's just because I'm getting old."

"But you're not calling me about him."

"Right. I want you to know that I'm very happy with my situation with Alan just as it is now. I am fine with it. Very happy. But Alan … he says he'd like to go further."

I tried to figure out how she wanted me to act. Was she hoping

I'd be all happy and chatty like maybe a daughter would be? Did she just want me to tell her she was doing the right thing? Before I could come to any conclusion, she told me what she wanted.

"What I'm calling you about – and I want you to be completely honest – and I will be fine either way – would it be all right with you if I married him?"

"Go for it, Mom."

My original Rumpled Suitskin voice had been my own, with just a hint of a Southern drawl that was maybe inspired by the straw fedora. But I kept thinking about what Eileen had said about the problem she was having hearing my voice on the phone, so one day I switched, and for the rest of the semester I used a high, fey, gay voice like Truman Capote's. I used that voice when she once again brought up *Coriolanus*.

"You keep bringing up that play," I said, raising my hand in as effete a manner as possible. "Could you tell us what the plot's about?"

She grimaced like she was sorry she had brought it up again. "There's a lot of fighting, political intrigue, *etc.*, but it's basically a psychological study. Coriolanus is a victorious Roman general. The citizens want to make him ruler. There are just two things he had to do. First, he has to get up in front of the crowd, tell them how great they are, and thank them for their support. Second, he has to open his shirt and publicly show them his wounds. But he doesn't really believe the citizens are that great, and he's too proud to display his wounds to the crowd. He won't do it. The citizens turn on him and he joins an enemy army and is then killed by the Romans in battle.

"Coriolanus was willing to die for his principles, but after you read the play you wonder what those principles were. Today, we might look at those principles and interpret them as psychological problems. But it's just a play, a work of art. Let's get back to our discussion of Chapter 12."

As my situation got weirder and weirder, I thought about calling

Alan for advice, but I decided it would be a bad idea. Alan would never be in a situation like mine. Maybe the key would be to figure out why Alan would never be in a situation like mine. I had known somewhere in my soul, from that first instant I saw Eileen coming down the stairs in that house in the pizza district, that she was the one. If that happened to Alan, he would never have messed around with another woman, even once. So that made me feel great about Alan, but it didn't make me think Alan could have any psychological insight that could help me now.

I made a real effort to act like an *A* student again. I did a little better focusing on the material. My courses were so scattered in so many different directions it wasn't easy. Back in my community college days, I had always jumped in, determined to get an *A* whether I liked the subject or not. But now I was stretched over too many fields, and my test grades were already checkered with low *B*s, and I still had a hard time concentrating. I just couldn't get the community college focus back.

It was getting close to the end of the semester and I knew Kit was coming again sometime soon. Eileen was now trying to get the students interested in taking the more advanced psychology classes, emphasizing the many branches of the subject that – you could tell – she thought would be appealing. "Some of you might be interested, for example, in personality psychology. We've been studying cognition, and the general concepts of perception, thinking and memory. Personality psychology comes at it from a completely different angle, by studying the thoughts, feelings and behavior that make an individual person unique."

"So would you take that course, like, to try to understand yourself?" This was from a girl I had never seen talk in class before.

"No. I didn't mean that. It would be a mistake to take psychology courses to try to learn about yourself."

"Really? Why?"

"The instant you start analyzing yourself, you've changed. The act of analysis changes those thoughts and feelings that you are trying to analyze. Once you start to look for yourself, you aren't there any more. So as far as self-analysis goes, it's just like what Mr. Suitskin said earlier in the semester: you can't even step in the same river once."

She waited until the auditorium had emptied out to speak to me.

"Kit's coming this weekend," she said.

"Why are you talking about *Coriolanus* in class, and quoting me?"

"I don't know." She looked flustered. "You used to talk about it when we were together, and .... Are you going to use that ... voice, and wear that disguise, when she comes? You are coming, aren't you?"

"I'll leave Rumpled Suitskin at home."

The intramural basketball season was over. This was probably fortunate for Slide, because it took away at least one excuse for not studying. His friends were in our room all hours of the day and night, so I convinced him to leave the room and study in the library two or three nights a week. He didn't tell me what carrel he studied in, but I had a feeling it was 542. I helped him a little bit when I realized he was worried about flunking out. I had the feeling he was doing what Jeremy had been doing the year before, just bumbling along, waiting for someone to have faith that he really had something to offer.

I gave Slide the box my father had given me for my birthday. I thought he needed to crack some codes. He thought it was hilarious and started playing with it the minute I gave it to him. I had learned a few things since my father first sent me the box. The box had led me directly to Eileen – and she had led me in a roundabout way back to my father, a journey I should have taken when I was ten or twelve. But the box was clearly not going to be able to tell me how to handle a twenty-year-old's problems, problems like betrayal, feeling worthless, pop-ups, stalking.

I stalked her the night we were supposed to meet Kit. I was

suspicious because I was supposed to meet them only at a very specific time, between 7:45 and 8:30, on the Friday night that Kit arrived. I watched from far away as Eileen stepped out on her porch with a handsome dude with blonde, movie-star hair. I made sure she didn't see me. I followed them as they went up a hill, silhouetted in the twilight. They weren't kissing or anything, but they were talking and laughing as they walked along toward the town. There was a nervous tinge to their laughter like this was a first date. I guessed I was supposed to go in there an hour later for the purpose of being introduced to my replacement. I was wondering if I could handle it. Then my phone rang.

"Tim, hi. What are you doing?"

"Dory?"

"Of course. Are you okay?"

"I was having a bad dream."

"It sounds like you're out in the street."

"That too."

"What about the news? It's so cool your mother's getting married to Alan."

"Yeah. That's great, isn't it?" I started to walk. I thought I'd go to any bar and order a burger and a beer to be fortified against the shock, just in case Eileen was getting ready to blow me off.

"There's kind of a problem. They want to have a very small wedding, in the courthouse. Your mother is so shy. They want only two witnesses. And they want them to be you and me."

"What are you saying?"

"I'm saying I love your mother, and I'd love to do it. But I can't be there, just me and you, if you have the slightest chance of getting back with Eileen. That would ruin you getting back with her, I know."

I went in the first restaurant I passed. I asked her to hold on as I went to the back and sat down at a table and ordered a beer. "My mother has every right to have whoever she wants there."

"This isn't anything about *rights*. You still don't know how people think, do you? If you have any chance with Eileen this will ruin it forever."

"Are you saying … you want me to tell you right now if there is any chance of me getting back together with Eileen?"

"Yes. Well, I have to tell your mother something soon."

"Call me next week."

"And Tim, I'm really sorry if what we did has now screwed up your life. I got so mad at Jeremy over those Diamond Service Girls, but what I did to him was much worse. I can't even apologize to him because he doesn't know I did it. So I'm apologizing to you. Sorry."

"Forget about it. You guys are both good guys. My best friends. Call me next week."

Just as I was gulping my second beer, Eileen walked in with the blonde guy. They both quickly turned back – I thought at first because they had seen me. But I was wrong about that. They hadn't seen me. They turned around because they were both busy ushering another person inside. Kit.

I sat there wondering what would be worse, to barge my way into their conversation and show Kit that Eileen had yet one more good reason to dump me, or to hide out like a coward at my back table until one of them had to come past me on their way to the ladies room. I had never realized that losing Eileen would mean losing Kit too. Kit sat with her arms at her sides, hands close together, palms down on the edge of the table. It looked like she was answering Blondie's questions one or two syllables at a time. Blondie was a slight, young-looking guy. He was talking familiarly with Eileen, but he seemed to have a hard time talking to Kit. Eileen was watching the two of them.

"Hey, Kit! Hi, Eileen."

Kit seemed flustered by my stepping in so suddenly. Eileen was calm.

"Tim, this is Henry. Henry, Tim. Henry is Diane's brother, up for a tour of the college himself. They're going on a blind date tonight that we arranged."

Ever since the first moment I saw Eileen walk out of her house with Henry, an invisible hand had been clutching my chest from inside. The instant I found out that Henry was not Eileen's date, the hand let go. I could suddenly breathe freely. I sucked in half a roomful of air and started laughing and could not stop. Kit and Henry, I could tell, both thought I might be laughing at them. They were both very nervous about the date anyway. I smiled, shook hands with him, touched her on the shoulder, smiled, but there was no way I could convey to them how happy I was that they were each other's dates.

"So you two split up?" Kit focused the attention back on us.

"Yeah. Guess it was all that baggage. Step-sisters always hanging around, needing babysitting, slowing us down."

Kit and Henry started to loosen up a little. Kit was an avid tennis player, but it turned out that Henry wasn't into sports at all. That didn't look good, but then Kit started talking about books, and Henry's face lit up. Kit was really pretty skillful in keeping him talking. She was managing the conversation, but in a very subtle way. I couldn't tell if she was enjoying herself or if this was work for her.

"My prediction," I said to Eileen as soon as they left for the movie, "is that they will both say it was a fine blind date, but Kit will never want to go out with him again."

Eileen smiled. "That's why I thought a movie would be a good idea. If the talking gets too hard, they'll have two whole hours when they don't have to say anything."

"But we," I said, "have a half hour. It's nice to talk to you without being in disguise or anything."

"It is. Regular face, regular voice. I've missed that."

"Did you tell Kit why we broke up?"

"No. She really likes you. I don't want to mess that up."

Eileen not telling Kit the real reason we broke up was one of those woman things that I used to call lies. I could imagine hearing Eileen's voice as she talked to Kit on the phone, saying that "things just didn't work out," or "I felt I needed more space," or "we're not ready to commit," or some such female claptrap. The blatant truth was, I "boinked another broad," as Slide's friend Greg put it.

"You covered up for me with Jen too."

"Jen was the only other person you knew on campus." She looked at me like it was obvious that she wouldn't want to mess up my relationship with Jen, or anyone else. The nicer she was, the more I knew she had way too much class for me.

"Why did you read *Coriolanus*?" I asked her then.

"I probably shouldn't have brought it up in class. It's not that related to psychology."

"You're a good teacher."

"I'm doing what I did my senior year in college, nothing but studying and running. And now, teaching. It's not, like, a complete life, I know."

"You're not going to those auditions for the role of faculty wife?"

She shook her head. "No. I keep thinking I'm too young for that. But maybe I'm not. I have to do something. I can't go on like this forever."

She didn't mention that I was even an option. I figured I deserved that position below the bottom rung of the ladder.

She asked me how I was doing. I told her I was fine. When I mentioned my *B*-minus average, she looked concerned. I shrugged it off, saying this was the best I could do. I didn't tell her about standing on the rail on the bridge over the ravine. Not telling her, I realized, was a man's kind of lie. If she knew about the ravine, she would think less of me. If we ever got back together again, I would worry for the rest of my life that she did it out of pity. If we didn't get back together, and she knew I had tried to jump, I would always remain a pathetic loser in her eyes. No, this was a male secret. No one would ever know but me, the police, and the Three Wise Men.

"Actually," I said, "I think I was worse off when I took eighteen credits and got all *A*s. I had no reason for that except ego. I was just trying to be something special. I'm not special. *B*-minus is about what I am."

"Please don't say that."

"You don't think *B*-minus is what I am now?"

"No. And I won't ever think that."

The pre-arranged drop-dead time of 8:30 was fast approaching. Would I be better than a *B*-minus person if she were mine? I thought so, but that was just an academic question. She wasn't mine.

"Oh, just one more thing," I said as we stood up to go. "Don't worry about Kit tonight. I kind of did the big-brother thing. To Henry. In the restroom. I guarantee you she's going to be very safe in his hands tonight."

She laughed. "Damn, Tim. That might have been a bit much. Henry's not exactly a scary guy."

"I don't know. I feel like I have some kind of, you know, brotherly duty, to protect her."

"That's so sweet. It really is. But I think you might have an overly idealized view of the brother-sister relationship." Then she lost her smile, and a thoughtful look came into her eyes. "There's a lot of that going around, I guess."

Chapter 26

> Suit-Skin, Rumpled, Mr.:
>
> Your attendance has been very poor over the last few weeks. This is not the type of attendance record we like to see in a student who desires to come for advanced instruction. In order for you to have any chance of coming in the future, it is imperative that you meet with the Graduate Assistant immediately after the last class this Friday.
>
> The Faculty

I told Slide this would be my last Rumpled Suitskin. He shook his head. "You gave it a good shot, man."

"But she still sort of wants to see me," I said. "What's that all about?"

"There's a name for women like that. It's politically incorrect. Here, let me write it out in code. Wait, is it one word or two?"

"I know what it is. One last tease can't hurt me that much."

"Mr. Suitskin? You have a question?"

She was wearing high heels, silver earrings, and a tight black and white silk print dress that contrasted with the iridescent sheen of her hair. I knew she wouldn't end the last class without calling on me.

"Why are you wearing that beautiful dress?"

"That is an inappropriate question." She held herself straighter and her eyes flared. She wasn't the kind of girl who blushed easily.

People were listening, though. I had the feeling I had asked the question most of the class wanted the answer to.

"If you must know, I have some place to go, a faculty reception, right after class. In fact, let's just wrap this class up. The final will focus on Chapters 11 through 16. If you haven't read them, read them before next Tuesday. If you have read them, think about the questions at the end. I think this is a fascinating field of study, and the 200-level classes go into some amazing concepts. I really hope this course has kept your interest, and some of you will want to go into this field. If anybody wants to talk about that, I'll be available after the exam. Thank you all."

There was first a little smattering of applause, and then it picked up some, and then it picked up a little bit more, and then she really did blush.

"You were great." We were walking towards her house, her high heels clicking on the sidewalk. "I don't mean just today. The whole semester. You're good at this. You know what you're talking about. You have charisma."

I thought maybe she wanted me there to say a final goodbye before she went back on the faculty social circuit. "You're going to do well," I blurted out. "Not just academically. Every guy who's got any sense can see you're the class of this whole joint. I wish you the best. I ...."

"I got this note," she interrupted me. "I think it's from your roommate. Here." She handed me a folded piece of white paper.

"What? This is in code."

"I know. He wrote something in English on the other side. It says the note is actually for you. It says to give it to you after class. And something about a hat." I put the thing in my pocket and we walked on. "What did you tell him about me anyway?" she asked.

"That you are out of my league."

We had reached the bridge over the ravine. She was complaining that her high heels were hurting her feet. Right in the middle, right on the spot where I never wanted to be again, she stopped and looked down over the rail. It was like looking through a tunnel of evergreen fir toward the dark bottom 100 feet below. You could feel the dark dignity of the giant fir trees that survived the deep shade of the ravine. The little stream at the bottom was down so far below you just had to have faith that the tiny sparkle you saw was something alive.

"You never asked me …." she started.

"Okay," I interrupted. "I'll ask. What does it mean, your going to this faculty affair?" When I said this, she half rolled her eyes and looked away and down into the ravine, her shimmering hair catching the spring sunlight. "I didn't ask," I went on, "because I was afraid of the answer. I'm still afraid. But I'll ask if you want me to. Does going to this faculty affair mean you're going to start dating again?"

"The problem is," she started, without answering my question, "you treat me like some sort of special person."

"You are."

"I mean like a special person you can't question. Until now, you never asked me if I was dating again. Last weekend, when you thought I had brought Henry as my date, I could tell you were going to just stand there and take it."

"I have no rights over you." Even as I said this I knew it was in some weird way a man-lie, and that she wouldn't understand. I remembered telling Dory on the phone that my mother had the right to invite whoever she wanted to her wedding. I remembered being told that rights had nothing to do with it. Eileen seemed to think the same. The talk about rights annoyed her, and she looked away again.

But then she turned back. "Do you love me?"

"I do. I thought you knew that. Psych 101 isn't *that* interesting."

I couldn't read her eyes. "Stalking isn't the same thing," she said. "Stalking is an obsession with an idea in your head, not love for the real person."

"Maybe people stalk because they're not allowed to interact with the real person."

She pulled back. I was trying to really see her now, not just idolize her. Okay, she was still gorgeous and competent and confident – in general – but the look on her face right then was contrite. "What I told you once on the phone," she said, "about how I couldn't talk to you because just hearing your voice, even on the phone, made me ... affected my body. That was really unfair. I knew the minute I said it that I shouldn't have, but it's not something you can take back."

"That really put my head in a weird place."

"I'm sorry."

I had learned something in the past year about talking to women. I wasn't supposed to just brush off her apology, like you would an apology from guy to guy.

"Apology accepted."

"Thank you."

That was nice. We stared down into the ravine. I knew the "do you love me" conversation wasn't finished, but I didn't know how to get it started again. "Really," I said, "why'd you read *Coriolanus*?"

"I don't know. You were so interested in it. I just had to know what it was."

"I read it again last night myself. Coriolanus was a complete asshole."

"He's not your hero?"

"I never said he was my hero," I protested. We seemed to be getting farther and farther away from the desired conversation. "But I read the play in kind of a different light last night." She didn't seem interested in talking about Shakespeare. She lifted her foot and took off one shoe, rubbed her foot, then put the shoe back on. Then she did the same to the other. My bad memories of the ravine didn't seem so strong while we were idly looking at it together on this suddenly lazy day. She seemed to be waiting for the conversation to continue too, but she wasn't in any hurry either. It seemed like we were going to stay here until whatever had to be done was done.

"You know," she said, "you have a piece of paper sticking out of your hat."

"Slide?" I guessed. "What does it say: *Kick me*?"

She pulled it out of the hatband. "It's just the letter *E*."

"Oh, that's the key to his coded message. I know why he picked *E*. That's for you. He's a real fan of yours."

"Why don't you read his big secret message? He obviously wanted us to read it together."

"Okay. It will take me some time. Okay, the first part of it: CK BKN EP PEI. No, I can't do it without a piece of paper." We used the back of the other paper. "It's really pretty simple. You just go four letters down. *A* means *E*, *B* means *F*, *etc*." I felt a little sheepish when it was done. "It says 'Go for it, Tim.'"

She laughed. "I think I might like this Slide guy. What does the other one say?"

I started doing the other one: PDA LNEYA EO PK WOG EP GEJZHU.

"It's a quote from *Coriolanus*," I said. "Slide must have seen me highlight it last night."

"What's it say?"

I wasn't worried about the few other random students who were crossing over the bridge right then, but I did do a quick check for the police and the Three Wise Men. They weren't there. Then I got down on my knees in front of her and said, as clearly as I could, "I love you with all my heart. I'm sorry for what I did. Will you forgive me?"

Slowly, deliberately, she threw the high heels she had worn for the faculty reception off the bridge, one by one. We started walking toward her house, but the rough concrete surface hurt her feet.

"Just this once," I asked, "can I carry you?"

The answer to that was yes. The answer to my previous question was yes. I carried her all the way to her house. She said she had been in love with me for a long time. She said that had never happened to her before. She said she was a little afraid, because she knew she wasn't as perfect as I thought she was. She asked me if I would be patient when that reality sank in. She said she had hated seeing me in so much pain. She said she would have forgiven me long ago, if only I had asked.

A real nice final line to remember would help!

pg. 82, not interested in the boy's house
chat, nor in Tim's father – nor
the box – but why not? Still, pg. 87,
pg. 86 another unfathomable line.
See 87,

CPSIA information can be obtained at www.ICGtesting.com
Printed in the USA
BVOW04*1916160615

404899BV00001B/1/P